For a united kingdom

Al Ponte'

For a united kingdom®
Oregon USA

Acknowledgments

While this tale of a time of conflict and downfall of the Stuart Monarchs tries to follow the events and timeline of the true story, other parts have been dramatized to enclude Scottish and Irish legend; a work of fiction presented by the author. Based on a true story some parts of the actual timeline has been condensed to fit into the restraints of the fictional story line constructed by the author and so should be considered as a work of fiction rather than a true exposay of history.

LCCN# 2025927305

ISBN# 979-8-9937486-0-3 Hardcover Edition
ISBN# 979-8-9937486-1-0 Paperback Edition
ISBN# 979-8-9937486-3-4 EBook Edition
ISBN# 979-8-9937486-2-7 Audio Book Edition

For a united kingdom is a Registard Business
in Oregon, USA

A First Edition Printing
2026

Dedication

Dedicated to Dr. Gene Scott, PhD
Stanford University California

He opened my eyes to a lost generation of my family who only knew that they had come from Ireland. And since the last two generations had red hair, they figured that they were, in fact, from Ireland. But when checking the surname, it wasn't considered Irish at all; who would know?

Out of the blue Dr. Scott sent me a genealogy chart that showed a ancient family member that showed an Irish linage, and this was contrary to what I had found out; how could this be? This started me to research and with the help of my cousin started me on a quest to find out the truth.

Even though I had an older Irish relative; my fore-father had moved to America in 1715. He had been raised by his grand-parents who were Scottish in Ireland, but there was a Scottish lineage that had gone back over 500 years. His father had married the daughter of the burgess of Aberdeen. before moving to Ireland. His great-grandfather was not only crisened as a child, but would at the end of his life in 1657 would be inturned in the Kirk-yard of St.Nicholas Church in central Aberdeen.

For a united kingdom

Cardinal Cona'eus - Counsel to Charles King of England, and The Bishop's War; the prelude to the English Civil War.

For a united kingdom by Al Ponte® is a registered Business in Oregon, U.S.A.

ISBN# **979-8-9937486-0-3**

In 1637 George Conn returns to England and travels up to Scotland with King Charles, and together they try to win the support of the Scots who are set on rebellion. What they don't know is that the Scottish Assembly the equivalent of the Parliament in England has already voted to reject the King's wishes. Before they know it they're on the run and try to raise a local guard. King Charles calls on the Scottish Privy Council to answer to what has happened to a Royal reserve treasury which also contained the Deeds and Titles of the Scottish Earls and Land Barons. Because of their rejection, the King threatens to take their titles and lands back unless they show the support they promised when receiving their Titles. With the Titles and Deeds missing it's a race on to find them. George though has his own agenda.

Steve Conn
Chief Editting Oficer

FOR A UNITED KINGDOM

by Al PONTE

TABLE OF CONTENTS Page #

Acknowledgments ii

Dedication. iii

Introduction ix

Interlude xv

A place in time; back to the beginning

Guardian Defender of the faith Part One

1. **Gifts from Across the Sea** 1
2. **The Confirmation at Kells** 23
3. **The Search for the Relics Begin**. 35
4. **On to the Isle of Iona** 53
5. **Spirits of the Chapel** 63

Court of Charles I of England Part Two

6. **Henrietta Maria**. 79
7. **Old Friends Unite** 87
8. **A Redemption for Marie**. 105
9. **The Work at Westminster** 117
10. **Testing the Stone**. 135
11. **At the Queen's Chapel** 145

FOR A UNITED KINGDOM

by Al PONTE

TABLE OF CONTENTS (Continued) Page #

Scotland and The Bishop's War
Part Three

12. The Quarry Secret 165
13. A Treasury uncovered 177
14. The Turriff Trot 189
15. Building the Kingdom 201

Escaping to the Continent
Part Four

16. A Hasty Convenient Truce 221
17. Escape to the Continent 233
18. Visit to Glastonbury 245

Epilogue 267

The Treaty of Berwick and the Liturgy;
An out and out rejection of the English hypocrisy

Acknowledgements 271

Introduction

To have you fully understand the depth of what has been taken to be seen as a destiy, we have to go back to the first book of the Bible, Genesis, and the patriarch Jacob, to whom God had given the name Israel.

The slab of rock that Jacob had used as his pillow was consecrated as the cornerstone of God's house of worship. The Stone, also known as Jacob's Pillow Stone, or the Stone of Destiny, and the Stone of Scone, in biblical times, had traveled throughout the desert as the center point of the Tabernacle, the portable tent used for worship. Later, the Stone would be set up as the altar stone in the Temple of Jerusalem by Solomon, the son whose namesake would follow Jacob as the House of David.

The attributes of the Stone, which we also find in the book of Genesis, describe it as somewhat of a portal between heaven and earth. Known as Jacob's ladder, it's described as having God's angels ascending and descending a ladder rising back into the heavens. According to an old Irish legend, the Stone first made its way to Ireland's shores shortly after the destruction of Solomon's Temple, when the tribe of Israel were taken off in bondage as captives into Babylon.

The Stone had arrived in Ireland along with other holy relics and what would be called the Seed of David, King Hezekiah's daughter. She had escaped with the help of the Holy Prophet Jeremiah; she survived and eluded capture, and with a small entourage, came to Ireland.

The Irish High Kings could have also been considered as High Priests, continuing a tradition followed by the tribe of Israel. In the annals of ancient Ireland, we are told of a dynasty of High Kings who would eventually bring the Stone over to Scotland and then on to Scone Abbey.

In a Traditional Coronation ceremony with the Stone, the Scottish King John I would be the last true King to be crowned at Scone. Robert the Bruce, King John's grandson, would eventually crown himself at Scone. By then, the Stone had already been carted away, stolen by Edward I of England, otherwise known as Edward Longshanks, Hammer of the Scots. Edward would subjugate control over the Scots by having them submit to being a Vassal to his English rule, and for Edward to be fully recognized as Scotland's feudal Overlord.

When the Scots could not decide on a ruler of their own, Edward would support John I (Balliol). Then, after his coronation, he would take the Stone back with him to London and set it under a throne chair that he had built and put in Westminster Abbey. For centuries after, right up to the present day, this chair, now referred to as 'King Edward's chair', someday will again take its place, front and center, at each and every subsequent coronation of England's next monarch.

Scotland, though, for several times, as in the present, would go without having its own King. It would seem that to be a King of Scotland would almost ensure one, the promise of an early death. The fighting amongst the Scottish Lords at this time and the various claims to the Crown were constantly at hand. Around the time of the first millennium, the Scottish Kings had made it a habit of inviting English gentry to Scotland, giving them land and title in part to appease the English King.

In the first century of the new millennium, things got so bad that the Alban Lords, the founders of the Scottish nation, felt that something must be done to realign the culture and bring back the Scottish heritage to the Scottish people. King Fergus, who had first brought the Stone to Scotland, was from the family of the Irish High Kings. The Alban Lords would go back to Ireland to look again for a Royal family member to help. Their candidate would be the son of an Irish warlord, recently killed in the Western Isles, fending off a Norse invasion.

His son, at first being so distraught over the loss of his father in battle, was reluctant to return to Scotland. The Irish legend has it that when emissaries sent by the Alban Lords approached and made their offer, the son known as Somerled was fishing in the lake. So distraught he was and disinterested in returning to Scotland, he made a counter-offer based on chance; 'said that if he caught a fish, he would return. The story goes that shortly thereafter, he landed a most wonderful and beautiful trout. And even though reluctant, he would return to Scotland and take up the task, much in part that his father had started. But of course, it would turn into much more than that and end with him leading a great army into Edinburgh to claim the Crown.

His endeavor, though, would not come to light; betrayed by a rival Irish cousin, one who had given his alliance to the present King. Only years later, Robert the Bruce, who himself was a descendant of those Norman English lords, who had been given lands and titles, and Kingdoms too, would hence turn the tide on English domination himself. If only his efforts could have restored Scottish cultural sovereignty in Scotland. It would seem that it was still a very dangerous job to be King.

Scotland would again go without a King, for a time. So, in place of the King, a panel of Lords would act as Regents.

And Scotland still being a dangerous place; the Regents would act in secret chambers and take great efforts to hide their identity; in what might be considered as an act to preserve Scottish culture, the title of Protector: Defender of the Faith; Guardian of Scotland, would be somewhat arbitrarily handed out in the years without a ruler. Later, the King himself would hold the title of Defender of the Faith. Guardian?. . Protector?. . The Defender of the Faith?. Guardian of what?. . Defender of what Faith?. . If it was to guard Scottish sovereignty and culture, well, that had been lost before the first millennium, according to the Alban Lords.

A Defender of the Faith?. . . Was this the Faith that was in connection with the Stone, and perhaps the direct relationship with the God Almighty? Truly, by the time of John I; having a Scottish King of Norman descent, and the Stone being taken off to reside in England, perhaps the Faith was that God would still stand by his Chosen People. So, Scotland had no choice but to rule by a Regency of Lords. But for acts of State, they soon decided to elect a spokesperson; identifying him as the Steward of Scotland, and the main Regent, or otherwise the figurehead King of Scotland.

As it was the custom, the stewardship would be handed down, just as any other title. Steward quite quickly changed to depict a family name, that of Stewart. Robert the First, or 'Robert the Stewart', began the great dynasty of the Stuart monarchs. As the monarchs would continue to be Coronated at Scone, whereas the Stone itself would remain in England.

The Stone, though, held a prophecy, written in Latin, that would later be translated by Sir Walter Scott; the famous Scottish author and poet: . . "*Unless the fates be faulty grown, and the prophets voice be in vain, wherever it is found this sacred Stone, the Scottish race shall reign*".

Imagine all of the elation, jubilation and joyful celebration when, finally, King James, after almost three hundred years, is coronated King of England; the prophecy had finally been fulfilled! And could this be a part of a much older prophecy; the manifest destiny of Jeremiah's commission?

Let's take a step back; the Guardianship, some believe, goes back to Ireland; and the titles held in conjunction with the High Priest and King. Some believe that the Guardian was the High Priest and, because of his great position of authority, was given the additional title of King. So, what was he guarding?

We know that the High Priest would be in possession of certain relics, including the Stone, and others that were brought out from the East along with the Stone to Ireland. There was also given a "revelation to a dynasty" that is said to have happened as the king did a playful jig upon the Stone.

Such a revelation in connection to the Stone had not happened or been recorded since Jacob in the Holy Lands at Bethel. The name Bethel translates to House of God in Hebrew. Such a revelation, therefore, would've been held as a true treasure and confirmation of the covenant that Jeremiah had made with God. In Ireland, the keeper of the holy relics and any revelation conveyed, and knowledge of the covenant, be it High Priest or King, would have been naturally handed down through time. One theory concerning the monk Columba, who was of the Royal family and in line to be King, he had written down the dynasty that had been given by this earlier revelation on the inside cover of his Book of Kells.

The Book of Kells was thought to have been taken by the Norse invaders, who would often raid the East Coast of Scotland. It appears once again at the monastery in Kells, only to be missing its jewel-encrusted cover.

Legends of the holy relics that were once kept in Ireland abound. St. Columba was the building founder of the church and monastery on the Isle of Iona, where a majority of the Scottish monarchs are buried. Some believe that the true Stone of Scone was moved to the Isle of Iona shortly before a copy of such was given to Edward I to take back with him to England.

Before Columba left Ireland, he founded the fortified city of Derry on the northern tip of Ireland, said to be the last standing fortified city in western Europe. The big question is, why a fortified city?

And why, if such a stronghold was in place, why move to the Isle of Iona? One more thought, on these holy relics believed to have come from the holy land with the Stone; going back to Somerled; might he have been given a relic that could have been used to raise the army of men that he would need? After failing to advance on Edinburgh and losing his command, Somerled's vast army of men were all dispersed and told to go back to their homes.

It's quite a coincidence that the next monarch in line appears to present a battle standard so similar, and resembling that of King David of Judah. A battle standard that his father, King Malcolm the Fourth had given him. And in fact, despite the time the monarch had spent in England, up to that time; William I or 'William The Lion'; had the longest reign of any Scottish King. Could it be that the standard was recognized by the people, and that they knew what it was and what it represented? If it was recognized, that might explain why such an abrupt change in the longevity of the monarchy.

For a united kingdom

Interlude

A place in time; back to the beginning

My story begins with another Scottish King, that of James IV, and how he maneuvered his descendants' destiny to coincide with the traditional King's destiny of Scottish culture. True, it took a generation, but building that legacy began with James IV and his observance and respect for the traditions that had passed down through the generations in Scottish culture.

Like William St. Clair of Roslyn, James IV looked to honor God by constructing a Temple Church based upon the plans used by Solomon and the Temple in Jerusalem. Although Roslyn Temple would never be completed, James IV Chapel in the old King's College in Aberdeen would be built under a Papal bull. Construction would begin and coincide with the day Solomon began the building of his Temple in Jerusalem, as noted by an inscription on the left of the North entrance to the Chapel.

It was also James IV, who would arrange his son's marriage to the daughter of King Henry VIII, which would eventually lead to, at long last, the tradition of the Scottish destiny to be fulfilled by his grandson James VI: King James I of England. Try to imagine what elation and sense of fulfillment that King James must have felt in fulfilling the prophecy of the

Stone of Scone. It had been over three hundred years since a King of Scotland was crowned using the Stone of Scone as part of the coronation ceremony.

This was a big deal; James was seen as a new messiah. Many of his Scottish advisors tried to convince him to celebrate the coronation ceremony at Scone, and that it would strengthen his support in Scotland. James thought quite differently, considering he had ruled Scotland from Holyrood, moving his throne to London is what he needed to gather up support there in England.

The Stone of Scone itself had a long and storied history. According to legend, it was the very stone upon which Jacob had rested his head in Bethel and was brought to Ireland by the prophet Jeremiah. It was then transported to Scotland by Fergus, the first King of the Scots, and has been used in the coronation of Scottish monarchs ever since.

James IV's reign was marked by efforts to centralize power and assert the monarchy's dominance over the fractious Scottish nobility. He was a patron of the arts and sciences, founding the Royal College of Surgeons in Edinburgh and supporting the University of St Andrews. He also built up the Scottish navy, commissioning the construction of the Great Michael, the largest ship in Europe at the time.

James IV's marriage to Margaret Tudor was part of the Treaty of Perpetual Peace between Scotland and England, but the peace was short-lived. James IV was killed at the Battle of Flodden in 1513, fighting against the English.

His death left Scotland in turmoil, with his infant son James V inheriting the throne. James V continued his father's efforts to strengthen the monarchy, but his reign was also marked by conflict with England. He married Mary of Guise, a member of the powerful French family, in an effort to secure an alliance with France against England. This alliance would later lead to the "Rough Wooing," a series of wars between Scotland and England during the 1540s. James V died in 1542, leaving his six-day-old daughter Mary, Queen of Scots, as his heir.

Mary, Queen of Scots, faced numerous challenges during her reign, including conflicts with the Protestant Reformation and political intrigue. She was eventually forced to abdicate in favor of her son, James VI, who was raised in a Protestant court. James VI would go on to unite the crowns of Scotland and England in 1603, becoming James I of England and fulfilling the prophecy of the Stone of Scone.

The union of the crowns marked the beginning of a new era for Scotland and England. James I sought to create a united kingdom, though his efforts were met with resistance from both English and Scottish factions. He promoted religious tolerance and commissioned the King James Bible, which remains one of the most influential translations of the Bible to this day.

James I's reign laid the groundwork for the eventual political union of Scotland and England in 1707, which created the Kingdom of Great Britain. The legacy of James I and the symbolism of the Stone of Scone continue to resonate in the history and culture of Scotland and the United Kingdom.

So elated was James that he wanted to share God's word with his subjects, he had the Bible translated from Latin into English. But of course, by having Holy relics to show his subjects, James would try to further establish his legitimacy in ways not so uncommon with the rest of Europe at that time and to show that he was in God's grace.

Even though it could be claimed he was already sitting on what could be considered the most important relic of all, that of the cornerstone of God's Kingdom, Jacob's pillow stone, the symbol of God's house on earth. But there were other relics that came with the stone upon its arrival, long ago, to Ireland. And this is where we go back to the monk Saint Columba, who certainly must've known of the relics, and of the guardians that protected them.

In ancient Irish kingship, the High Priesthood and guardianship were all entwined. It wasn't until the unrest in Ireland that Fergus thought it best to move the seat of power to Scotland, so that the roles of Guardian, High Priest, and King would be separated. And so, some of the relics would stay in Ireland under guardianship; only the King knew who in Ireland was considered to be the Guardian, who had the secret knowledge of where the relics were. Over time, all knowledge of who the Irish guardians were was lost or held tightly in Ireland.

King James had an early interest because of the years he had served as the Scottish King. He thought that it entitled him to be considered a guardian. Others thought differently, and that not having been coronated by the Stone, James did not have the proper access to approach the other guardians. Interestingly though, his dynasty would be written along with the Irish lords; shortly before he would become King.

As Elizabeth the First lay dying, an English envoy and close ally to the King, who would later claim to have helped directly in King James's ascension to the throne, came to her with a plan to approach the stronghold of the Earls. Only then would James be able to deal directly with the Irish lords.

Still at war with France and Spain, but with the marriage of the French princess Henrietta Maria to the English Prince, son of James I, Charles Stuart, the political situation would dramatically start to change; probably too fast for the rest of the country. With the threat of French involvement as a French contingent was sent to see after the needs of the Queen, married at the age of fifteen, she had a full host of servants follow her over to England in 1625, including seven catholic priests.

This wouldn't set well with many of those in Charles' Court, and by 1628, most of all had returned to France; even the Queen's main lady in waiting, Jeanne de Harlay, also known as Madame St. George. Charles even went as far as to jail one of the priests, Robert Phillips, worried that he might give away the true identity of his new stable master, whose family is well known in Scotland. Phillips, who was also from Scotland, thought that he might be recognized. It didn't help that a large percentage of the King's Privy Council were also from Scotland.

It wasn't just the Scots who were seen invading British soil; the general populist would see a French Invasion, not realizing it was in support of the Queen. The French Court had given the young princess Mary Stewart the utmost reverence when it was ever in procession or 'On Parade." The future wife of the Dupain would always lead the procession, showing how much respect they had for the long-lasting Stewart Dynasty, or more importantly, their position with the Church in Rome.

For a united kingdom

Part One

Guardian Defender of the faith

Al Ponte'

First folio - MMXXV

Iona
Aberdeen
Londonderry
Dublin
London
George's Travels
Scots College
Paris
Rome
Madrid
Lisbon

Gifts from Across the Sea

Chapter I

Late in May of 1636, a Portuguese cargo ship waits just outside the convergence of water that separates England and Ireland. Commonly known as the Irish Sea. Spring always brings up the weather and storms this time of year, and unexpected patches of fog along the coast can be extremely dangerous. Despite the danger, the ship has dropped its main sails as it is approaching a bank of fog, and on the ebb tide silently enters the white blanket of cover it provided; and comes almost to a stop.

The Captain had become quite good by now at using the fog and ebb tide to elude the Coastguard, running the blockade enacted by the English Parliament. They were trying to stop any sort of contraband arms and ammunition, a trade that is better known as gunrunning, from reaching Ireland, and fueling the revolt brewing there and in Scotland.

The people were feeling increasingly ignored by their government officials in London. Unrest and riots have now fueled notions of a civil war happening, while the King was feeling more and more distrust in Parliament, which had formed a divide that would lead the King to dissolving Parliament in 1629.

Charles, not able to have Parliament's ability to raise the money for his return to Scotland, had to rely on only what he received from the domestic taxes known as Ship's Money; it first started as a remittance for shipbuilding and expanded to finance Naval bases and training. With the ever-growing need for more money, the Naval authority would eventually cover all of the existing coastline in England.

……And so, the ship sits in wait, ebbing in the tide, in and out of a great blanket of fog, and waits for an escort ship to appear. Having dropped its main sails, the ship sat vulnerable, and if it were spotted, it could easily be overtaken. Making matters worse was the fact that the ship itself was a liability, and identical to the most feared warship of its time, the Portuguese Man of War. The ship does its very best to stay hidden. For them to go any further, and enter the Irish Sea, would make them vulnerable and they could be shot at. It would be much safer to wait for their escort and only hope that they will not be spotted before their escort arrives.

Earlier that day, at Caernarvon Castle, on the southern tip of Wales, Charles I, King of England, looks out towards the straight that separates the mainland from Ireland. The King has a worried look, next to him stands one of his merchant fleet Admirals, who tries to assure the King that the mission is going on schedule. "Your Majesty, your flagship, and the escort frigate have only been gone now some forty minutes and should be nearly approaching our friends in wait."

"I worry because I know that the Parliament's Navy suspects my activity to involve Irish allies and is looking for anything to raise a contention with Parliament. I've gotten word that its cargo is coming my way, and I would hate to see it commandeered. They should be heading for the docks at Dublin, and I don't want them stopped and harassed, so I hope that your orders were clear to your Captains, Admiral."

"They know what's at stake and were told to take every effort to see that the Galleon makes port in Dublin without delay. Your Flagship, along with an identical Galleon that sits in wait at the Dublin docks. It's ready to sail at a moment's notice as fast as they could sail to keep up and follow the Flagship directly to Beaumaris Castle, where we should be waiting. Your presence there will only lead them to believe that it is something to do with Your Highness and know to leave it alone."

"We shouldn't act too quickly and show our hand. Let's wait until we know that their escort arrives and hope that they're not stopped before then."

"Your grace, nothing can go wrong; our plans are foolproof, and even if our friends are intercepted, there's nothing in their ships' manifest that presents any danger to Parliament, and the identity of its true cargo is well disguised. But if there is trouble, they'd know not to dock in Dublin as planned and head towards the mainland to Beaumaris Castle, which is where we should be heading towards soon, so as to support our deception and divert any suspicions that may arise".

Charles sighs; forcing himself to relax. "Very well; I suppose there is little we can do but wait." He stepped back from the parapet and turned to face the Admiral. "Have them prepare the carriage —just in case."

The Admiral, a seasoned man with a weathered face that betrayed years of navigating both waters and treacherous courtly affairs, nodded solemnly. Charles shifted his gaze, focusing on the distant horizon where the sky met the sea, blending blue into a stormy gray. He murmured, recalling the whispers of dissent and mistrust that filled his court. "I fear the treachery that lurks beneath the surface, both in the waters and in the hearts of men."

"You can trust in your plan, your Majesty."

The Admiral placed a reassuring hand on the King's shoulder. "Your intelligence is sound, and your choice to send the flagship was wise. The wind is favorable, and they should make good time."

"And if they do not return in a timely manner?" Charles's brow furrowed, picturing the scenarios that danced through his mind like phantoms. "If they encounter trouble, or even something worse if they're intercepted."

"Then the ships will act swiftly to regroup and escort the freighter straight away across to Beaumaris," the Admiral said firmly, his voice calm with a faint hint of uncertainty. "But for now, we must have faith in our crewmen and the mission, that it will succeed without any trouble."

Charles managed a small smile, grateful for the Admiral's optimism. "And what is a King without hope?" he remarked. "God willing, our mission shall bring peace, not just to our kingdom, but to the lands beyond and for the good of all humanity. Don't underestimate my friend, he is very clever. Catching him out of step will be almost impossible while he has my protection. And there are many who would gladly go out of their way; to offer protection, to him. This is how he can freely move around Europe and thinks nothing about breaking the blockade Parliament puts in place."

As they walked back around atop the castle's rampart, the horizon off in the distance loomed ominously, a reflection of the turbulent times ahead, yet within Charles' heart beat one of a leader, determined to navigate through the storm. But there was a real danger, the Portuguese Galleon had a similar appearance to the most prevalent warships of the day; the Portuguese Man of War, and to find it having dropped its sails and sitting off England's southern coast was sure to attract any Coast Guard vessel on patrol in the area. The Captain had dispatched lookouts forward and aft, and up on the highest trees on the main mast with orders to keep a sharp eye out for any approaching ships.

The Galleon now nervously looking out into eerie banks of fog that seemed to be ever-changing clouds over the surface of the ocean. The sun was just rising and now would reveal the banks of fog even brighter and showing the eastern horizon, where any bank of fog now behind the Galleon would make it stand out and be easily discovered. All the Captain could do now was to slip back into the fog and hope not to be detected.

The Captain orders to raise the spanker and jib sails to move this ship back into the fog. Then, off the starboard side, one of the lookouts from the cross trees up top of the main mast sees a ship approaching at full sail. "Captain, a ship approaches off the starboard side, shall we make sail?"

The Captain shouts out: "Do you see one or two ships? Two ships were sent to escort; if only a single ship approaches, we can be sure that it is most likely to be one of the Parliament's naval warships that patrol this part of the sound."

"Only one ship sighted!" calls out the first mate.

"Look hard mate, look towards the horizon; do you see our escorts?"

Looking towards the horizon and into the sun made it hard to see if a ship was there, but once there was a bank of fog behind them, they were much easier to see. "Yes Captain!; on the horizon, perhaps a mile behind the first ship."

"Is it one ship on the horizon, or two?"

The second mate shouts: "I think, two; Captain!"

"Are you sure?" Asks the Captain.

"Two sets of masts Sir, it must be the escort at full sail and moving in fast. Now one of the two is breaking free and making up distance behind the first ship out in front."

The First Mate asks: "Shall we make sail, Captain?"

"No, but make sure that our cargo knows that we might soon be boarded by the Coast Guard. Maintain the jib and spanker sails to make sure we stay covered by the fog for now."

King Charles, just a year earlier, had been given a gift of his own new flagship, a magnificent ship with 120 cannons aboard. It was said that all of the elaborate gilding on the back of the ship; cost as much as the total cost of a regular warship of the fleet. The Sovereign of the Seas was a 17th-century Fleet Warship of the English Navy. Launched on the Thirteenth of October 1637, she was ordered as a 90-gun first-rate ship of the line. When she launched, she was armed with one hundred and two cannons at the insistence of the King. Later, it would be renamed just Sovereign, and then; Royal Sovereign. Designed and built in 1636 by the Master Shipwright Mathew Baker, after the revolutionary new concept of a lower setting and a much faster ship; which was launched back in 1577.

The whole back outside area section, where the Captain and officers' quarters, the ship's Galley and kitchen were; was painted black and gilded in solid gold; and it was said to have been designed by the Flemish Master; Anthony Van Dyke. Known more for his painting, he is the Royal portrait painter during this time.

This new design of warship, referred to as a 'Race-built Galleon', would dominate warship building for the next three hundred years. The Sovereign, adding another twelve cannons, made it the most heavily armed ship in the fleet. In its time, it was the largest ship in the known world, and it was fast!

The Second mate shouts: "The escorts are closing their distance to the first ship sighted, and all three ships are at full sail and approaching fast."

The quickly approaching ship, now less than a mile off, sends a warning shot across the bow; clearly stating its intention to the freighter to lay way, and prepare to be boarded. As a boarding party sets off in a launch towards the freighter, the escorts finally catch up behind the Coast Guard vessel. Charles's flagship is clearly recognizable, as it sends off a flare indicating to the boarding party to heed to, and for the patrol vessel to stop any further action. Whether or not the flare was simply ignored or just not seen by the approaching boarding party, they were now making their way up the side of the freighter and boarding the ship.

Admiral Roberts from Charles' flagship was also wasting no time and had also set off in the flagship's launch towards the freighter and was quickly crossing the distance to board the freighter himself. The boarding party was now organizing itself on deck, insisting that the Ship's Captain present his manifest and make for the arrangements for his cargo to be searched.

Admiral Roberts now makes his way up the side of the freighter. As he reaches the railings, he begins to express his disapproval of the Coast Guard vessel not complying with the flagship's instructions to stand down, with the understanding that a boarding party would be contrary to any action on their part. By now, the first boarding party's Coast Guard Captain is standing on deck and looking very surprised and somewhat guilty, as he sees the Admiral now climbing up and over the railings to get on deck.

The Coast Guard Captain now pleads, "Admiral Roberts, if I had known that it was you who had come to escort the freighter, I would not have made such an effort to detain and board this ship."

"And so what are you waiting for then, Captain, take your boarding party and leave now, I want to see your vessel making sail in ten minutes, is that clear?"

"But Admiral, what am I to say in my report?"

"What would you like to say in your report, Captain? That you disregarded instructions from the Flagship of the Admiral of the King's merchant fleet? Captain, I would suggest that you get back to your ship and forget that you saw anything this morning."

"I'm sorry Admiral, but I have my orders. May I see the ship's manifest please, and I will have to search what is in the hold; those are my orders; you understand that Parliament has a blockade on trade of any munitions. You understand that our country is now in a state of civil unrest. This is all in part due to a maritime blockade done in force by the Parliament, instructing the King's navy to enforce. You can see, Admiral, that I'm only doing my duty."

"The Admiralty will certainly hear about this; I will personally bring this up before a hearings board. You will be held before the board to answer for your actions here on this day.

Back at the Castle, a shout comes from the high lookout: "Ships flares seen beyond the horizon, your grace."

One flare signal's only a warning, but it could mean that the ship has been discovered by the Coast Guard.

"We shall wait and see, have the lookout keep a sharp eye out to see how many vessels come over the horizon, we shall wait and see."

As it was starting to get light, the bright blanket of fog could now be plainly seen, and any ship on the horizon would stand out like a fly on a windowsill. Back on board the ship, the Captain seems nervous. The picture of a true gentleman, dressed smartly in a black and crimson coat, white blouse, and pants. His boots are shined, and he has a black sash around his waist holding two pistols and a Cutlass on his hip. He looks more like a war Admiral than a tradesman, although it wouldn't be uncommon to see a ship's Captain armed on the high seas.

It had only been a few decades ago that the Spanish Armada had tried to invade, and relations with Spain hadn't gotten any better. Pirates and Privateers that had flourished under Elisabeth's reign continued into the beginning of the seventeenth century. Pirates such as Nathaniel Butler and James Riskinner, or Charlotte de Berry, a known woman Pirate, raided French and Spanish ships looking for spices from East India and gold from the New World of the Americas. By 1610, under a new King's rule, the numbers had dropped off, in an attempt to make peace with France and Spain, something not too popular with the Parliament

"Captain, may I see your manifest."

The ship's Captain then, reaching into his coat, pulls out a folded piece of ledger and, handing it to the Coast Guard Captain, remarks that they are just on a regular trading mission from Lisbon, Portugal, to the Irish port of Dublin. "Captain, we carry only trade goods of olive oil, Sherry wine, and animal hides. We have no contraband aboard."

"We will not be sure until I have had the opportunity to inspect the hold". The ship's Captain to his first mate: "See that the Coast Guard Captain has full access to inspect the hold".

As the first mate leads the boarding party off to inspect the hold, the Coast Guard Captain wonders why such a cargo could be of such importance to the merchant fleet Admiral.

"Admiral, is it your custom to greet all foreign merchant vessels this way?"

"Captain, you yourself have admitted that a blockade is in effect; this trading vessel sails under a Portuguese flag, and the merchants of Lisbon have much to offer in trade. I would not like to see the Captain of this vessel get the wrong idea and turn back with its cargo not reaching its destination. The Portuguese are not Spanish and are not our enemy. Goods like olive oil and port wine are valued commodities and make for good trade. You will find no contraband aboard this ship."

"Admiral, I hope that this is true, and I have no intention to disrupt any legitimate trade mission.

With the state of unrest in both England and in Ireland, Parliament has put out a blockade to stop items listed as contraband from entering into the country. If what is stated on the manifest, matches what is in the hold; then there is no problem, and the ship will be set on its way."

While the two sets of boarding parties' armed marines are left on deck, exchanging odd glances at each other, the two Captains, the Admiral, and their first Officers descend into the belly of the ship's hold, with the shipping manifest in hand. The Coastguard Captain looks around and says, "It has been very well organized down here. Captain, very clean and orderly. I'll have my men open one of these crates. . . I would like to see what's inside."

"Very well,. . .

"As you see, they are all clearly listed on the manifest."

"Yes, these printing supplies. I'll have to have my first officer go through the manifest if you don't mind."

The Captain replies: "Not at all, we can then return to the deck where the air is better, if that's OK with you."

The Captain then instructs his first mate, "Please stay down here and give them any help if asked."

A prompt "Yes Sir" from the first mate, as both Captains, along with the Admiral, make their way back to the main deck.

The Coastguard Captain remarks, "I noticed that along with those listed printing supplies, there was also a printing press included. As not specifically listed as contraband, it is on the watch list of items to take note of."

The remainder of the search team then returns to the main deck. "Captain, all is correct according to the manifest; with the exception of the deck below, of three horses quartered with a stablemaster."

"Horses? There are no horses listed on the manifest, and as horses are listed as contraband.

I'll have no choice but to take further action and commandeer this ship."

The Ship's Captain tries to explain; "They are not on the manifest because they are ships property; one is mine, one is for the first officer, and one for the procurement officer, they are needed ashore to arrange for our return journey, to arrange for supplies and the goods of trade that we will be taking back with us."

The Coast Guard Captain complains, "Procurement is all I hear nowadays; I was recently told that the Navy's area of procurement is nearly the whole bloody coastline now."

The Admiral helps to explain, "As it has to be if we are to patrol our coast. These horses seem to be of a common arrangement for the Captain and his officers, surely, three horses do not justify the commandeering of this trading mission, Captain?"

"Oh, . .I guess ship's property would adequately explain their presence, and therefore, no further action will be taken, and Captain, you and your ship may be on your way."

Despite the tense nature on board the freighter, the seas have now become calm. The once dense fog had now cleared, revealing a bright and sunny day. The sea was flat, reflecting every bit, gleaming as if it were glass Back at the Castle, the lookout now reports to see four ships coming over the horizon; "four ships now on the horizon, your grace, it does seem that the mission has been intercepted and we should now make ready for our alternate plan."

"It does look as though the Coast Guard has spotted the mission, and whether it follows along to see it into port or not, the Admiral knows to implement our alternate plan".

"Your grace, we should be off then quickly to Beaumaris Castle, and make ready our plans to see the ships make port without delay."

As the four ships make their way towards the Irish Sea, and the port of Dublin, the Coast Guard ship slows and now seems to have taken an easterly direction. It would seem that they were successful in fooling the British patrol, and as for now, the mission is still going along as planned.

The alternate plan though would still be in effect, as the ship, and its cargo has now been discovered by the. As the three ships now sail into the narrows between Ireland and the English mainland, they make their way towards the port destination of Dublin, the shell game, of ships at sea, begins. Even though the Coast Guard has thus so far allowed them to slip through the blockade, it is relatively clear that they could at any time be stopped, reported, and the ship, commandeered by the Parliament's naval forces.

So as the three ships get closer to Dublin harbor, two of the ships one of which will be the larger flagship of the Admiral; The Sovereign, will cut sharply to the East, making full sail to Beaumaris Castle. The other ship will make its way into port making sure to mingle with ships of a similar type to confuse its identity, making it difficult for the Coast Guard vessels to recognize. Meanwhile, the King and his Admiral make their way towards Beaumaris Castle by way of carriage.

The Admiral puzzled by all the attention focused on a single cargo, and asks the King why? Admiral the King explains, "This cargo is but a small part of plans that were set in place by my Great Grandfather; the King James IV of Scotland. As a young man and heir to the throne, he had seen the Knights returning from the Crusades.

The Crusades led a great adventure into the Holy Lands and started mainly as a Marshall plan to protect those on their pilgrimage to Jerusalem. But as the Crusades developed and Knights of the Holy Order were finally able to secure Jerusalem, they chose to make their camps on the Temple Mount, thus becoming known as the Temple Knights of Jerusalem or the Templars.

Once they had secured Jerusalem and offered adequate protection to those in transit, they were able to focus their efforts in another direction. The Knights being of a Holy Order, many have been to Rome, some even had an audience with the Pope. The Knights became steadfast at finding Holy relics to bring back, if not to the Pope, then to their own parishes, fixed on erecting their own venerated temples of worship.

One such Knight was Sinclair of Rosalyn. The Temple Knights were 12 years in searching out the Holy relics of the old Temple in Jerusalem. They searched in and around the city and even went as far as to dig into the catacombs of the Temple Mount trying to find the sacred articles of Solomon's Temple.

For years they searched and found only a few scripted stone monuments and a handful of related first Temple artifacts. Frustrated, they sought out, the local clerics, in hopes that they could tell them what had happened to the Temple relics. Finally, they found an old cleric from Crete, who spoke the language of the book, and was happy to tell them what he had learned.

The cleric, who was a very old man, was a monk on the isle of Crete and had come to Jerusalem on a pilgrimage. He was very surprised to find that he was so accepted by the Moslem overlords. The old monk, it seems had been free, to come and go as he pleased, and so decided to stay and to study the Gospels; one of many that had come to Jerusalem at this time to study the scriptures that could still be found in circulation.

The old monk, became well-versed, in many of the Gospels, and stories of the old Temple Mount, and the history of the Jewish nation. And so, the Knights were able to ask the old man about the relics of the First Temple. The old man when asked smiled and his eyes got wide. He then lifted his arms up into the air and said that the Temple had been destroyed, and what relics could be found in the Temple then were taken off along with the Jewish nation into captivity in Babylon.

The Knights asked, "you mean, that they took everything?". The old man again smiled and told them: "you need to better study the Scriptures; the books of Kings, the story of Jacob, and Jeremiah. You need to understand the promise God had made to his people, then you will come to realize, not all was taken. You English crusaders search high and low for the Holy relics of the Temple, don't you realize, that one of the greatest of all relics, you already possess, and is in your backyard!"

Study the book of Jeremiah, and you will realize that God had plans for the future of Israel and the House of David. But his intention should be no surprise and were in line with the promises to Israel that he had made in the past. "Have you not realized that our Lord keeps his promises and intends to guide his promised ones towards a closer life with him."

What the old man was trying to explain was something more valuable than any relic that they could find, and so the Knights returned to England, yes with a few dated relics of the time, but more importantly returned with the precious knowledge, and understanding of God's future plans for his people, the nation of Israel, and the House of David.

William Sinclair was one such Knight who returned and wanted to build a temple to the precious knowledge he had brought back from the Holy Land. Sinclair and his Knights had found what looked like a plan or a layout of Solomon's Temple, and so this would be what he would base his own design for a new Temple at Rosslyn.

But as the Knights returned, there was a sense that they would never fully control the city of Jerusalem, and therefore never really be able to rebuild the Temple there. Sinclair's rendition of Solomon's Temple would be a grand monument to the knowledge that was brought back from the Crusades. Sinclair's Chapel though would never be finished; and suppressed because to now be taken as the manifest destiny of God's commission to Jeremiah, making such an assumption was not to be made lightly and, to be sure of the all important timing; would it be too soon, and not yet knowing of Jerusalem's fate.

And so, with Jerusalem now back in the hands of the Moslems, it was soon realized that the Holy Lands would most likely be forever lost, and as written in the book of Jeremiah, forever forsaken by God.

God had intended a new beginning for the tribe of Israel and the House of David, not all was lost at the destruction of the First Temple. God had instructed Jeremiah to direct the remnant of the House of David, to escape, and to rebuild the tribe of Israel in a place of sanctuary, and safety. Ancient legends and Irish folklore point to an Eastern Princess arriving in Ireland soon after the destruction of the Temple.

Folklore tells of an entourage from the East, who had brought with them Holy relics, some of which were from the House of David, suggesting that this was the remnant that God had directed to Jeremiah to help to escape, and rebuild.

As the King and his Admiral approached the stronghold of Beaumaris Castle by carriage, the Sovereign was heading there too, towards the inland coast of England.

The other two ships were now pulling into Dublin Bay and heading for the main docks. It seems like the first part of their plan had been successful and that they had arrived at Dublin unsuspected. Having the escort of the merchant fleet there to guide the ship in, it was easy to arrange for them to dock so that they could unload their cargo and be on their way without causing any suspicion.

Fortunately, the boarding party of Cromwell's Parliamentary Navy had mistakenly seen only three of the seven horses hidden in the hold of the ship. The three horses found forward were there to act as a diversion to make it look as if they were boarded and searched; as there were only three horses aboard. Something as large as a horse, though, would be hard to hide and would be quite noticeable because of the smell that they would have had coming from the stalls. The four other horses were placed in the back behind a false wall.

And so, their plans now would go off as scheduled; at the docks, they would present their manifest, as goods to be delivered to the Abbey at Kells. There was nothing really secret about what they would take to the Abbey: five barrels of wine, two barrels of refined olive oil to be used in sacrament for the monks. Also, there were two bundles of fine calfskin, and the latest in bookbinding, five reams of paper made in Lisbon, with a bundle of lambskin parchment.

They were also bringing a gift from the merchants of Lisbon for the Abbey, a small printing press. All this would be loaded into a lorry that would be hoisted off the ship, along with all seven horses. George's wagon of books, along with his personal items, would stay aboard during his tour of Ireland. Four of the horses would be needed to pull the lorry loaded with the goods destined for the Abbey, the other three would be ridden by the Captain, his First mate, and a third rider, the one who would accompany the horses to their destination, the Stable-Master.

The Stable Master, who would act as their trainer once they had arrived, or sort of the three would travel in disguise, where their normal attire would surely give them away. There was nothing, then, out of the ordinary for all these goods to be loaded up at the dock and driven off. Even leaving with all of the horses;. that four of them pulling a wagon would look out of place. The ship was then to cast off and head further north, where it would wait for the Captain and his party for two days in the northern city of Londonderry.

The Captain and the two other riders now take the lorry loaded with goods, making their way through Dublin. The Captain, knowing the city, knew to stay clear of the Archbishop's house on the edge of town. The best thing that they could do was to stay on the main streets and head northwest and do not stop for any reason, that if anyone asked to simply tell them the truth; that we are heading towards the Abbey at Kells carrying the normal supplies to the monks there and try to avoid any and all other priests and clergy; to simply say that you're late and have to press on.

The Captain explains, "Even if we run into the Archbishop himself, though trying hard to avoid him, be sure to wave him off and hurry along, only saying that we should call on him on our way back through town".

Our group really had nothing to do with the Archbishop; not that they wouldn't be invited; to the contrary, they would probably be asked to stay, and then for dinner. But there were questions that they couldn't answer, and really didn't have the time or the where to be, answering any questions right now. His mission at the moment was to see that they all made it back to his ship and see that the cargo and his two other riders made it to Kells Abbey by tonight.

So, looking to dodge all distractions, the three made their way through Dublin, heading West towards Kells, looking for the Navan Road. The Captain had left his uniform and had opted to dress in ordinary attire, the rest of his party, or now donning monk's robes so as not to attract attention, as they were on the road to the Abbey at Kells.

Little did they know, but they had been followed ever since they had left the docks, and the very thing that they thought would keep them safe, had actually given them away. It was the Archbishop's need to control every aspect of life in Dublin that led him to post agents at the docks who would report on who had come or gone. If anything did not look quite right, the agent knew to investigate and dispatch a spy to find out more. Seeing a party coming ashore with Monks in tow would have sent up red flags.

The Archbishop was at odds with the Church of England and especially was against the King's recent addition wanting to revise the church service by including a revised version of his father's Book of Prayer; as it included too many similar traits found in the Catholic Mass and thought that it was done as a way to help convert those that while Catholic wanted to fully support the King.

When it was reported that the Captain and the wagon had no intention of visiting the Archbishop, they were suspected of maybe being from the English Church and followed. Remarkably no one bothered them, and upon finding the Navan Road they headed out of the city, and on towards Kells, not knowing that they were being followed.

The Captain, though, knew about the Archbishop's agents from the various times his ship had made port in Dublin. He had been looking for them since they had docked. He knew that they were there and wanted to see who the agent might send off to follow them. If he could identify the spies behind them on the road to Kells, there was a good chance that they were being followed. Sure enough, the Captain watches as the agent instructs his spies on the dock, but as the agent had many spies, the Captain alone couldn't be relied on to remember all of them; so as they would usually go out in pairs; each member of the landing party would have to remember two or three sets of the agent's spies to hopefully remember as many as they could.

Unfortunately, the agent had talked to nearly a dozen sets of men, where any or all of them could have been the agent's spies. This was too many for just the three of them to remember all of their faces; they would have to think of a different plan to set the agent's spies off of their trail. After much thought, they decided that if they waited at the crossroad and quietly asked; "what road would take them to the abbey" and identify themselves as Catholic Priests. Thus, insuring that they were not taken as members of the Church of England. That would be enough to have the spies give a satisfactory report back to the Archbishop; saying that they intended to stop and visit the Archbishop's house on their way back. So as to relieve the Archbishop, of any fears that he may have; of odd-looking strangers.

Their plan would take little time, as it wasn't long after they had stopped at the crossroad that two men rode up, and were clearly the only other riders that could be seen coming down the road, that they had to be the two spies that they were waiting for. By now, the Captain had changed back into his regular attire and was quite a surprise to the two approaching horsemen to find that he had gotten behind them when they finally caught up with the wagon.

The plan to ask for directions and identify themselves as Priests went well at first, but when the two riders, after identifying themselves and insisting that they return to Dublin to check in with the Bishop, the Captain appears and with both pistols drawn.

The teamster at that moment also brings out from under his monk's robe a blunderbuss loaded with shot. The Captain informed the two that theirs was a race against time to get their shipment to the abbey, unload, and make it back to the ship, where, if time allowed, they would stop in at the Bishops on their way back. At that, the two shadow riders turned back around towards Dublin. The Captain now was satisfied they had put off the Arch-bishop's spies and could make good time reaching the Abbey.

Kells Abbey Ireland

The Confirmation at Kells

Chapter 2

When they reached the Abbey; the monks greeted them with much surprise. The monks had not ordered supplies recently, but when told the shipment had been arranged by the Vatican, they were most pleased and welcomed them in. The Captain and his party were then directed to the Abbey stores; the Captain says he must talk to the Abbot and will send along the lorry driver to arrange for the goods to be unloaded. The Captain, his First mate, and the stable master then dismount their horses, tied them to the lorry, while George and the Captain made their way inside to talk with the Abbot.

"Hello, I'm Abbot McMurray. . . I would like to thank you for your gifts; how can I help you? "

"Abbot McMurray, I am Captain Sandoval of the Portuguese freighter the San Sebastian.

I would like to introduce the Monsignor Cardinal Father Felipe Castillo of Rome, and the Rector of San Lorenzo in Damasio, at the Piazza della Chancelleria in Rome; Father Georgio Cona'eus."

The Abbot, upon hearing this, now looks very surprised: "Please tell me how it is my pleasure to have a visit from a Roman Cardinal, and the English Bishop? . . I was led to believe that San Lorenzo no longer occupied the English college in Rome. It is a extraterritoriality of the Holy See and the office of the Vice Chancellor. . . You are the Vice Chancellor!! "

As the Abbot spoke, the two removed their robes, revealing their black priestly attire that they had been hiding.

"Cardinal, give the Abbot the Papal letter, please." The Monsignor smiles and reaches into his front pocket, and presents a piece of parchment with what appears to be a Vatican seal.

"Abbot McMurray, we bring a communication from the pontiff, Urban the eighth, at which I was present at the time that it had been made. It is an affidavit signed by the Pope acknowledging the statements made by O'Neil of Tyrone before he died.

"Is it so now, about O'Neil you say? Have you read it then?"

"Oh no, noone has read it yet, it is for you; you can see the Vatican seal is intact."

"Yes, I can see that; the seal looks too beautiful to break, wouldn't you agree?"

"Here, give it to me." George takes the parchment, and with one quick stroke of his knife, one that he kept in one of his tall stockings, he opens the letter, leaving the seal intact, and quickly hands the message back.

"After years of working in Rome, opening a letter becomes second-hand. Leaving the seal intact, so it looks as though no one has touched it, is a slightly more difficult task."

"So, . have you read it?"

"Of course not; it is addressed to you!"

"Father Cona'eus is one who is highly regarded and a well-respected secretary, that of the Pontiff's Nephew, the Cardinal Barbini.

"For the sake of our lord, open the thing, we have carried it across the seas to give it to you; please don't leave us any longer in suspense."

The Earl of Tyrone was one of the Earls who had fled Ireland thirty-one years ago. King James I had made arrangements to lure the Earls away and open the door for the arranged settlements in Northern Ireland. King James, knowing that his royal predecessor, Queen Elizabeth, was on her deathbed, had sent emissaries of the Queen, who were now secretly working on behalf of James, to negotiate with the Earls.

It seems that for years, the Kings of Scotland had been negotiating over what they felt was their right of guardianship. In Ireland, questions persisted as to the right of guardianship, since proper coronation had never been performed, and the King had not been presented before the Stone. This had also been true with James VI before his ascension to the throne of England.

But now, for King James, the tide had changed, and it was thought that now his right to guardianship could not be denied. Though in the past negotiations with the Earls, his requests were rejected, he was now in a better position to offer a substantial reward for their cooperation. So, James, knowing that he would soon take ascension to the English Crown, was able to now deal, although somewhat indirectly with the Earl of Tyrone, and chief of the McDonald clan; arranging what appeared to be an exchange of power between the two, and that would form a grand alliance between Ireland and the West Coast of Scotland.

In reality, it was nothing of the sort, and more collusion on the part of King James to take control of Northern Ireland. Every indication pointed to the holy relics being hidden away in that northeast upper section of Ireland.

St. Columba was known for having turned down his right to be King to pursue his priestly endeavors, but had not given up his position of Guardian, and was known to have possessed the relics. He had taken great lengths to fortify the city of Derry and to build a church there before leaving Ireland. Next, he went on to build a settlement among the Western Islands of Scotland and build a monastery on the Isle of Iona.

What exactly he had done with the holy relics is not known, guardianship being retained there in Ireland. The Irish Clans, those of the Earl of Tyrone, and the MacDonalds of the Isles, were related by blood and were cousins. Their relationship was estranged, mainly because of not wanting to share control and power over the territory. King James, knowing this, used this to his advantage. It was easy enough for the crown to simply take charge of a small island off of the Isle of Atoll and offer it up in exchange as what was to appear as an attempt to unify both families or clans. In truth, all that was promised was a position that would include a land title central to the McDonald's holdings along the West Coast.

The Earls, believing that the arrangement had been made through an agreement between Elizabeth and the Highland Lords, made such a deal attractive. But when Elizabeth had died, and James VI was now the first of England, he started moving in and setting up plantations of Scotch-Irish in Antrim and County Down,

O'Neil realized what they had done and what could have been considered as abandoning the northern territories, in which he would be obliged to also have handed over the guardianship. So instead, O'Neil sought his only alternative, that's to establish a so-called leave of absence, and fled to Rome. And as long as he stayed in Rome, the guardianship was not obliged to be forfeited. And so, O'Neil officially retained the guardianship while he was a guest of the Vatican in Rome. O'Neil would stay there until the day he died and had made arrangements that when he did so, the guardianship would pass to the next appropriate recipient of the title.

O'Neil knew, of course, who would next be in line with the McDonald's regaining a stronghold at Dune Luce Castle. The only question was whether they had kept the inherited line intact. Of course, only the Abbot of Kells knew for sure, for it was one of their jobs at the Abbey to keep track, in accordance to the prophecy that was given many years ago.

The McDonald's had built a little too close to the cliff's edge, and their castle fell off into the ocean. The McDonalds would nonetheless have an abrupt calling to return to Scotland when their Clansmen there took up arms against the King.

In or around 350 A.D., the High King of Ireland was said to have done a jig upon the Stone, whereas a prophecy was given of a dynasty of future Kings. This event would eventually call the name or one of the names used to identify the stone as "The Stone of Destiny or Destiny Stone". This destiny was said to have been recorded by Columba inside both the front and back book covers of a transcribed record of Gospels he had done.

This book was very precious and traveled with Columba as he made his way to the East Coast of Scotland, to the Abbey outcropping of Lindisfarne; a common spot for the Vikings to raid. It is said that during one such raid, the book covers, which had been by this time heavily adorned in gold and jewels, were ripped from the text and taken as booty by the Viking Raiders.

The gospel text, though, remained, and eventually made its way back to Kells Abbey, where it gets its name, "The Book of Kells". The common opinion is that Columba had written the Gospels there at Kells, but then there are those who believe that it had been produced earlier when Columba had visited the Abbey at Lindisfarne. Somehow though, whether it was from the original text, having been produced at Kells, or a copy of the dynasty prophecy that had been given to the Abbey by Columba; the Abbot there, whose job it was to keep track of the guardianship, knew.

The Abbot, given the communication, looked at the papal seal with amazement. "I wonder, what it is that could be so important a communication that it is hand delivered by no less than a Cardinal and a Bishop."

The Abbot takes the communication and slowly walks to his desk and sits. "Please gentlemen, have a seat. I have the strangest feeling that this communication has something to do with your mission. And one that has taken you so far from the Vatican, in Rome."

As the two messengers find their seats, the Abbot has now carefully opened the letter and has unfolded it, and now has begun to read. As he reads, about halfway through, he seems to pause and glance up at George, only momentarily, as he continues to read the communication. The Abbot finishes reading and leans back in his chair and looks up into the ceiling of his office, pondering or questioning what he had just read. He puts down the communication on his desk and now as to pause, looking at the Monsignor again, and then to George, while with his right hand he rubs his upper lip; while all along looking quite amazed.

"Gentlemen, I am all too pleased to be of such service to our Pope and will try to do all that he requests. You know of course that the Guardianship will be challenged by all those who think they have a claim and will try to discredit its recipient. It has been known to have happened time and time again once the transfer of guardianship happens. But it seems that the communication is quite clear and that the Earl, before his death, had communicated its transfer to the Pope. They were both able to confirm the recipient, which I guess is George here. Well, you're at the right place, and I will start transcribing the transfer and confirmation of guardianship immediately.

"As for the relics I'm afraid I can't be as much help there, of course, the harp had been long agreed to stay in Ireland, as for the rest as far as I know, or as much as I know, they were in charge of Columba, and you will have to visit the Monsignor Columba's church in the fortified city of Derry, where I could only speculate they are there, only they could have been taken on by Columba to Iona, and somewhere there on the island.

"Anyway, I only keep track of the Guardian, where the actual relics are, you will have to speak to the Monsignor.

"My hunch, though, is that they were on Iona, as there was much to do, as to leave the harp in Ireland. So, Ireland has the harp, Scotland or England has the stone, this much I know, as to the rest of the relics I do not."

George then blesses both the Abbot and the Monsignor, "May the Lord bless you and keep you. May the Lord make his face shine upon you and be gracious to you. May the Lord lift up his countenance upon you and give you peace."

The Abbot now arranged for their lodging. They would be able to clean up and dust off the dirt of the day's travel. Meanwhile, a meal was prepared for their dinner, where the conversation would be centered on the situation in Northern Ireland. The Monsignor asked how they felt about the new settlements. None of the other monks knew about their true mission, only that they were concerned as to how safe it would be to travel in the Protestant areas of the North, and whether they would find much loyalty towards The Stewart Kings up there.

The Abbot assured his visitors that they would find overwhelming support for the King, being either Protestant or Catholic in their beliefs. There wasn't much faith in James's forces that would make them believe that anything would be made better, only that if King Charles's forces prevailed, they could expect more taxes while losing control of their lands. George, though, knew better, insisting that Charles, like his father, would reward Ireland; bringing them a better life of wealth and prosperity in a country unified under God.

When they had finished dinner, the guests found their way to the rooms the Abbot had arranged for them. After a good night's rest and a hearty breakfast, the horses were hitched back up to the wagon, and the group set off towards the northern provinces. Just as they had set off from the Abbey, they came across three mounted knights. The Knights greeted them and told them that they would be their guides to the North and that even though there was an overwhelming support for the King, tensions were high among the Protestants and Catholic regulars.

The Knights said that the Abbot felt that it would be in the best interest to have more of an escort if they were to venture into the northern provinces. They said that they would travel Northeast, to Monea, where a fellow Scotsman, Malcolm Hamilton, had recently constructed a stronghold which would allow for a comfortable night's stay, before heading further north.

Hamilton, the rector of Devenish, an alumnus of Scots College in France, was well known as a supporter of the Stewarts, who had always been patrons of the college. Upon hearing this, George, traveling in the group, seemed very pleased, saying, "Hamilton, I know him well; it will be good to see him again."

Just a day's journey and a short distance from the town of Monea was the fortress that Hamilton had recently constructed. Previously a castle stronghold of the Maguires, it had been taken during the recent conflicts and has now been re-fortified and taken over by Hamilton. When they arrived, the two Scots immediately embraced with joy, having been reunited after so many years.

There was much to talk about, as to how their lives had changed since attending Scots College. George, it seems, had gone on to Paris, where the college had another branch, and he had written a biography of Mary Queen of Scots, published in 1625.

He had also met the young Prince Charles on route to Spain with his friend Buckingham; the Prince traveling to Spain in hopes of marrying the Infanta Maria, daughter of Phillip III. Born in 1602 at the San Lorenzo de El Escorial palace, northeast of the King's royal palace in Madrid. Maria, just nineteen at the time, would go on to marry King Ferdinand of Hungary-Bohemia.

He would later be crowned Holy Roman Emperor, making Maria Empress and the sovereign Queen. George spoke of an instance at the French court, where he had introduced the Prince to one of his patrons, Henrietta Maria, and he thought that they had good feelings towards one another. And was pleased when things hadn't gone well in Spain, the Prince would later choose Henrietta to be his bride.

George also wrote of the Scottish royal court, and about the ascension of Scottish Kings, and the divine right of rulership. He said that he had supported James I, in his cause, and that both himself and King Charles persist in the effort, that was really started long ago, by Charles' great grandfather King James IV. 10 years after Sinclair's effort in Roslyn, the King would build his own rendition of Solomon's Temple at what would become King's College in Aberdeen.

For years, the Papal authority had considered Scotland as a special daughter of the church, this after having been reconciled through the Declaration of Arbroath. Having such an arrangement, James IV would build his chapel at King's College in Aberdeen under a Papal bull. His great-grandson Charles I was aligned in this effort, raised as a ward of Alexander Seton at Fyvie Castle, where George Conn had also been a ward.

And it was to be the next stop before they would meet back up with the ship, they would visit John Leslie at his stronghold overlooking Rohoe Cathedral, the site of a sixth-century monastery, superior to the monastery founded by Columba on the Isle of Iona.

After a night's rest and a hearty breakfast, the newly installed Guardian and his troop, along with the two escorts they had picked up outside of Kells, continued North towards Derry.

The escorts had given warnings of traveling in the northern area; tensions were still high since the earlier uprising, which led to the flight of the Earls and the settling of the plantations by James I. The escorts thought it best to skirt the northern boundary and avoid conflict. Leslie's Castle in Rohoe was newly constructed and not more than 30 miles outside of Derry, and only a short distance from Locke Foyle, where the ship had been positioned in wait for the men and the horses to return. It was almost dusk when the group had finally made their way to Leslie's Castle.

The Cathedral of Rohoe Ireland Known as the smallest Cathedral city in Europe. Named for the Abbott of Iona; St Eunan's was the mother church of the Abbey on the Scottish island of Iona.

The Search for the Relics Begin

Chapter 3

The Leslie family, one of the most prominent of Scottish families, and trusted by the King, Leslie had held many positions at court, even to oversee the Royal coffers, holding the purse strings of the Royal treasury. They had been major benefactors and patrons to the city of Aberdeen, King's College, and also to Scots College in Dubai, and Paris France.

Both King Charles and George had been wards of the Leslie's as boys growing up at Fyvie Castle. James Leslie, still in service of the King, had only recently come over to settle in the northern plantations, building his stronghold, adjacent to the Cathedral city of Rohoe, the site of the sixth-century monastery. As the group arrived, Leslie came out to meet them, saying how he had been awaiting their arrival and was pleased to see that they had arrived safely before dark.

The group was ushered in, as for their horses, Leslie had them taken to his stables to be cared for. Leslie quickly escorts the two into his library, where they can have a formal greeting and a toast to a good friendship.

Leslie says that he had received a most secret message from King Charles. "Only two days ago, the king informed me of the passing of the Guardianship. He did not say who it was to be, and I'm not sure that he even knows. I can say that I am most pleased to see that he now stands before me. As the Monsignor, whom I don't perceive as being a Scott, I therefore believe that it must be you, my old friend from France, and the good family of the Aberdeenshire.

"It has been many years since we last talked in Paris. I have read and cherished the works that you have done about Scottish history and the life of Mary Queen of Scots. Her son James, I knew well; as well as his son, too; whom I hold most close to heart; King Charles had let me know of his dealings with the Earls, and the plans of his father, and grandfather, to restore the greater monarchy of Scotland.

"You did have Hamilton, witness the Abbot's decree? I shall want to assign to that, as a witness also, right away. I know that King Charles would like you to bring back what relics you can find that would enhance the new monarchy. It might have been your thought to search in Derry?"

The Monsignor answers, "We both had talked to the Abbott at Kells about what relics do exist. He had told us that he did not know where they would be, but the knowledge of such was held by the Rector of Columba's church in Derry."

Leslie adds, "It must've slipped the poor Abbot's mind, that Columba's church is no more, it was literally taken apart piece by piece, searched by every stone. Phillips, you may know, was commissioned by the King to fortify the city of Derry, and used the stones in reinforcing the old city's ramparts. Church records, documents, along with any artifacts that were there, were taken with all of the vestments and transferred to the Cathedral here in Rohoe. I had informed the abbots there if he could make himself available upon your arrival, if you wish, I will send for him now."

"Very well indeed."

"Great, then, we will have another guest for dinner."

The Abbott is a very knowledgeable man, having served in the crusade, after which he sponsored education, and he decided to join the church. It would definitely be in your interest to quiz the Abbott on relics that may still be here in Ireland. In Sir Thomas Phillips' employ, a Thomas and Robert, George, were you aware?"

"My uncles, no, I would have thought, they would be back working with their father, the deputy sheriff in Aberdeen, you say that they were there when Columba's church was dismantled and searched? I would certainly like to know just what they found."

"I believe they found nothing, but you can ask them yourself in the morning. I have arranged for them to act as your escorts through to the end of your visit, and to see that you get back to the ship and are on your way." "How great, thank you, it has been years since I had seen them last."

The Abbott from the neighboring Cathedral now arrives at the library, greeting Leslie, and seeming pleased about having been invited to dine with them this evening. The Abbott curiously asks, "Is it true that you both have traveled here from Rome?

What business have you here now in such a turbulent state of events that seems only to get worse, not far from here in the North? I don't understand, what could be in the King's interest involving Vatican secretaries?"

"Abbott, you know that the church has considered Scotland as a special daughter; going back to the Declaration of Arbroath, the Vatican has seen to side with the Scottish interest. These two distinguished clergymen are also here in regard to Scottish affairs. It seems that the Earl O'Neil has passed in Rome, and has now passed the guardianship, to hence, we now have before us, the new Guardian."

"Glory be to God, this is something great, not just for Scotland, but for mankind as well."

"Well then, gentlemen, it seems as though our meal has been set in the hall. Let us go now, and enjoy some refreshment as we continue our conversation."

As the four make their way into the Grand Hall where an evening meal had been laid out, the Abbott seems full of joy, to be taken in, and the thought of sharing meaningful conversation with a fellow clergyman who had come all the way from the Vatican to visit. "So, tell me, George, what does the new Guardian of Scotland want from me?"

"The King has made an appointment in his court for my presence, and he would like to have me bring back a relic to show a legitimacy and right of guardianship".

"Sinclair of Roslyn once related a story of the crusaders who were sent searching the Temple Mount for relics. Not being able to find much, they asked an old Greek cleric what had happened with the relics of the Temple. He said, the greatest relic, the

English already possess, and that most other relics of the Temple were lost when sacked by the Babylonians. Then, after their release from their captivity for some 40 or more years, they returned to rebuild what they had lost.

"The King of Babylon wanted to destroy the culture of the Jews; he killed the King and his sons, and all the priests sacked the Temple and took whatever relics remained. After years of captivity, the tribes of Israel returned to Jerusalem and set about rebuilding their Temple. But they had nothing, all the holy relics had been taken, and the high priests killed, and that lineage destroyed. So they developed the Sanhedrin, a chosen group of elders, who would take the place of the priests that they had lost. They also chose to replicate the one relic that they thought would work in part of their worship in the Temple. The old Greek cleric, whom Sinclair had mentioned, had said, "Find the key, the key, find the key.

"At first, it was thought to be some type of metaphysical reference, as perhaps an answer to a question, but then, what if it was in reference to a physical object. There is a reference to early rituals of the Second Temple, and how the priests would light incense of frankincense and myrrh, using a vessel suspended by chains from the ceiling. This incense burner could be raised or lowered over the congregation. This was the relic that the builders of the Second Temple chose to replicate to be used in their service. It is called a Thurible, and is used by many of the Judeo-Christian houses of worship.

"The original example that was used in the First Temple was the altar incense, positioned just outside the holy of holies, lit to invoke a portal to the heavens. The special Thurible used inside the Holy of Holies went by the name: The key of Solomon or

Solomon's key. This gentleman is what I believe the old Greek cleric from Jerusalem was trying to tell of, and it was thought to have been the original of the First Temple.

"And this is why the clerk wanted the Temple Knight to seek out the key; there from under the Temple Mount. But of course, we know that the Babylonian invaders who had sacked the Temple had carried off what relics they could find. Strange though, how it is expressed in the Gospels, that after the fall of the First Temple, that Jeremiah was in possession of the Ark, we can surmise that before the Babylonians arrived, there were relics that were taken from the Temple to be saved. And so this brings us to the Jacob Stone, and its appearance in Ireland shortly after the first Temple was destroyed. Thus, hence the Guardianship is the protector of the relics that arrived along with the stone."

The Monsignor asks, "So yes, this much has been surmised, only that a reference to the key, and that the existence of a Thurible as a relic was not known, is there any reference to an incense burner of record at St. Columba's church in Derry?"

The Abbott responds, "Not specifically, but there were items that were requested by the Abbey on Iona, to be sent to be used in the funeral Chapel; that is adjacent to the Abbey. When they recently went through the church there in Derry, most church records were directed to here, and such requests from the Abbey of Iona were sent here also, as this Abbey is father to the Abbey built there on the Isle of Iona. I'm sure that you are aware that for hundreds of years, the Scottish Kings and that of the Isles, are interred there, adjacent to the Abbey and the funeral Chapel.

"It's my guess, though, and I don't know for sure, that any relics are there. Stories abound of how, as Kings, their reign had been consecrated upon the Stone, and upon their death, done also. Stories talk of a funeral service where the Stone would be set as an altar, of course, this hasn't taken place in many years, since the Stone had been taken to London. In many ways, Richard Lionheart must've gotten word, during the crusade, deciding he was going to have a holy relic after all, and so he built a great throne and encased the stone, but interestingly never seemed to want to sit upon it. You must therefore go on to the Isle of Iona, I will send with you my decree, saying that you are the Guardian, and have all rights to whatever relics that are there.

"Not far from the monastery, you will find the small funeral Chapel of St. Orrin. Originally, the Chapel was built by Saint Columba himself, in honor of his predecessor. It is said that this is where the Stone of Jacob was housed and kept there to be used in part of the funeral service. The Stone would be taken and used in the formal coronation ceremony, but would be returned to the Chapel. Later, the Chapel was rebuilt by Somerled, who is himself buried there alongside no less than 60 other Kings; 48 of whom were Scottish, eight Norwegian, and four French.

"The Chapel is very nondescript, only having a small ornate Cove where The Stone was set. Used as an altar, and along with the incense burner, Key of Solomon, this would facilitate the fallen one's soul into heaven, and summon Jacob's ladder, opening the portal to heaven. Whether or not the Key of Solomon is still there at the Chapel, I do not know. But as Guardian, you will have the Right of Ownership if it is found.

"Tomorrow, as you head north towards your awaiting ship, you will be heading into the northern plantation territory.

Be on your guard, I am sending with you an escort that I am sure will help you to your destination safely, as your two previous escorts have returned south."

The group awoke that morning, and as to be prepared for any trouble that may arise on their way north, it was decided to now go in more normal attire, so as not to draw any adverse attention. They had all gathered in the Great Hall before breakfast and stood before a great fireplace. Leslie appears with two knights, the two escorts who would lead the group North to meet the awaiting ship that would take them to the Isle of Iona in Scotland.

"I hope that you all slept well," Leslie asks. "And are ready for a fine breakfast, as it will be soon set before us. To my pleasure, let me introduce you to your two escorts, of whom I know will be a rejoiceful reunion. George, your two uncles, Thomas and Robert, who have been in service to the King, working with Sir Thomas Phillips; with your Uncle Thomas, acting as his armed servitude."

At once, George happily embraces his two uncles; "It has been a very long time since I've seen you two, I am so very pleased. I am assured that we shall not have trouble on our journey North. What have you two been doing with Sir Thomas?"

Thomas then quickly answers, "Sir Thomas has been commissioned by the King to fortify the city of Derry, of which has been financed by London merchants, a stronghold to serve the plantation, and a place of refuge in case of trouble. We have heard that you had taken favor with King James, and now with Charles. We've also heard of your commission in Rome, strange bedfellows, and what could be considered a dangerous alliance, even treasonous by the parliamentarians and by those in London."

Robert adds; "Cromwell is anxious to seize control, here in Ireland, the Irish, who didn't much like the Scottish plantation settlers have even, much more hatred of the English, I feel that soon Ireland, and especially the plantations to the North will become a powder keg and could be set to go off at any time."

"I think it would be wise", the Captain comments. "If we left the wagon here and continued by horseback, we could make better time and attract a lot less attention. We can have a couple of teamsters to attend the wagon and bring it to the encampment we have set up. Also, I think it's well advised that we stay clear of plantation settlements, the best we can, for the rest of our journey here in Ireland. We will stable the horses for a couple of days of rest, just this side of Greencastle, while we wait for our ship to arrive."

The next morning, they said their goodbyes to Leslie and, with the horses, headed north towards Greencastle. The escorts, now not having to look after a wagon and cargo, keep with the group as they make their way. The escort, George's two Uncles, are very interested in what their Nephew had been doing, and now felt free to ask about his life spent on the continent.

"Sir Thomas has a nice collection of your manuscripts done in Paris," Comments Thomas. "He says that King James and King Charles have a great interest in your writing. I, too, have had the chance to review some of your work and find it remarkable, and it is no wonder why the Stewarts have such an interest."

"King James had known of my study concerning the life of his mother, Queen Mary. I was very much engaged in correspondence with the King, who helped me to clarify many issues I hadn't questioned about her life, both in Scotland and France, and her relationship with that of her stepsister, Elizabeth of England. But it was the work of his great-grandfather that interests me the most, and the ambition that he had to bring about traditional belief and history of the clans, the formation of the Dalriada and the early Alban Empire."

Robert says, "I can see how there might have been an inspiration in your other works; which detailed the ascension of the Scottish Kings."

George then replies: "James then insisted that his son have detailed knowledge, and it was arranged through the King's invitation that he visit me in Paris, France, where my latest works were published, and receive copies of the history of his grandmother.

"It was brilliant to see Charles again after so many years, and remember the times spent at the Leslie's Castle at Fyvie; close to the Templar hamlet of Turriff. When I saw him then, he had made the appearance as if to have gone off looking for a wife, although now, he had preferred to be in the company of his chief advisor, his father's dear friend, George Villiers; the first Duke of Buckingham. Though while at Court in Paris, I did introduce them to one of my loveliest supporters, the beautiful Henrietta, who would soon become his queen, and is more or less responsible for me being here, and my quest in England.

"Charles though, was not hard to convince, but could not say so in court. The church, I mean those in Rome, are somewhat indifferent, due to the state of the English college there, but then having an altogether different opinion on Scotland. Charles very much liked what literature I had published in France, and was intent on collecting what volumes else that he could find on the continent, to take back to London. Such is a confidence he has given to the Archbishop, that allowed, now seems to finance through the University at Oxford, a grand new library. I too, hope to contribute to the shelves of such a library in the future."

The group, now approaching the Foyle Inland Sea, could start smelling the ocean breeze as they got closer to Greencastle. From across the sound, they could see Londonderry with its fortified docks and trade guild. The bay, though quite foggy, showed Londonderry and its shipping activity relatively quiet, though we imagine quite a center of activity at the time.

And so, this was the time that, naturally, the troop could move gingerly north without drawing suspicion, hurrying towards Greencastle, to get there before dark. Actually, they did not have too much further to go; to a place where they could stable the horses, and they could all rest awhile as the ship would load-up on the supplies they would need to take them on to their destination. I was good to have the horses on dry-land after the long voyage from Portugal, and give them some time to recover before taking the last voyage over to England.

These horses were, actually, of excellent stock; Portuguese, Spanish warhorses, raised outside of Granada, and a gift of the Spanish King. The horses would now need a nice rest before going on to England and being presented to King Charles. Although not exactly what King Charles really had wanted to bargain for while on his visit there with his adversary, Buckingham.

As the group makes their way up to the North, along the bay of the Foyle, they finally see the harbor lights projecting through the fog in front of them, the small harbor town of Greencastle, in the distance. George, speaking somewhat under his breath to his uncle's remarks; "By the way, uncles, as we approach Greencastle, and our ship, I am now assuming the alias, of the stable master, I traveled in secret till I reach Iona, and then not till I meet up again with my friend King Charles."

As the group now approaches Greencastle, on The Main Rd.., Thomas and Robert now ride ahead and soon return in the company of six mounts.

"We now turn towards inland and have a camp, where stables have been arranged. Hurry quickly as we turn up promptly; I have six loyal to King Charles, who will block our exit off the main road and ensure that we have not been followed."

The whole group then gallops off on the main road towards their camp. As they reach the designated intersection to the West, inland, they veer off and charge up and over a small pasture as the light of the day diminishes, and their camp for the night awaits. Thereupon the pasture in the hills above Greencastle, there had been constructed a camp composed of five wooden buildings, comprised of a blacksmith shop and shed, a barn, a cook shed, and one arranged for the comfort of six travelers, who by now had become the best of friends. George and his uncles would soon have to say goodbye, as their Nephew left by ship, on his way to England. There he would find his friends, King Charles and his queen Henrietta.

The camp had been constructed, though hastily, had a look as though it belonged, and had always been there. Inside the camp, the group now came upon 50 more men loyal to the King, who would now, until the time that they would again board the ship, guard over the group and provide their protection.

"This is quite the reception." George remarks to his uncles, "I do hope we haven't missed dinner".

Uncle Thomas replies, "George, it's all the courtesy of St. Thomas Phillips."

"And these are all your men," George asks?

"Yes George, these are all of our men. We are both the servitors of lord Phillips, and as such, all of these men work for us; and are completely loyal and trustworthy."

Thomas replies, "Loyal, to me and, to the King; thanks to Sir Thomas Phillips, and his efforts here in Ireland."

George asks, "What, if anything, do you hear about my brother, Patrick? I've been constantly traveling, it seems, for so long, I haven't been able to keep in touch with them. Is he still working with his father?"

Thomas answers, "We thought you knew; He's the sheriff's deputy of Aberdeen. The High Constable made him Commissioner to the Earl of Erroll. And our brother Francis is back in Scotland; Titles restored at that."

George: "So Francis and Patrick made it back from France. I was worried that there would be trouble when they returned; I guess I worried over nothing."

The Captain then comments; "It would not be good for those on the other side of the sound, to know of what documents and the nature of the correspondence you carry. You have; signed letters from two abbots, two magistrates, and a written introduction from the Vatican;... the Pope no less; and in the company of their constables. All of which would raise a certain amount of suspicion, and our mission questioned. So, the men though, know you only as "stable master". Although the men are not likely to question your uncle Thomas."

As the horses made their way to the stables, the group found their newly constructed quarters. With Thomas's men, now stationed about the camp, the four travelers could relax and look forward to an evening meal and quiet rest.

The horses could now also rest, be fed, and put up and stables for the night. Beyond the stables were some of the finest pastures of grassland in that part of Ireland. The horses had been raised in the hills of southern Spain; in the upper meadows where there was always an abundance of fresh green grass. The smell of green grass, after so much time abord ship, made the horses a bit uneasy, but still eager to hit the stalls and be brushed and put up for the night, a place for the horses to recuperate before continuing on their journey aboard ship; a journey that had taken them from the far coast of Spain, through to the Atlantic seacoast of Portugal, across the Spanish Main to the coast of Ireland.

In fact, they were but halfway home, and still had a long way to go, to where their journey would end. For they had a new life awaiting them at the royal court in England. George and his fellow travelers, relaxing a while in their smartly constructed quarters; after a few drinks of refreshing ale, arranged for their enjoyment, the new group of friends sent for their food.

Thomas stood up, raised his glass, and said, "We shall find it all safe and comfortable here, now till you board the ship. Let us now, all share a meal, I with my good brother, and nephew George, The Stable Master, I wish the rest of your journey to be safe and hold to the King, our good friend Charles I".

As the day ended, and the group of friends shared a fine meal, the horses too were to be attended. That night, the horses would be watered, fed, and groomed, and put up for the night in stables. The next morning, the horses would be again brushed and groomed, and a blacksmith would service their shoes and see to their needs.

Robert would take the captain down to the wharf at Greencastle to make arrangements for the ship to make port there, later that week, after the horses had time to rest.

The next day, the captain and Thomas traveled to the docks at Londonderry to send the message to the merchant Fleet Adm. saying that they were ready to again board ship and make their way across to the Scottish Isle of Iona. The wharf along the fortified city walls were busy, and it did not take the Captain long to find an advocate to relay the message. Still, it might be a week or so before the admiral's ship will arrive at Greencastle, but it would provide ample time for the horses to rest before traveling on to England.

There were also supplies to be arranged for, provisions for both the ship's company and their cargo of horses. The merchant ship that had brought them to Ireland still had some of the provisions that were intended as gifts to the Abbey, these had to be unloaded at Greencastle, to be put aboard the admiral's flagship when it had arrived. As the group waited for the admiral's ship, there was time for the uncles and their nephew to talk about what had taken place in the plantation settlements, and what they might find on the Isle of Iona.

"We did find one particularly odd feature," Thomas says. "Going through the old church at Derry, there appeared to have been a small side chapel that would have been facing the cemetery. We think that it was a funeral Chapel which has described would seem similar to what would be found at Iona."

Inside, it was unadorned except that on one side, there was a place where there could have been an altarpiece, except there was none, only a small pillar in its center about 3 feet in height. We thought that this could have been a podium and a place where funeral rites were given, only it was too short in stature. We came to the conclusion that it must've been a support pillar for the Destiny Stone when used during the funeral ceremony. There was also an underground crypt, which allowed an entry from each side, to allow for a procession of mourners to enter and exit, as the deceased had been laid in state, prior to the formal ceremony that would've been held above."

George asks, "And you saw nothing strange or what you thought to be out of the ordinary?"

Thomas replies, "The only thing that I felt was strange was that back above the area that we presumed to have functioned as the upper altar place, there was the symbol of David, the six-sided star carved into the stone wall."

"Was this a large carving?, "asks George.

"No, and almost unassuming, only about 18 inches across, and thereabouts in height."

"Well, that would not be so strange, taking into account the ties that are connected to the tribe of Judah and that of Israel, and that we suppose a connection with the ancient High Kings. This would also greatly support the notion that the Stone of Destiny was definitely used during the funeral ceremony. It is just these traditions that King Charles, and also his predecessors, his father, grandfather, and great-grandfather, were trying to resurrect and to be realigned with God's will, and his Kingdom arrangement on earth."

Of course, the tribes, after their captivity in Babylon, tried their best to do the same. Those, though, found upon their return to Jerusalem, that for them to resurrect the traditions of the Temple and Kingdom would not be so simple. Not only have they lost the Temple to destruction, but the Temple hierarchy, their High Priests, the lineage that had been promised by God to remain in service to God, and the Temple were gone. The Babylonians had not only wanted to destroy the Temple, but also the culture of the early Hebrew tribes.

What they did not know, is that God had made arrangements to Jeremiah, to reestablish, thru the seed of Judah, a sanctuary, where the seed could flourish, In this way, God kept his promise that he had made to the earlier generations, that his servants would receive his help and protection, through time eternal.

Three days have passed, and Thomas is now returning from the docks at Londonderry with news that the Admiral's flagship has left the port of Dublin, and within a day's time will reach the Foyle and the port city of Greencastle. The merchant's vessel had a day ago, unloaded its cargo at the Greencastle docks, and arrangements were made to have freshwater, hay for the horses, and also eight sheep, some to be used as provisions, but the majority to be presented as gifts to the King's kitchen when they arrived in England.

With everything in place, and the site of the admiral's ship now making its way towards the deep water port of Greencastle, it was time for George, who was once more masquerading as the stable master, to say goodbye to his Uncles.

Thomas now reluctantly says goodbye; "Good luck and Godspeed, nephew, and our best regards to King Charles and his efforts for greater Britain. Please let us know about any news you get from our father in Spain."

Robert then adds, "I hope that it won't be long until the situation here in Ireland allows for you to return, have a safe journey to England, and may the Angels look after you and keep you safe."

Iona Abbey Scotland

On to the Isle of Iona

Chapter 4

The Admiral's ship was able to dock in deep water, allowing for all the provisions to be loaded straight away, along with the horses and sheep. With good weather, they would make their way to Iona within a day and be dining at the Abbey that night. Iona being a small island, with no Deep-water Port, the Admiral's ship would have to lay anchor offshore during the stop.

The short trip over into Scotland made George reminisce about his childhood and what he could remember; it seemed so long ago. There would be some goods to come ashore: two small casks of wine, and olive oil, two reams of fine sheepskin vellum, and a bundle of finely tanned calfskin. They also brought three sheep to make as a gift to the Abbey. The Abbey had not been notified, and not knowing the situation ashore, they would have to approach with caution, Cromwell's parliamentarians were about and there was always a question as to who were loyal to the King, or who had taken up sides with the English Parliament and the forces under Cromwell. No doubt, that he would have informers placed about the Isles of the Highlands, and the mainland of Scotland.

A monk's robe might have worked well here in Ireland and not attracted too much attention, but England would be another story. The sad truth was if they were caught after setting foot in England, they both could be killed. George would have to carefully hide anything that might give him away. Of course, George had planned for just this weave of deception. There were many things that could give him away; items that taken alone seemed quite innocent, but seen together could mean his life. His robes and slippers, along with his stoles that now wrapped around as a belt for the robes, would be packed together with a pair of Scottish English pajamas, where he would do his best to hide as much as he could in plain sight.

Scotland who had officially sworn their allegiance to the Protestant Reformation that had engulfed much of Europe, and England, there were still a few powerful families in Scotland, that had remained faithful to the old traditional religious values, and even though the King was professed adherent to the Protestant factor, there was a feeling that he was still sympathetic to the old religion, and the old families of power in Scotland. Most knew that the new Queen was a practicing Catholic; in line with the King's sympathetic feeling, and given this fact, the King could set aside religious differences and give consideration to those families of the Highlands who had for centuries retained some control in Scotland. The Admiral's ship was now stationed offshore, where they could see the lights of the Abbey, for the sun was just setting upon the Western horizon.

The Captain, the Monsignor, and George were now ferried across towards the island in one of the ship's longboats, towing an additional one behind loaded with provisions to be given as gifts to the Abbey. As they made shore, they noticed the outline of what appeared to be three monks, in light-colored robes, one of whom held a lantern and swung it back and forth slightly, as to signal where the longboats should come ashore.

As the boats pulled to shore, they were helped by two of the robed monks, both longboats being pulled up to the shoreline, the one monk, who had been holding the lantern, now turned and raised the lantern to signal inland.

The Captain tells the others, "Be on your guard; we don't know who they are yet, better to know that they're from the abbey first, after all, they could be anyone."

George asks, "Should I quiz their skills, their biblical knowledge?"

"I presume I will know, when close to them; I've been here several times, and they should know me. I've noticed that all the monks have a familiar smell about them. Must be the soap that they use." With that, the monk standing next to the one who held the lantern spoke: "I am Father Carmichael. We have signaled your arrival, bringing supplies, whereas some of the brothers will bring a cart to convey your luggage and supplies up to the Abbey. Now, if your party, will please follow me, I will take you to see the Abbott."

George asks; "That would be Father Michael, of course?"

"No, it's Father O'Reilly

The Captain responds, "Of course it is. You remember what Father Leslie said; Father Michael is at Derry, and that Leslie had sent us here instead."

As the group now made their way up to the Abbey, they could see more of a commotion, as the windows and doorways of the Abbey started to light up. As they approached the bank of the shoreline, they stopped for just a moment as Father Carmichael instructed a group of monks, who were on their way back down to the boats with a cart, to retrieve the luggage and supplies and to bring them to the center courtyard where they could be received. The group now made their way up to a small set of buildings, and churchyard, and led into a house opposite the Chapel.

Inside was the Abbott, Father O'Reilly; " I have been told that you bring supplies, we have not ordered any, and this seems a strange time in the evening to be bringing such. What may I ask, is your mission here?"

The Captain replies, "We bring letters for the Abbott, and some supplies, gifts to the Abbey. We bring greetings from Ireland from James Leslie, as he too has written a correspondence to be given to you, Father O'Reilly."

And at that, the two clergymen remove their robes, revealing their priestly attire.

"Abbott, Father O'Reilly, I am Captain Sandoval of the Portuguese freighter the San Sebastian. I would like to introduce the Monsignor Father Felipe Castillo of Rome, and Rector of the de facto English College, Father Georgio Cona'eus, Canon of San Lorenzo in Damaso at the Piazza della Cancellara in Rome.

"Father Cona'eus, I know of you and have read several things that you had published in France, I wasn't aware that the English college in Rome was active, but I am pleased to meet you now, I know of your well respected family in the Aberdeen shire, but tell me, Father Felipe, what brings such a ranking member of the church to Iona, surely it's not to just deliver supplies to the Abbey?"

The Monsignor adds, "We bring several letters of important correspondence that will fully explain our mission, but briefly, let me explain; the Earl of Tyrone, upon dying in Rome, had revealed Fr. George to be next in line as Guardian. The Pontiff has seen that it's in the best interest of the Church, and that of Britain, that the rightful Guardian comes forth to take his place. We make our way to the Court of Charles I. The correspondence we carry is from the Abbott of Kells, who has just recently confirmed the transfer of Guardianship."

George adds; "We bring you gifts of oil and wine, to be used in the sacrament, as well as some fine sheep. We too are looking for a relic of faith, that we think might have been brought here shortly after the founding of the Abbey. Or maybe among things recently transferred from St. Columba's church in Derry.

"George's two uncles are working there now; for Captain Phillips." Monsignor Castillo adds. "But they couldn't say what might have been found, or rather where anything has gone, only that Father Leslie might know, which is where we met George's Uncles: Thomas, and Robert."

George states, "There's only a slight mention of the relic being used during a funeral ceremony. We would like to inspect the funeral Chapel to see if there are any clues to what it might be, or what has happened to it."

The Abbott answers, "Well, there is Oran's Chapel that is traditionally known to have been where funeral services were given, only it has been closed off, and I don't know of anyone who has been inside; it's been locked up as long as I have been here. Many Kings, including those from Scotland and Norway, are buried in the Chapel's cemetery.

"Of course, it has interested us, and I remember looking for a way in, but we couldn't even find how it is locked; there are no locks on the doors, so we assumed they were locked from the inside; it's very puzzling. As Guardian, you have the right to any relic you may find, but I don't think there are any of the relics here at the Abbey. If there's anything, it must be inside the Chapel, and that is why it's been locked up as such.

"You must understand that the Chapel and a traditional funeral service have not taken place in almost a century, but we will have a look in the morning when it's light. So, for now, may I offer you a meal and some refreshments while your accommodations to stay are being prepared for you.

And with that, the group, along with the Abbott, made their way out and into the courtyard, across and to the Abbey's kitchen, where a table had been set to provide refreshment for the guests that night.

As the four reclined in the dining area and drank some of the wine that had been brought as a gift to the Abbey, the Abbott was shown the correspondence from the Vatican, and the letters sent from Kells, and Leslie in Ireland. The Abbott was told about George's relationship in Scotland with the young King Charles, and that when they were just boys, and both wards of Alexander Seton, at Fyvie Castle.

"The Queen having been raised at the French court," George says. "She had been an acquaintance and patron since the time that I had spent at Scott's college in Dubai. So as to make my appearance at the English court seem less intrusive, it will be made to look as though I have come on the Queen's behalf, herself being a practicing Catholic.

"Only when the time is right, shall the truth of my true mission be revealed. So until that time, and especially now during my transit to England, I will act incognito; as the Stable Master to the string of Spanish horses being brought as a gift to the King. And only later, when we can arrange a solidarity within greater Britain, shall my true identity and that of the Guardian be revealed. As to that end, we seem to have gained the support of the Archbishop, as well as many lords, and those of title, who stay faithful to the King. But there is much of a resistance that is given towards separate denominations, whereas denomination should not be the central issue, but that of the Kingdom, and one's personal choice to enter into, or remain outside of the Kingdom."

Just like the King's father James I, as he tried to unite the realm into one Kingdom, even his attempts to bring forth the word of God so that anyone and everyone in the Kingdom could find the knowledge of God's promise for themselves. So much has denomination worked as a distraction towards establishing God's Kingdom once again. For whom is to say what denomination is true and correct, is it not only just a form of worship? Do not all represent the Kingdom that the Lord, through the house of David, had established?

"And therefore, can there be separate forms of worship to be represented by different denominations within the Kingdom? That's our dilemma, and whether to allow separate denominations, or force a type of worship, in its own domination upon the people. These are things that of course, must be decided and acted upon for our plans to come together, and God's Kingdom be established."

At that, the Abbott asks: "I can guess that this idea goes beyond greater Britain, in that other denominations around the world would naturally want to be included. So, should they be made to abandon the denomination and type of worship they practice to be included?"

George answers; "This is why, at this time, until I am again to meet up with my friend the King, I should travel under the guise of the Stable Master, and keep my identity secret. We have brought with us from Spain, five of the finest breed of Spanish war horses, as a gift to the King's stable."

The Abbott states, "We'll make sure that you don't have to stay in the stables tonight, although you might find them more comfortable than the hard wooden beds here at the Abbey."

George says, "It's what I'm used to, and I'm thankful to just spend the night on dry land."

Now a fine meal was placed upon the table for guests to enjoy, as more of the monks, brothers, and all those there at the Abbey came in to share in the meal.

"Abbott," the Captain says, "I'm sure you know that all that we have discussed, should remain secret, until the Kingdom is made known to all."

The Abbott states, "I am honored to keep such a secret, I shall keep the knowledge of your plans to myself alone."

As more of the monks and brothers came to be seated, the food started to arrive. The Monsignor from Rome was then asked to bless the meal, and so recited a short prayer, after which the meal began, as the Captain summoned for more wine to be brought up. No more was said of George's plans, and he had returned to wearing the garments of the Stable Master. That night, the whole Abbey would celebrate all of the fine gifts that they had received. The revelry in the dining room, was to last well into the night, whereas the Captain and his party had decided to retire early, and so said goodnight to all and retired to their arranged apartments to rest the night and sleep with the hope; dreaming of finding something of what they were after, in the morning, that next day.

The morning came, drenched in fog and cold. The Captain, knowing that such weather would be of advantage, as the next leg of their journey would take them off the coast of England. And though it would be dangerous traveling in the fog, and they would have to travel quite a distance before reaching their destination on the Southeastern end of the English mainland; whereas any fog they find would help to hide them along their journey.

George was anxious to find what relics they were after quickly, and that they all could be on their way again, worried about having to expose the horses to another sea journey, even with the break they got in Ireland. George, the Monsignor, and Cardinal were then taken into the dining area and given a breakfast of oatmeal and bacon. A tea was served, where the captain saw a chance to voice his concerns on this final leg of their journey, and how it would be to their advantage to cast off sooner rather than later. The Abbott, saying that he had expected the weather to change, as they could see storm clouds breaking high up to the North.

Al Ponte

St. Oran's Chapel isle of Iona

Spirits of the Chapel

Chapter 5

The Abbott assured them that what they were looking for must have been in the funeral Chapel, and that the Chapel wasn't very large and had no unknown crypts associated with it. Since the Chapel had not been in use, the Abbott could not be altogether sure of what they could find, but assured the group that the Chapel would not take much time to search out any objects that lay within; it had been closed for as long as he could remember.

The Monsignor says, "I am Glad to hear that the day was starting off on such a promising note," insisting that, "Surely there is time enough for another cup of tea. "

"Do you have any idea of what you are looking for," asks the Abbott.

The Monsignor explains, "it is an incense burner that is used in connection with the Altar Stone of Jacob. "At the time of the

Second Temple in Jerusalem, it was given the name 'The Key of Solomon', but that is all we know and have no description of it. As it was not found still in Ireland, the thought was that it had been taken by Saint Columba and used in the founding of the Abbey here on Iona. So, if it's here, it's here, and if it's not, it's not, either way, this shouldn't take us long, and we should set sail shortly."

"If you will follow me out," says the abbot, "I'll take you to see the Church and Chapel, it's just across the road."

The Captain said that he would look after the ship and make plans to set sail, and so would meet them later back aboard. The Abbott led the Monsignor and George then across the road to where the Church, a small graveyard, and Chapel stood.

The Abbot asks, "the small funeral Chapel sits just behind the Church; shall we check their first?"

Back behind the Church sat an old graveyard, and in the center, there was a small Chapel that was said to have been built originally by St. Oran, and then in the 12th century, to have been refurbished by Somerled. Its location inside the cemetery could have been seen as being a small mausoleum, or that of a somewhat large memorial; that of the McDonalds, with several McDonald Chiefs interned here on Iona.

Maybe it was just luck, or prearranged by the Abbott, that they were to inspect the Chapel just as the morning sun had come up over the eastern horizon. This allowed the morning sun to shine upon the doorway, just enough to put a bit of light into the inside of the Chapel.

"We have never been inside," the Abbott went on to explain,

"It seems to be locked from the inside, and we have never figured out how to get in. Looking it over, and in through the small windows on each side, we could see that there was little to nothing inside and concluded that it served as somewhat of a mausoleum or a memorial to be left alone. Though as you're the Guardian, you have every right to break down the door, if you felt to do so."

"Not so fast," ..cautioned George, in an easy way he would often question something that might be out of place, or something that was vaguely familiar. "I recognize something odd; up there on the left-side of the doorway. I noticed the large stone halfway up; it looks out of place, the one with some writing carved on it; do you know the one I mean? Abbot do you know what it says?"

"We could never quite make it out," the abbot states, "Some think it says House of David, named after the first temple."

George replies, "Well, let's take another look, shall we?"

George walks over to take a closer look, and with the light of the sun now lighting up the front of the Chapel; George attempts to dust off the face of the stone in question.

"This isn't Latin at all; it's written in French."

"Can you read it" the Monsignor asks. "What does it say? Can you make it out?"

"Well, if it's in French, it says something like, 'Destiny of Man' ;which would seem to be an appropriate saying for a funeral Chapel; wouldn't you say?"

"That's what we supposed," answered the Abbott,

"But there's something odd about it," George says.

"It doesn't look like a load stone; it actually looks loose. Has this stone recently been put here?'

"No, it's always been there, as far as I know."

"Let's try something here; Let's find a couple of downed branches, as straight as you can find them. Two to three inches wide ." After a few minutes, they each collected a handful of branches.

The Monsignor asks; "we will burn through the door? But that will take too long, wouldn't it be better to just break down the door?"

George calmly answers, "No, no, we won't need to do either of those to get in if I'm right."

George then begins to push the stone and is able to wiggle it a bit, just enough so that he can get his fingers along the bottom, and lifting upwards, he is able to inch the stone forward. Enough now to grab it, George moves it forward and eventually out from its place in the Chapel's wall, and then is able to bring it to his chest, holding the stone and moving it away.

"Good God-man," cried the Monsignor. "I hope that does not collapse the Chapel. Isn't that heavy? Are you in need of some help? Maybe we should put it back, quickly, before the chapel collapses."

George says: "Relax, if this were a load stone, I could hardly move it, let alone remove it from its place. Its dimensions are very close to a standard outside building block; most journeyman mason would have no trouble moving it. It can be a little awkward, but don't let anyone tell you that Masonry is easy."

George sets the Stone down on an arrangement of some of the branches they found earlier.

"now do we burn it?" . asks the Monsignor, "I'm confused."

"Don't be. . The branches are there so when I need to move it again, I can get my hands under it, it makes it much easier to lift than if I'd put it on the ground. Don't be afraid of the doorway collapsing; these walls are almost four feet thick."

The Monsignor adds: "I hope that you're right and this Chapel doesn't come down around us."

"Now I can understand why masons have such upper body strength," The Abbott says, "You sound experienced. And the way that you were able to man-handle that stone out and carry it inside. One would think that you have a second job back in Rome as a builder."

"Oh no, I come from a family of Master Masons; my father and his brothers are all Masters. They own and work out of a quarry outside of Terriff in Scotland."

"Yes; the Builder. We have all heard of the Builder," says the Abbott, "and how he is going to build up God's Kingdom here on Earth."

"And such is the job of the Guardian," George adds . "To build up God's Kingdom, and ready the Throne, where his son will sit in judgment of all mankind. I'm not sure, but this block might be a relic. I will take it, and present it to King Charles, and at least have something presumed to be an actual relic, or at least to have appeared, as one."

George then goes back to inspect the now void, made when he removed the stone. And just like he knew what he was doing, he reaches in towards the door. "It's just what I thought, the loose stone was there to hide a door latch. An old masonry trick." And with that, George reaches in, and with a pull, unlatches the door, and the door then swings open, with a loud; 'Squeak'.

Just like they were told, the Chapel was essentially empty, the diffused light that came through the two side windows didn't do much to light up the interior, and there seemed to be more light coming through the open door. What there was; was a small stone pedestal in front, which looked as if it was to serve as part of an altar. George gets the Monsignor to help him bring the Stone and carry it inside the Chapel, resting it perfectly upon the pedestal that they found.

"It seems to fit perfectly like it belongs there," remarked George.

And so, just as they were making their way towards the doorway to leave, George noticed what seemed to be a small Star of David, carved into the stone just above and to the left of the enclave. "What do you make of that, Abbott?"

"What is it? What do you see?"

"It appears to be a Star of David, carved out upon the wall to the right of the enclave."

"Really, I have never noticed it before."

"Bring me the lamp, Monsignor. I would like to have a closer look."

George goes back and picks up the Stone, saying, "Someone place a couple of those branches we cut, down by the Chapel wall, in front of this star, so I can get a better look and get high enough for a closer inspection." He then places the Stone on its end; up close against the chapel wall underneath the Star of David, that he'd noticed. Now he could step up to it and have a closer look.

"It looks like only a vent; it's just covered with soot," Says George.

The Abbott asks: “Is there anything special about it?”

George says, “At first, I thought it to be a carving there placed in stone; but now, I’m not sure, there’s a lot of black soot, up here. Abbott, might I prevail on you once more, and ask if you have something to wipe this off with?”.

As George wiped it down, what he thought was a carving of the Star of David on the Chapel wall was more of a mystery.

“What did you find, George?” Asks the Monsignor.

“I’m not sure, but it appears to be metallic and set into the stone wall. Not the carving I thought it was. I am looking to see if I can find what secures it to the wall. Behind a vent would be a right good place to hide something.”

George begins to clean off the dark soot. As he rubs, the star comes loose, and he desperately tries to catch it as it comes away from the wall, fumbling as it seems to be breaking up and falling apart. As the object falls, it hits the Stone as it tumbles to the ground, making a terrible racket. At that, what seemed to be a flock of silver-colored birds, like a trick of the light, suddenly flew up and in an instant were gone. All except one that stayed for just a moment longer, and then, like the rest, in the blink of an eye, was gone.

“What was that?” George asks. “Did you see that? Where did all of those birds come from?”

“I’m not sure,” Says the Monsignor. “I mean, I’m not sure they were birds. Did you notice one off to the side, that seemed to have lingered?”

“I noticed it too and had a strange premonition that it was the Archangel Gabriel.” States the Abbott.

The Monsignor adds, “Strange, I thought of the Archangel too.”

George explains, "Gabriel the Archangel, waits to announce the coming of Christ to sit on his earthly throne."

The Abbott adds, "If this was a vision of angels, and of the one who waits; the Archangel Gabriel, the fact that he is seen just off to the side of the altar, could signify that the time is close for the return of Christ."

The object now lies on the Chapel floor in a jumbled metallic pile of soot. A sweet smell of incense now filled the Chapel.

"Oh no, I think I have broken it," Cries George. "No, wait, it somehow, someway, has managed to stay in one piece, but it surely seems to me to be broken."

George now noticing that his hands were covered in black soot.

"Wait a minute, do you smell that? George asks. "It's the smell of incense. Let's see what we have here. There is no vent up there, and it doesn't appear as if it has been filled in; I don't think there ever was a vent. So what we have here is a Star of David covered by soot and assembled in such a way could perhaps be something to burn incense on."

Lying it down on the chapel floor, they soon noticed that the outer triangles of the six-sided star were hinged to a six-sided quadrangle. George, having been somewhat scared thinking that he had broken the star, one which had long ago been set in stone to adorn the Chapel. As he examines the star and lifts each of the hinged triangles, the object has now turned into a small pyramid.

George asks, "Monsignor, Abbott, please tell me if I'm wrong, but is this not, a Thurible? Could it be, one of such relics that we are searching for?"

"I think it, must be," exclaims the Abbott. "If you notice

overhead, in the ceiling, there is a hook. I have noticed it before, but never gave it any attention."

"And look here by the door, this must be the chain which was used; although now it is in pieces."

"That all makes perfect sense," Says the Abbott, "an incense burner, when lit, would be swung by the cable chain over the attending congregation."

Just such a type of incense burners that were used in the traditional church service, called a Thurible, and when used in conjunction with the Stone would help to draw open the portal to the Heavenly Kingdom and would allow God's angels to descend Jacob's Ladder. The more they handled it, the more soot came loose, and now seemed to have created a cloud; a sweet-smelling cloud, now filling the small Chapel.

Perhaps it was in the Chapel's design, and what they saw was just the cloud of soot being drawn up through vents in the roof. Secretly, no one wanted to admit that they saw what looked like a tight grouping of Angels twisted around together, and like a whirlwind, climbed up towards the top of the Chapel; then, disappearing up high in the rafters of the Chapel's roof. Then just like a wisp of wind, the cloud gathered together and rose up towards the rafters of the Chapel.

But there was no wind outside the Chapel; it was perfectly calm. Not a single breeze could be felt by anyone. The phenomenon was so extraordinary that no one dared to speak, hesitant to comment on the strange occurrence they had just witnessed. As it had happened so fast, like an afterthought, the fleeting vision that vanished as quickly as it appeared leaving them uneasy.

The Chapel with its ancient stone and stained glass windows, seemed as if it was holding its breath as the soot cloud ascended. The intricate carvings on the ceiling seemed to come alive in the dim light, and was casting eerie shadows that danced along with the rising cloud of dust. For a moment, it felt as if time had stood still, the very air was charged with a sense of mystique. However, a sense of awe lingered among them, as none wanted to admit what they had seen. The silence was palpable, each person lost in their own thoughts, questioning the reality of what they had just experienced.

George, still holding the mysterious star that had transformed into a pyramid, felt a shiver run down his spine. The relic in his hands seemed to hold a faint sense of energy, as if it were a living entity aware of its own significance. As the sweet-smelling cloud dissipated, the small Chapel once again felt like a sacred space, with a sense of divine presence. As they exchanged glances, their eyes reflecting a shared realization that they had stumbled upon something truly extraordinary.

"I will bring this to the King," George exclaimed. "Abbott, would you have your monks crate up this stone, I can show them how I'd like it done and include the incense burner."

The Abbott then directs the monks to follow George's instructions. George tells the monks to gather up five pieces of firewood that they would use in the kitchen. George tells them to split four pieces in half, placing two halves at each corner vertically. Take the last piece of firewood, split it into quarters, placing one of the quarters at each corner; then bind with some strong twine, making sure they go around several times at the bottom and top of the vertically placed split halves.

George explains, "For the incense burner, simply put it between two frames tied down tightly together at each corner.

Please have them ready to go aboard ship, when we are ready to leave."

After the two pieces are crated and ready to be put aboard, George flattens out a small spot on one of the wooden braces of each crate just large enough to carve out an inventory number with his knife. This is done so he can then add both items now to the ship's manifest; listing the stone block as a sculpture stone blank, and the incense burner as a spare navigational compass. Everything on board must be accounted for, because if they were to be stopped on route, it would be better to hide things in plain sight, rather than try to hide something away, only for it to be found and not identified on the manifest.

So as luck would have it, the relics that they had sought had now been found. Now the next leg of the journey would begin. George showed the monks how to signal the ship and light up a signal fire, telling the Captain it was time they had left the island. The group headed down to the shoreline to receive the longboats that would transfer them back to the awaiting ship.

It was now, that George would say his goodbye, to his friend the Monsignor. It would be very dangerous for the Monsignor to continue on the journey to England. As for George, he would now resume his disguise as stable master, and if either of them were to be caught, they could easily be killed. Also, if any of Cromwell's men found out what documents or religious artifacts they carried, they could also be arrested and just might be killed too.

So now at the shore, the two said their goodbyes as George would have to continue alone. He's asked as to what is to be done with the new crates and where he wants them put aboard ship. George tells them, "There's a wagon painted a shiny black with crates of books in them. That is my library, you can stow them away together there."

George then walks over to speak to the Monsignor Father Felipe Castillo, "I do think it best Monsignor, that we now go our separate ways; take the letters of correspondence we have gathered along our way, and see that they make it back to the Vatican safely. Please give my regards to the Captain, and I hope that my mission in England goes well."

"We shall pray that you are successful in England, your mission means more to humanity than anyone knows, and of course, the Vatican and the church support your efforts and will be there if you need us." As the longboats pulled up to the shoreline, the two embraced, shook hands, and said their goodbyes to the Abbott. The Monsignor would embark on the ship that had brought them, the Portuguese freighter, which should have no problem getting past the British navy.

The King had redirected the merchant admiral's flagship to take George on to England. Since most ports were now being guarded by Parliament's coastguard, the fleet admiral decided that it would be better to go around towards the East Coast of England and make port at Rye.

Rye, which was known for its illicit world trade, was a port that was not unfamiliar to foreign vessels, and ships would often use Rye to smuggle goods into England. The cargo aboard the Portuguese freighter now had to be transferred over to the admiral's ship at Greencastle before they had left Ireland. The large amount of heavy cargo made the ship to sit low in the water.

St. Oran's Chapel as it is seen today missing its Stone

St. Oran's Chapel

For a united kingdom

Part Two

Court of Charles I of England

Al Ponte'

First folio ~ MMXXV

Henrietta Maria

Chapter 6

On July 16, 1636, George's escort ship, disguised as an ordinary freighter, makes port at Rye, East Sussex, England. Rye was a most unusual and busy port, the actual port being well inland and mostly cut off at the tide. For years, the city had profited from the smugglers' trade, but now, due to the situation and conflict between the parliament and King Charles, the port served as a major port of entry of trade goods that were needed to support the royalist cause.

George, now disguised as the stable master, had discarded all letters of correspondence, but one that identified him as his position of the stable master, which included the bills of lading for his cargo he would transport to London. It was an easy thing for the ship to inconspicuously pull into port and unload its cargo. The merchant Admiral had arranged to have wagons ready to transport the cargo as it was unloaded from the ship.

The cargo, besides the horses destined for the King, was a collection of books and manuscripts totaling over 1200 to be sent to Oxford and added to the newly constructed addition to the library there. The Bodleian Library had suffered during the reign of Henry VIII; many of the older books and manuscripts were ordered to be burned, though many survived, either clandestinely gathered up or sold by collection.

The Archbishop of Canterbury, now Provost of the University, took it upon himself to now update and expand the library. George, throughout his time on the continent, was able to collect a vast library himself, but also inherited one that once belonged to the pope's nephew, to whom George had worked as his secretary. Upon the nephew's death, he had willed not just a great estate, but also his vast library collection. The books were to be contained in Loud's new addition, under the pretext that they were on an indefinite loan from Scots college.

The docks were so busy that nobody seemed to notice or care about the cargo being unloaded. The five horses put ashore; four, would be hitched to the wagon that would carry the books, the other horse would be ridden alongside as they made their way to London. After the cargo was unloaded and in the wagon, the bill of lading would be switched to show the cargo as books to be delivered to Oxford, care of John Payne, to the Archbishop's library.

The Archbishop, having been made Chancellor, assured that the cargo would make it to London unhindered; the cargo being the relic they had found at Iona, the incense burner, and George himself. George would remain in disguise for his journey to London, for if it were known that he was a Catholic priest, his very life would be in danger. If he were to be found out, he would immediately be brought before Parliament and sentenced. With the wagon loaded and the Teamster at the reins, George, still the stable master, saddled upon one of the horses and started towards London. They would travel north to Leeds Castle, about 36 miles, where they hoped to arrive before sunset. Lord Culpepper, who was a quiet supporter of Charles in Parliament, would provide lodging and protection as they stopped to rest on their way to London, another 42 miles.

Leeds Castle, the home of Lord Culpepper's cousin, Sir Thomas Colepepper, who was also a loyalist and supporter of the king. He had first walked into the Middle Temple in London when he was just sixteen, and would keep an office there up until 1627. Active in Parliament in support of the King, this caused a rift between Thomas and his eldest son Cheny who would later be disinherited and see his younger brother Thomas Jr. inherit the family fortune.

Young Thomas idolized his cousin and would have done anything for his cousin John, known as Lord Culpepper. The castle was built on a small island; it had a natural, deep water moat around it. Both John and Thomas were the support the King needed in the House of Commons in Parliament. He was also involved in another plantation colony; The East India Company, which took a lot of his time.

It was Thomas Jr. who would welcome George at the castle, his father living more in their London house. With Parliament closed, most of the business is done at the several men's clubs, guild halls, and even in a Public house or tavern. More often, dinners were followed by an after-dinner social, which could include gaming such as billiards and cards. Thomas Jr. shows George around to the kitchens, as he asks George, "We have been asked to provide for your meals on your way into London. I'll let you talk to our chef, so he can get started with that. And any preferences you have for tonight's meal, by all means, let the cook know.

George, left standing in the kitchen and looking at all the commotion, asking himself, which one's the cook? He hears a voice behind him, "So, what will it be?" George answers, "You know that we should be in London; well before noon."

"No, I was only asked, as a favor to the Queen, to have plenty of food made up for guests. Are you part of that earlier group that came in? The Queen's Guard?" George, feeling a slight tinge of fear, asks, "Just here, for the night; are they?"

"Monsieur, I was only told to have an early breakfast ready for them. I presume that they will go into London tomorrow. You, too, are traveling to London as well." George then asks, "Your French. Were you a cook there as well?"

"Oui; I was a Chef, and I worked in one of the finest establishments; in Pear rie."

"In all of my travels, from Herring in Norway to grilled octopus on the Mediterranean, over all my most favorite meals were from Naples. Tuscan with some added spices, and what they call Pizza."

"I know Pizza, and you're right; there's nothing like the food in Naples; we will have pizzas tonight! What will you have for tomorrow, any requests?" "Just make an extra pizza or two, we can have them for a snack on our way to London."

George's interest was stirred; hearing about the four riders of the Queen's Guard arriving before him. He had noticed them upon leaving the port of Rye, and was worried that he was being followed. The fact that the guards had arrived before him; put doubt in his mind that they were following. Then they might have known where he was going, and based on that assumption, could he take the guards at face value, knowing that the Queen has no reason to do him any harm. Therefore, he could assume that the guards were there for his protection.

The next day, George awoke to the sound of riders, but they were not approaching the castle, but leaving. Worried about the horses, George was able to get to a window just in time to see the four riders of the Queen's Guard ride off. George wondered, "So maybe they were not following me yesterday."

The morning meal was planned to be served on the terrace outside of the Grand Ballroom, where last night's banquet was held. There, George meets Thomas Jr., who tells him that the cook had put together an assortment of sweet rolls and made some coffee as requested. He apologizes for not being here to say goodbye, and left me to tell you that he has wrapped up a couple of the pizzas from last night for you to take with you on your way to London.

As the two sat for their morning meal, George was able to ask more about the riders who came in before George the night before. "Thomas, what can you tell me about the riders who left here earlier this morning?"

"Not too much I'm afraid, about as much as I got when questioning them last night. My father did say before leaving for London that they would be around, and to expect a visit from the Queen's Guard, and not to worry, they were sent to make sure that you make it to London safely. The Queen must think a lot of you to send out her personal guard, to see that you safely make it to London."

"I have known the Queen, her brother, her elder sister, and mother for many years. It's not surprising that she would send out the guard; but want to keep it a secret."

It was still early morning when George sets out for London. He was amazed to see all of the morning traffic both coming and going on the London road. Along the way, try as much; he could not see the Queen's Guard anywhere in sight.

With all the traffic around, it gave George a sense of protection; at least it was a well-traveled road with a lot of witnesses around if anything were to happen. As they got closer and were finally approaching London,

George decides to ride the stallion, with the mhares along with the fold; trailing along hitched to the back of the wagon. There were two of the guards standing stationary by the side of the road. George was told to keep close to the wagon, soon to follow, as they made their way across the city to St. James's Palace, where he would finally see again his childhood friend, King Charles. As the wagon approached the palace, the Teamster signaled the guard and was shown in straight away and directed him to the King's stables.

The wagon, now safely inside the palace grounds, made its way to the stables where the horses would be unbridled, and each given separate stalls that had been prepared for their arrival. A page had been sent to show George his quarters in the palace, and told that his arrival would be announced. Though George now felt safe and able to relax after such a long journey, he still could not reveal his true identity, and so even in the household of the Palace, everyone would know him as the Stable Master, and Groom to the King's newest set of horses, a breeding pair; in hope to produce fine- quality stallions.

George, only in his quarters for a few moments, was then met by another page and told to follow him across the yard, but first to change into the garments he had been given. Having now changed his clothes, George made his way across the courtyard and into the main Palace and was taken to a bed chamber, where he found waiting a valet, and two maids, one of which was a kitchen maid who asked what he would like to have from the kitchen to eat or drink.

The valet now asked George if he could dispatch the other maid to make up a warm bath so that he could clean up; or would he prefer some refreshments from the kitchen first?

George said that he did need to clean up some and that he was thirsty, as if they could bring him some refreshment right away. With that, the valet dispatched the two maids to arrange his needs and showed him into the bed chamber saying that there would be hours before dinner and that he would have enough time, three hours and a half, to clean up, have some refreshment, and time to take a nap before he was to meet the King at dinner. His room was situated three flights up and overlooking a great expanse of gardens toward the West. From out his window, George could see the gardens clearly and to the northwest a pond.

He found a fire had already been set in place to warm his room, and now the valet was attending to the bed that was centered on the right side of the room. As the valet asked if his trip had gone well, a second valet entered the room; with a wardrobe of fine garments As he placed the wardrobe down; he asked George,

"Does the gentleman know his shoe size?"

"A medium size, I think, maybe an eight or nine? Nines will work fine thank you." As George bathed, the valet brought in a tankard of ale and then asked George,

"Do you have the pleasure of smoking tobacco?" George thanks the Valet, and in reply asks, "Have you a pipe?"

"Yes Sir; at once," answers the Valet.

Once George had time to clean, he retired to his bed chamber to rest before dinner. King Charles, who had earlier this year, without a sitting Parliament, had signed the People's Bill of

Rights, but without a sitting Parliament, decisions on just how to initiate new laws pertaining to the bill had put the King in a tough position, and at odds with trying to raise taxes. But on the other hand, the existing laws, such as how King Charles could raise funds or levy any new taxes, fell within King Charles's prerogative and his personal rule. Even though there were those parliamentarians who would run the risk of questioning the King's powers to raise taxes on the people.

Still, the King had open discretion on the levees he would set up on commerce, shipping, and transportation. And of course, there were local taxes collected to house a garrison and the maintenance of their quarters that were mostly connected to a Royal property, or a fortress. But still, generally, the populace of citizens supported the King and his right of personal rulership. It had been six years since the King had called for a sitting Parliament.

Since the last Parliament's attempt to discredit the royal court, and charging its members of some sort of dereliction of their duties; of course, they would have been acting upon Charles's favor, the King decided that he would support the members of this court over that of Parliament and decided that he would rather dismiss Parliament, which was in his right, and rely on the Privy Council to direct his personal rule.

Old Friends Unite

Chapter 7

Charles's advisers, such as Hamilton, and the Archbishop of Canterbury, certainly found respect in both the House of Lords and the House of Commons. But Hamilton, having much business in Ireland, was frequently unavailable, as was the Archbishop; now the Chancellor of the University of Oxford. He was busy working to expand, adding to the library, and establishing new colleges within the University. The problem King Charles had was that the Scottish members, though they had influence in Scotland, however had little in London.

Although the King himself had a direct influence upon the Scottish lords who still lived in Scotland, the Scottish politics was starting to fracture as it had almost a century ago over religious beliefs. This the King found it difficult to believe, but Scotland had now for many year, had been removed from their spiritual center, their ritual of coronating a King in the traditional manner. Such were the consequences of trying to work as a King, so far removed from the people he ruled over.

Charles's father, James I realized that he had to do more to unite with Ireland so that they might take their rightful place in the union of the three Kingdoms into one.

The plantations established in Northern Ireland James hoped would bring about a stronger bond between Ireland, and the Scottish Highlands; a bond that had long ago fractured. James had hoped that the two nations, regardless of what sort of congregation they held, would come together in tradition as a Kingdom under the Guardianship and proper leadership by the King. James had figured if he settled the plantations with Highlanders, who showed much faith, they might set the example for the Irish people, who over time faith had dwindled.

And even though, the situation about the northern plantations were presently not as the King would have expected, the emergence of the Guardianship being present at the Royal Court, along with the fact, that there had been a proper coronation of the King; that the Irish as a nation would come together and realize the presence of the United Kingdom. In the same way, James had decided to deal with the lowland Scots; the large percentage having ties with England, would accept an English approach to worship. This he would accomplish through the conception of the Book of Common Prayer.

Whether or not they would accept the Guardianship, though not being brought up with the same traditions that Ireland and the Highland Scots had in common, James felt that they would eventually come into line with the idea of the United Kingdom, whose will it was from their King.

No sooner had George finished his bath and now was about to retire to his bed chamber, the King appeared at the door alone. King Charles came in looking very happy to see his visitor, "I just heard the news that you had arrived. George, my old friend, how good it is to see you again. I know you must be tired from your travels, but I could not wait till dinner to see you".

"It was a long journey your highness. I'm happy it has gone so well, and I hope that the Council will meet me with as much enthusiasm. I assume that you have told them of our plans?".

"George, you are not the one who should worry; I am the one who worries whether my counsel shall see fit and readily buy in with our agenda to further the union in Scotland and Ireland".

"And what does Henrietta say to France and Italy? My brother, stationed outside of Madrid, eagerly waits for his turn at the Spanish court".

"Henrietta too, is anxious to see you again. I'm sure she will let you know how things stand in the French court. As for Italy, I would think that you would know yourself how they stand. But I'll let you rest now, we are so glad you had a safe journey, you will bring us both joy at dinner tonight. Have a good rest, I will see that your Valet wakes you for dinner"George awoke to see the valet tending the fireplace, and the room was dark. He must've slept later than he thought, and hoped that he hadn't missed dinner. "Valet, I hope I haven't slept through dinner."

"Your grace, I see that you have awakened, good, the King and Queen, will be pouring refreshments before dinner on the patio, you have forty minutes or so to rise and dress, the King, has sent what he thinks would be appropriate attire, please take your pick, and I will be just outside in the next room if you need me."

George got up from his bed and sorted through the garments that had been brought to his room. They were of a fine quality, but of course nothing in the style that he was accustomed to, and certainly nothing that could be taken as the garments of the stable master. As he dressed, he spoke out to the valet, "Will there be many attending dinner tonight, with the King and Queen?"

The Valet enters the room to reply, "Your Lordship will be dining with the King and Queen alone; you must be of much importance to receive such an audience to dine privately with his Majesty and the Queen. The court has been very busy since the King dismissed Parliament. The court has grown tenfold since then and is always quite busy in the evening during supper."

"I hope that I have not put many away to go hungry tonight?"

"Not at all, supper was hours ago, and everything went quite as normal, the Queen also, took a nap".

George, now dressed, found a comb on the side table, straightened his hair, and from a large bowl filled with water, splashed some on his face, using the palms of his hands. He turns to the valet and says, "I believe I'm ready, or it might be that I am very hungry and anxious for some food and drink."

"Then, if you would follow me please," the Valet asks, "I will take you to where you might find the King and Queen." George follows the Valet down the passage, which opens up to a courtyard where on one side, seems to be a Chapel, and next to it, another building where the King and Queen, were waiting before a set of large, open doors.

"Thank-you Randolph," says the King. "Please arrange for the kitchen to start bringing in the food now." As Charles now gives the Valet some more instructions, Henrietta moves to greet George, showing much delight. "George, it has been too long, how very nice it is to see you again; you look well."

"Yes, you too look well. What a fine palace this is. You don't miss the French court?"

Charles adds, "Henrietta, you remember, it was when we met in Paris in 1625."

"Yes," George says, "I had just published the biography of your grandmother, Mary Queen of Scots. I hope that your father enjoyed reading it. If it was not for his input it would not have been possible to finish."

"We both were moved and enjoyed it much," answers the King, "but I have to say that it was your other work that my father most enjoyed reading, your manuscript on Scotland and the ascension of their Kings in regard to a divine right. And now I understand why my father had made it clear that Buckingham and I travel to Paris to receive copies of your work, before going on to Spain. As a matter of fact, I believe that was his intention, and that my audience before the Spanish court, with the intention of finding a bride, was more of a diplomatic mission instead."

"The news of Buckingham's demise weighed heavily on my heart," answers George, "I know how much he meant to both of you, and it still must seem as a great loss."

"Yes, and this is what it has become, where Parliament is free to make its own agenda, and that is why I dismissed them, they wanted to take action against my privy counselors. And I couldn't interest you in the wardrobe I had sent? I'm thinking that you taking a low profile here at court would be wise for just a while."

"I wanted to be genuine at first arriving. It's been such a long time since we were all together in Paris. And there has been so much happening since then."

"I see that you wear the cross of St. John; may that be of the

Order of Malta?"; Charles asks?

"That is where we went first, before Paris. First, I should explain how I happened to be there in Paris; something that I had never told either of you when we were all to meet in 1625.

"While in my last year in college in Bologna, I had made a friendship with a fellow classmate when we were both studying canon law. At graduation, we both went to work for his uncle; Pope Paul V had made him the Archbishop of Bologna. He himself would go on to be elevated to Pope on the fourteenth day of February 1621. He then made my friend his nephew a Cardinal.""I remember my father seemed delighted for some reason, even though the majority thought it wrong that the Pope would bluntly promote a member of his own family."

"But of course that's naïve, don't think that it hasn't happened before. Firstly, when made Pope, he was rather frail and an old man. He needed someone he could trust and who would not be corrupted. Gregory had also taken canon law there in Bologna before he was made Archbishop, and I think that he was very proud of his nephew for following in his footsteps. He was also confident that he could give him an assignment where he could use what he had studied in college. And I have to have been blessed, as he made me too, co-vice chancellor, to look after his nephew."

"So he didn't completely trust his nephew either. So, you, too, were elevated to be so close to the Pope?"

"No, it wasn't like that at all, but a place for me to support both of them. But it all would end in 1623 when his uncle dies, and I was sent off on a diplomatic mission which had taken me to Malta, more of a stop-over; where we were given the Order; I felt was more of a gratuity, as we didn't plan to stay there for very long."

"Please," Henrietta asks, "May we change the subject? You have just arrived, and will have plenty of time to talk of policy. So, what other books did you bring us?"

"Your Highness, I brought you a boatload of books, to fill the shelves of the Archbishop's new wing of his library in Oxford, I was fortunate to inherit a great library from my previous benefactor, and I'm still searching for somewhere to put them all, first wanting to send them to the Scott's Library, of which his highness grandmother was great patron, but then heard, of the Archbishop being Chancellor of Oxford, and trying to replace some of the old manuscripts that had been disposed of by King Henry. I thought what not a better place, to receive such a gift. Though I would like it to be known that the collection is on an indefinite loan from that of Scots College."

"Would this not be somewhat of a bribe? Charles says jokingly. "I have wondered myself how to console the Archbishop, in accepting your presence at court. It seems, as though, as usual, you are one step ahead. I expect the Archbishop will be much pleased, and have little to say on your position at court, regardless of what the others may think, and with such a gift, might probably defend you against the opposition."

George asks. "Will the Archbishop be dining with us tonight?"

"Tonight old friend, it will be just the three of us, as you have just arrived; we have things to talk about and discuss. How will you safely reside now that you are here? So let us share a meal, let's go in; our dinner is waiting."

Henrietta asks, "So what have you been doing since we last saw you there in Paris?"

"I've actually been working at the Vatican. I serve as a business manager for the Pontiff's nephew, that is, until he recently died but in his generosity, he left me an estate and his library.

"A generous estate, you say?""I've always lived on a generous estate; I'm the eldest son of my father and so have a share of the rents from our land holdings in Aberdeen-shire. I've also collected a good-sized library myself; my only problem seems to be what to do with it now."

"So, will you then go back to Rome?" asks Henrietta.

"I think that they expect me to do so; so much of the Cardinal's work was tied into that of the Pontiff's, and I very much expect that they already have a place for me to work on Vatican business."

The King, Queen, and George then enter into the dining hall, where it seems just a modest meal has been prepared for the three of them. And since it is just them that dine, there is no need to announce their guest, and it is George's valet who is there to serve their meal.

"George," asks the King. "The least who know of you, the better, for now. Your valet is one of my most trusted servants, Sir Gerald Matthews, who's service in the palace is second only to myself. he is most faithful and will ask no questions. He knows, now only what you have told him, and even that, I have asked that he keep to himself." George, seemingly worried, asks, "And what of your other guests, are they not to dine tonight?"

"Gracious no, I have made available the banquet hall for my other guests tonight, on the precept that they are to hear a speech given by one of my ministers on foreign affairs. That is much, they do not expect my presence tonight, and as far as they know, I dine tonight alone with my Queen.""So, this is not the main dining hall?"

"Oh, it is, but quite recently, I built another, a Great Hall, one addition added by the architect Indigo Jones."

"Yes, as well as designing the construction here in Whitehall," answered Henrietta, "he also constructed, on Charles's father's commission, a most beautiful chapel. It is said to have been designed using the same dimensions as the First Temple on the Temple Mount in Jerusalem, the one built by Solomon."

"I noticed that there is a chapel next door, is this the one that you talked about?"

"No, it stands just a bit to the north and is adjacent to the old Palace; it's not far away, and I hope that I can have you perform services there for me."

"It stands, just far enough away from here, to be safe; Charles adds, "and a good place for you to perform mass. But it must be done secretly, unfortunately, because if it were to be found out, it would create such a stir, it could even disrupt the Council at this time. We will make arrangements to have your priestly garments and vestments kept in the chapel, for you to use when you are performing mass. I hope this will be okay, but right now, I can see no other choice; of how to handle it. With Parliament looking for anything they can use to discredit myself with my counsel and those who sit in Parliament."

"I know we take a great chance", adds Henrietta.

"But it would make me so happy, I have such fond memories of the services you performed while at the French court for me, and it would be such a pleasure to have them again."

The trio dined and then made their way to the outer courtyard. The Queen said good night, and King Charles wanted to walk George back to his room. As they walked, they talked about old times that they had shared, as young boys, in Scotland, and of the time that they had met in Paris. They talked, and laughed, and seemed to be happy to be reunited once again. As they got close to George's room, George asked the King: "Do you have the occasion of going riding before breakfast? If so, may I join you in the morning?"

"There you have done it again; I was just going to suggest that very thing."

The two men laugh and say good night, looking forward to more good conversation in the morning. George enters into his chamber, finding his valet tending lamps for the night, having drawn the curtains and turned down the bed. "Matthews, may I call you Gerald?"

"Thank-you, your grace. I have set out some nightclothes for you, will you be joining the King in the morning?"

"Yes, we plan to have a ride before breakfast."

"Very good sir, I will arrange boots for you; as well as some proper attire to ride in. If there's nothing else, I will say good night and have a pleasant sleep."

George awoke the next morning, to find Matthews there holding some riding attire, along with a fine pair of boots. Still quite dark, Matthews was going about lighting some of the lamps in the room, saying that the King would be coming by in half an hour and would have a morning snack before heading off towards the stables. George got up, started to dress, and asked Matthews how far away they were from the stables and what kind of day it was. Matthews commented that it was about a twenty-minute walk to the stables, and that he thought the weather to be clear and that it should be a nice day, and a good morning to be going riding.

George, having dressed and now having tried on the boots, found them to be a perfect fit; they were brown and came up to just below the knee. Matthews, the valet asks, "I hope the boots fit you well." George answered, "Yes, they fit quite well. It's the other pairs I'm having some trouble with. The other shoes that you brought, while the size was alright, I should have said I need shoes that are cut lower around the ankles, due to a family trait of having an extra bone down there, making it difficult to wear shoes that go above the ankles. Did you say that the King will have something to eat before we go off to the stables?"

"Yes," Matthews replies, "I have brought some scones and tea, you'll find it sitting over on the table by the door. You're welcome to start. the King will be here shortly and has instructed me so. I will work on finding some other shoes."

As George pours himself a cup of tea, King Charles enters. "George, I see that you're up and dressed, good, let us have a quick something to eat and some tea before we set off to the stables."

They finish their tea, leaving the room across the hall and through a doorway leading to the privy gardens, cutting across, they exit the garden to a path that leads North.

"When my father built the little chapel that we spoke of last night, that's adjacent to my father's older Palace, though seemingly plain in design, it showed a classical elegance. My thought, like so many of my thoughts, was to continue in this design; adding to my father's plans.

I was fortunate enough to be able to employ the same architect to design my Palace at Whitehall. The large hall, which we passed coming in, was the last of the buildings constructed; that of a large banqueting hall, which I just recently had adorned with a magnificent painted ceiling; this is where my other guests, whom you had asked about last night, had dined."

"A painted ceiling you say? How wonderful."

"Yes, part of the commission given to one of the Flemish artists I have here at court. Originally, he was sent here, a gift of the Queen's mother, who has been the patron and has commissioned the artist to work, sending her sketches of the Queen and myself. I felt that she was lonely in the Netherlands, and that she longs to be in better-touch, with her daughter.

The only problem is that he refuses to do a formal portrait of us, due to his abiding faith; he being a Catholic. So, I have him, along with his continued sketches, working on biblical themes, scenes representing biblical characters. The work that he has done on the ceiling of the banquet hall is truly magnificent."

The two then turn right and walk into a large courtyard, that being the entry to the stables.

"This is the stables, built in the same design, another magnificent effort; classic, and elegant."

As they make their way into the stables, George stops just as they enter, telling Charles that he has a surprise for him. "A surprise, how nice."

"Yes, it works quite well, serving the masquerade I used on my journey here."

"Now I am intrigued; you say a masquerade helped you during your journey here?"

"Yes, pardon me, just a minute while I talk to the real stable master."

George then goes into the stables and talks softly to the stable master, who points in the direction of the stables. George motions to the King to come forth, as they walk in the direction that was pointed out by the stable master. Down near the end, at the far side of the stables, are the horses that George brought aboard the ship as gifts to the King and Queen.

"Charles, I have some good news and some bad news somewhat; You are aware of the five most magnificent horses I bring?"

"I assume, that is the good-news. I hope that you're not going to tell me you stole them. Horse theft will land you in the toll house, unless they turn up to be Spanish; which at the present would be deemed more of a trophy I guess."

"Well, you're right in one sense, that is that they are Spanish horses, but I doubt they would keep me from landing in the toll booth because they're sent here as a gift from the Spanish Court; The Siete Marez."

"Well, if that's the good news, I'm not sure that I really want to hear the bad news now."

"Well it's really not that bad, you see they're not really, after all; all, for you. As King Philip hopes that you would accept these horses as a gift that shows there are no bad feelings towards you, when you came to Spain seeking marriage. Not finding so, he offers these fine horses in fair consolation. But actually, it was meant more as a gift to both you and Henrietta from her sister. She hopes to visit someday, when she and Henrietta can once more ride together as they did in their youth, in the forest next to the Fontainebleau Palace. The two would often ride all day when young. I assume that both still enjoy riding.

"They are truly magnificent," The King exclaims. "I have never seen such fine examples in their breeding. and this was your surprise, George? Well, you're right, Henrietta still loves to ride when she can. I remember her telling me about her and her sister during the summers spent at Fontainebleau."

"These horses are bred in the mountain region of southern Spain, in An-da-lucia." George explains. "Then only the best are trained at the Spanish riding academy in Herez de la Fon-tera. Five broodmares and a fold. The mhares are named, starting on your right; Anastasia, Valenta, Estrella, or Star in Spanish; She's the only one with a blaze on her forehead. Then there is Paloma and Angela. The fold has yet to have a name." "Yes, your grace, and they also helped me to travel undetected, where I posed as a stable master. So I hope that Henrietta may be just as surprised and pleased to have them"

"That's just marvelous; we shall all go riding tomorrow morning. You posed as a stable master, what a splendid idea, and it seems to have worked. But I thought you had brought just books."

"That too worked to our advantage, as I didn't want either to be confiscated. We had stabled two of the horses forward with the rest hidden behind the shipment of books. The freighter was certainly riding low to the water line. If ever questioned if they found the horses or the books, they could claim the other and keep the main shipment secret. And I too, could keep my true identity a secret, as well."

"So this masquerade you say has served you well, perhaps it now could save us both. I think it would be wise to remain a stable master, keeping your true identity still secret. How would you feel, if I arrange to have your quarters moved over to here, you would be safe, surrounded by my loyal horse guard, and better yet keep up the masquerade, as the stable master who is quartered here, and as my advisor at court, you could come and go, and still easily disappear."

"You mean to continue my masquerade, giving the appearance that I am quartered here in the stables. I think that plan would serve us both well, especially if things were to go wrong, and I did indeed need to disappear quickly."

"Another advantage would be that it is closer to Henrietta's little chapel, which is just a way to the North towards Buckingham's palace. Henrietta, though, also has a palace, another designed by the same architect, across the Thames to the south, a Palace that was built for my mother, I have turned over into Henrietta's care. A rather remote position that gives a great view of the Thames and Westminster, to the north.

"And so, I just want you to understand that when I say that you quarter here, I mean just in appearance, to lend credibility to you as a stable master. But as for general quarters, as a way of the bed chamber, you should feel free to go where you want, as there are plenty of places available, and depending upon where you are, we can certainly find a place for you."

George asks, "As for the Council, which of them knows of my true identity?" "They will see you as my private counsel and only become aware of who you are, as they need to know. Let's have the horses brought forth for our ride this morning. I shall have the grooms bring forth two for us to ride".

George still worried, "What about those members at Court from Scotland, do you think any will recognize me?

"All of them I recall are from the lowlands and the Border regions," Answers the King, "I have picked them due to all of the opposition I have in both. I really doubt that any of them will even notice you, and if we keep our personal communication when our fellow Scots are present, in Latin, your Scottish pronouns shouldn't give you away."

The King motions to an attentive groom, who then hurriedly goes to prepare two of the horses that George had gotten as gifts. "These are truly fine horses. Please tell me more about them," Charles asks.

"For decades, the Spanish have been breeding the stallions from the South of Spain. They are considered some of the finest warhorses ever."

The groom brings the horses out and helps King Charles and George to mount up, and they both head off on the road that borders the palace and stables, heading north.

"We'll head towards the old palace of my fathers, and I can show you the chapel that we had talked about. Just past the old palace, if we head northwest, we come to Buckingham's house, now occupied by his son."

"I had heard about his father's demise," Says George, "and can't help but think back to when you both had visited Paris, and we had such a good time, and when you first met Henrietta."

"Yes, I regret that I could not do more to save Buckingham, but he sealed his fate when he had gone in the wrong direction towards siding against the French in the Netherlands; there was little that I could do but try to delay what was destined to be his fate.

The King, looking to change the subject, comments, "These are truly magnificent horses. You did say a gift from Philip? And not from the Queen's sister? I know or have been learning how much the Queen and her sister loved to ride. Are you sure that their mother had nothing to do with it?

"I was told it was from Phillip, but then, knowing their mother, I can see how you might think that she had her hand in it. An amazing woman, their mother, I think there are many places where she has her hand in, and we'll never know. To describe these fine horses, I though, have a firsthand testimony,from my own brother, who greatly boasts about their prowess in battle, their breeding, and the amount of disciplined training they receive, where only those horses who have trained well, are selected to be ridden into battle."

The King answers, "And I trust your brother's testimony; my Father had told me of your family's great courage riding in a cavalry to protect my Grandmother Queen Mary in Scotland. Are you sure that they're not a gift from your brother?"

"I sense that you're having trouble believing that Phillip has sent them."

"No, it's not that; I'm just feeling a bit uneasy; You know that Henrietta's mother's here."

"No, but I had a feeling that she was, I don't know why, but she has that effect on others. I can understand why you're feeling so uneasy. So, if she asks to tell her they're a gift from Philip. But, if it will ease your mind, yes, they're from me, see it as a belated wedding present. I thought Henrietta's mother was held up in Flanders. Has she resolved the position up there?"

"No, but I'm sure that she has done just about everything she can to influence her son to make peace with Phillip, his own brother-in-law."

"Well, if anyone could influence them to find peace, it's her."

"Let me say thank you for such a great gift, it will stay a secret between all three of us ."

Maria de 'Medici; born at the Pitti Palace in Florence Italy in 1575 her father was the Grand Duke of Tuscany Francesco I. Her Grandfather Cosimo I was perhaps the greatest of all Medici who established firm control of Tuscany thru to 1737. Their power spread across Italy and into Rome where they had built a grand Palace on Pincian Hill in the center of Rome over-looking the Tiber River and Vatican City.

A Redempyion for Marie

Chapter 8

Few figures in history possess the complexity of Marie de' Medici, as she continued maneuvering in exile outside of France. After hearing the news of her eldest son, Louis, welcoming his firstborn, Marie makes then a momentous decision; shaking the foundation of the tulip market; selling short the vast amount of tulips she owned.

Now, with the birth of her grandson, she found herself at a crossroads, with all hopes of installing her younger son Gaston, who was up till then the rightful heir, to the throne, gone for good. Her youngest daughter, Henriette Marie, was now married to Charles, a king with mounting troubles of his own; fraught with conflict and poised at the brink of civil war. To support her, and her daughter's stability; Marie's plan would pay off substantially.The tulip craze swept across Europe, and Marie recognizing a chance to get back some of the wealth she lost when leaving her lifestyle in France. She had put together an extensive amount of tulip bulbs. The investment flourished. It would entice the European nobility and also commoners to invest. The tulip, became the symbol of status.

Marie sensing the volatility of the market devised a plan, deciding to sell off her vast collection of tulip bulbs. Unknowingly she started what would eventually crash the market and send ripples across the economic structure of the Netherlands. As the news of her sell-off of bulbs became evident, panic among the speculators intensified. As the market prices plummeted, causing many of the investors to also sell off as quickly as they could; in an attempt to save their investments.

So, with fresh cash in hand and leaving the tulip market to its own demise, she made her way across the North Sea to England to visit her youngest daughter. She hoped that her husband Charles would show her respect giving her room in the Palace adhering to the lifestyle that she was accustom to. Some believed it was her brothers in Florence that had planned the fallout. She feared the resentment of those whose fortunes were lost. All along she worried about her daughter, who could soon be all alone in London, as Charles went north to Scotland; a kingdom that was now discontented with the King ruling from so far away in London.

Reaching the shores of England, Marie longed for the sight of her daughter, Henrietta Marie, whose grace and poise belied all of the tension that was brewing in the royal court. The Queen's natural beauty had captivated Charles, and yet their marriage seemed powerless against the storms gathering around them. Marie having embraced her daughter, felt the warmth of family bonds overshadowing what political tension that plagued the King.

"Mother," Henrietta greeted her with a mix of grief and apprehension, "what news do you bring me, and how are my brothers doing, I hope that now they can put the past behind them and be friends again"

In the following days, Marie would delved into the matters of state with her daughter, facing down the challenges posed by Parliament and the increasingly fractious nature of English politics. Marie detailed her ideas for reconciliation, suggesting ways to calm Parliament. The two schemed, drawing upon their shared lineage of both strong-willed queens, and accustomed to wielding power defiantly; even in the face of adversity.

As they plotted and planned, Marie sensed the shadows of her past decisions creeping back. The tulip market had suffered greatly under her hand, and while this might have liberated her financially, it also threatened to drive a wedge between her son and the now resentful elite of the Netherlands. Was this unrest worth the serenity she sought for Henrietta?

One evening, as the sun was setting beyond the horizon, and casting a golden hue over the English countryside, Marie revealed her heart to her daughter. "I sold the bulbs to set you free my child, but perhaps I have simply sown discord instead."

Henrietta gently took her mother's hand, "we must establish our identity and purpose in this tumultuous world. Your sacrifices are not in vain, and we will be much stronger for it."

The coming months saw the Crown now tangled in debate and tension with Parliament. Charles worried that he'd be seen by others that he might be influenced by his Mother-in-law. He began to reconcile differences with the nobility, and members of Court, although somewhat reluctantly.

As Marie navigated this new chapter in her life, the legacy of her selfish indulgence resonated beyond the realm of a regent in exile. In an efforts to strengthen her own position, she inadvertently was to reshape the politics in Europe. Thus leaving behind a world both beautiful and seemingly overwhelmed with the complex of human ambition. And so, Marie's story continued; an odyssey shaped by the interplay of love, sacrifice, and the pursuit of power.

By now, Charles and George had reached the small chapel, which was also built by Inigo Jones, as an addition to St. James Palace, which was adjacent to the North.

"Here is the chapel I have appointed to serve Henrietta," Charles explains, "as she is still Catholic, it is a way of pleasing her mother, who was so opposed to her having to convert to satisfy Parliament, with their objection to the Catholic faith. I hope that you can, as you did in Paris, serve her needs of fate, and give her the religious guidance when she asks."

The King continues; "Of course, all of this must be done in the strictest of confidentiality. If any of the members of Parliament were to find out, there would be much trouble, not just for the Queen, but also; for us. I have made arrangements to have at the chapel, the vestments that you will need, and ready for you; when you need to perform a service. But I must ask that you remember to change back to stable master, when you leave the chapel.

"My father's palace is now a garrison of troops stationed as the palace guard. They are all faithful to protect the Queen, but still, you must try not to be seen at the chapel, either coming or going.

"Now we will head back to have breakfast. I have a full day planned for us.".

The Archbishop had told George that both he and King James had very much enjoyed his books, and how much the

King had relied on George's thesis on the Divine Right of Kings. He said that he was anxious to engage in a theological discussion with George. King Charles was anxious to hear what Hamilton could tell them about the situation in Scotland.

The next day, the four of them would return by carriage to London. The Irish Minister MacDougal, whom the King had relied on for information about the situation in Ireland, would be sent by messenger to London, but there was also the correspondence that George had collected on his way.

Because King Charles had dissolved Parliament, he would rely on such correspondence from such ministers and the advice of what was now his new Privy Council. King Charles knew that although Parliament had been dissolved, their representatives were closely watching him and would try their best to ascertain who he had as counselors. For this reason, he had not called MacDougal since he had left Scotland, his lands confiscated by the present minister, Campbell. The King knew that he could rely on his allies, faithful royalists in the Northeast, and the allies of McDougal, also faithful royalists in the Western Isles.

It was in the lowlands and central Scotland, where for centuries, land and titles had been handed out to English lords, that hence had made their way into Scottish society. The plan that King Charles and his counselors were about to enact would rely on turning the power base in Scotland, which was the central lowland, by proposing a deal that they could not rightfully re-fuse. The plan needed the full support of both Ireland and Scotland to be successful. The problem was that dissension had been building up in both Scotland and Ireland for the past 30 years, and to make matters worse, that dissension used the division of religious beliefs to strengthen their cause.

So if their plan had any chance to succeed, the divisions in religious matters would need to end. Since their plan was based on religious faith, it was essential that any differences there be eliminated, and a solidarity established. And so, this would be the first order of business, which would be taken to the Privy Council, where ideas on how beliefs could be reconciled between Scotland, Ireland, and England. This, however, was not a new endeavor; the King's father, James I, had also tried in vain to do so. King James had felt that there was a lack of understanding, and of course, it was no fault of either side; it was just the course of religious ceremony, where most of the differences lay.

King James felt that first, his subjects should be educated, or be able to read the Bible, just as it was that important that they should read and understand civil law, why should they not be able to read and understand God's will, from its source, the Bible.

So, James had painstakingly translated the Bible into English so that it could be read and understood by the masses. His next step was then to unite his subjects in the new understanding that they would be able to read directly God's will and proposed a pamphlet that contained a common prayer, and that would also provide further understanding of what was needed to bring unity to his newly founded greater Britain.

The Duke James Hamilton arrived that night, returning from one of his regular trips up north to Scotland. Tomorrow, the King and his three counselors would return together to London by way of carriage. While in route, there was much discussion about the central Lords in Scotland, and how they had rejected King James' attempt to standardize the religious customs throughout Scotland, even though they hadn't part excepted the King's book of prayer, but privately did all they could to nullify its effect in the lowlands, while isolating the Northern, and the Western Highlands, royalist supporters.

The Archbishop added that the King tried to make it known and wanted the people to understand that by his coronation to the throne, he had become head of the church and responsible for their religious guidance. King James was hoping to find their loyalty to the crown stronger than their affiliation with a certain denomination, but also the understanding that to reject his will would be looked at as treasonous.

He had tried to bring about solidarity, regardless of what denomination, and that this was evident by way of a book of common prayer and common practice, a book that both I and the King had worked on. It was most unfortunate, though, that he found so much resistance; whether it was due to the long-standing practices instigated by his predecessors, and wholly blamed Henry VIII for dismantling the institution of religious belief that had been thoroughly established in the Three Kingdoms.

He felt that it had led to a spiritual revolution that was strengthened by what was happening in Europe. Hamilton had a different understanding, and felt that many lowland Scots held a strong alliance with London, which separated them from those in the Highlands and the Western Isles.

The Lowland landlords relied heavily on their alliance with families to the south in England. Hamilton said he saw the lowland Lords were more easily influenced by what was happening to the south in England, and that was where their loyalty lay, even though it was not a royalist ally, but one that tended to support Parliament against the King. The Archbishop was then to add that he knew James figured that he would need to find a compromise in both lowland Scotland and central Ireland.

The King had made several attempts to have the Irish lords relinquish the guardianship to him, and that, as rightfully crowned as their King, the guardianship was rightfully his. Of course, this was rejected by the Irish lords, who simply saw him as Scottish and not Irish, and that the guardianship belonged in Ireland, even though the title had been earlier bestowed upon favored Scottish lords.

Also, the Scottish King had bestowed not only the Guardianship but also that of a Defender of Faith. This was to have been rejected in Ireland, where it seems that the church for so long had been absent from the concept, and so reliant upon guidance from Rome.

But of course, there hadn't been a King that had been properly coronated in decades, so such concepts, as a defender of the faith, and Guardian, had but almost been forgotten. This might be the basis of why the Irish lords had been so reluctant to relinquish the title. And of course, the true nature of those concepts had been lost by so many years, and the understanding of what it really meant had also been lost.

That afternoon, they made their way back to Whitehall, where they would wait for the other member, Wentworth, to arrive. Charles would then have his advisers and would go into the business of how they would proceed. Wentworth finally arrived early that evening and was drafted to the dining hall. George, who had now been settled in his new apartment at the stables, was anxious to meet with Wentworth, to find out how the Irish alliance was doing and who could be relied upon for help.

Randall McDonnell, the first Earl of Antrim, would be left in Ireland in charge of raising a royalist force. Not called to counsel in London, he could have been considered George's cousin, having the same grandfather, the second Lord of the

Isles, Donald. But after Donald's demise at the battle of Harlaw, his title as Lord was taken by the King (James I) and given to Randle's side of the family. It was not known what they knew about George, and sensing animosity, the King felt that it would be best for Randall to remain in Ireland and to counsel Wentworth instead, he being the King's minister in Ireland.

George, though, would dine in his apartment; his meal would be brought to him. Both King Charles and George thought it best for him to stay incognito. Charles was afraid that there were spies at court who would give him up to Parliament. It was decided that George would attend the Council, but careful not to show his face, and it would be best that he wear a mask to keep his identity a secret. He and the King could easily counsel together during the King's visit to the stables and while they rode together. He can also dine with the others, under the guise of the Spanish stable master who had come along with the stallions, a gift from the Portuguese nobles.

George, by living in the stable apartments, would be in a good position to serve the Queen, providing mass, arranged at her own chapel, adjacent to the older Palace, built by Charles's father, not more than 10 blocks away. Just such a service would be held the next day, it being the Sabbath.

Only this would be a special service, attended by the King's most trusted members of the Council, where they would give mention to their future effort, it being God's will, and about their mission to restore his Kingdom on earth. Even to those council members who were to attend would find it hard to recognize George as their equal and counsel, since he was to keep his face covered. And this, of course, was the only such service they would attend, and would most definitely have them wondering if they had recognized him also as the stable master, so familiar to King Charles, so often together on their horses each day. It was also thought best that George should hide his face and prevent anyone from recognizing him while he visits Whitehall.

Both King Charles and George feared that he would be recognized, not as a friend and advisor of the King, but as a Catholic priest, and that spies of Parliament would find him out. Only as his role as stable master, could you drop his disguise, but then even this would be taking a chance, that even then that he might be recognized. That Sunday, after the service that George conducted at the Queen's Chapel by St. James's Palace, there was a procession of those who attended back to the King's grand new banqueting hall, the procession would make its way back towards the stables, where across the street stood the King's Grand banqueting hall, designed again by indigo Jones who had also designed the Queen's Chapel.

That night, there would be a grand reception for what only a few would know. Those chosen to attend the service that was held prior to the banquet must've figured that it was in connection with the service, but not sure why. But of course, this was a grand event; the King's new grand Council would meet tomorrow.

The chatter was loud at the banquet, everyone wondering what it was all about; questions went out to the many high-standing dignitaries present, each having their own answer as to why the banquet. Each wanted to include themselves in reasoning why King Charles would hold such an event so grand and in such a fine appointed hall.

Of course, only a few really knew why the banquet, and the service, and that the Kingdom of God was not far from being a reality very soon. George assumed his role as stable master and so could easily mingle with the guests.

The Archbishop of Canterbury, who had attended the service, was very interested in the type of service that had been performed earlier at the chapel. He was quick to question about the incense and was told that it was frankincense and myrrh. The King added that the burner had come from the holy land and that perhaps it had even once been used in the great Temple at Jerusalem.

Members of the Privy Council were told that there would be a meeting of the Council in three days and that they were to make sure that they would be available to attend the Council meeting. There were a lot of things that needed to be done before their great plan could be made public, that is, a need for solidarity, much like that of which the King's father, James I, had sought to be in line with this concept of a Great Britain. But of course, political tension has increased and has been slighted for a hundred years towards that of English interests, which of course had now come in line with that of central and northern Europe.

As they continued to walk towards the King's banqueting hall, Charles asks, "I've been wanting to ask you, what success, you had, if any, at the service in the main chapel of Whitehall the other night. George replies, "I guess as much as any clergyman of thc faith would have at a normal congregation service. You did say that your father had this last little chapel built especially for his Catholic Queen?

Given what attention, any service, mass or otherwise I'd give, might just raise an eyebrow of those in Parliament, any further services held would be better done in this little chapel. The big test will be, and where you could be a service, you have little choice, is that just how we are going to move the stone from Westminster Abbey, without anyone knowing." At this, Charles replies, "We will have to devise a way to do just that, maybe, that is what you must first ask the Angels." (The King chuckles, under his breath)

The Work at Westminstser

Chapter 9

"Aren't you Charles, putting the cart before the horse?"

"What-horse? It's really quite simple, we just sneak in one night, remove the Stone with a wheelbarrow, replacing it with some facsimile. Then, to hide our work, we can put up a nice little curtain; something appropriate. Something made of silk, or crushed velvet, or that of sorts. I'm sure that I could find something that would do. Something from the King's wardrobe-maybe. Something that would never be missed.

"Very good," says George, "shall we say goodnight?"

And the next morning, at breakfast, they started to plan how they could switch out the stone, without anyone knowing. King Charles had invited his minister of northern regions, Thomas Wentworth, someone whom the King knew George would need to question about Scotland.

King Charles and George arrived first and had started when the queen and Wentworth arrived and sat down. "Wentworth, I need your help."

Wentworth replies, "Yes, your highness, but if it is about the plantations in Ireland, they are furious over the Scottish settlements. And it's not my fault if the Scottish lords won't give an inch; they have already deemed to classify Ireland as an exile, and simply won't agree to back down on the issue. Hamilton has tried, and I'm afraid, that they will only talk with you, for it is only you that they know and trust."

"But you're wrong," The King exclaims. "There is, someone else, but Wentworth, that's not what I need help with right now. Tomorrow, an hour before daybreak, I would like you to meet me on the East side of Westminster Abby. I have a task for you of much importance, and you are not to tell anyone of our plans, because the Queen will be with us. Do you understand?"

"Why of course, Your Majesty; an hour before daybreak; I will be there."

George speaks up: "And what is this, you say about an exile?"

"Wentworth, I'd like you to meet my Stable Master, George; George's brother is over in Ireland." George adds, "I always thought that he was over there building the ramparts of the fortress, and not that of a prison."

"Oh well, our friend Hamilton is a fine example of the Scott in exile," Wentworth says with some sarcasm in his voice. "The Irish want to make a case against him, and he certainly cannot return to Scotland, and I believe he already has a room reserved for him in the tower."

"I certainly hope not," says the King, " I'm depending a lot upon what influence he has left, or mainly his influence he has with our opposition in the North."

"So, can Your Majesty tell me your plans for tomorrow?"

"Thomas, I don't know what there is to tell. But George, I will have a Mason waiting for you at the river's edge just down from here to the South, and he will assist you to get what we want ready." "Your Majesty," George answers, "I won't need a Mason, an apprentice will do fine, as long as he will let me use some of his tools; for as you should know, once a Mason always a Mason, or the son of a Mason."

"You're right, I should have known this is your forte. So why don't I have Thomas instead of meeting up at Westminster, and instead meet you at the work site in the morning?"

Then at the Chapel service: "I seem to get the message to unite God's Kingdom on earth; under God as is in heaven. And I'm starting to see a pattern: first it was to use your father's prayer book and then to continue upon his work to unite the Kingdom."

The very next morning, Wentworth met George at the construction site as planned, although now finding him donning an apron and inspecting tools that had been left there. George had Wentworth follow him to where they found a large set of Stone, whereas George began to scribe a line across and continued to work in deeper with the chisel. All of a sudden, to Wentworth's amazement, the rock split, leaving a large rectangular stone, to which George now started to work the sides, shaving off the stone. It took George about an hour, and then he asked Wentworth,

"Thomas, would you get that side of the stone, and help me to lift it into the wheelbarrow? "Wait, let's tilt the wheelbarrow, and then we can both get behind the stone and just flip it into the wheelbarrow".

"Am I to believe that now we are to roll this all the way over to the Abbey?" Asks Wentworth.

"Not at all," answers George. "I had earlier met an apprentice who was arranged to meet me here this morning, and after helping me to pick out an appropriate stone to work, he arranged to have a barge waiting for us, just down here at the riverside; I have sent him along where he will be waiting for us upriver."

The King had also arranged to have four of the mhares pull a wagon just like the one those same horses had done earlier in Ireland. He made sure that even the wagon was the same size and with an identical harness and tack. George had told him that the horses would go through a lifetime of continuous training. The King, thinking back to growing up in Scotland and how George's father was a great horseman and a renowned Captain of Cavalry. The care and attention given at the quarry stables, he was sure that he would never forget, even if the two young wards were often called upon to help muck out the stalls.

"Is it a repair that you do for the King and Queen?" Asks Wentworth.

"Not exactly," says George, "but it is something that the King had promised the Queen that he would do. And I must tell you that this will be a test of your loyalty to the King and Queen, and that you should say nothing of what you do and see."

The two made their way down to the river's edge, where the barge was waiting. A plank had been laid out to easily wheel the wheelbarrow onto the barge, where seven crew members would take them upriver to Westminster where the King and Queen were waiting. The barge was manned with rowers three to each side and with the captain at the Rutter. Wentworth stood silently alongside the wheelbarrow as the barge then set off downstream on the Thames. Westminster could be seen standing off in the distance. It was just dawn and with the sun to our backs, it was just starting to light up the towers of Westminster.

The river seemed strangely quiet, being so early in the morning. As the oarsmen found their rhythm, you could see that it would not take them long to get downriver. The two men now found it easier to talk and not break the silence that was so overwhelmingly found as they first approached the river.

George asks, "So, you are the King's man in the northern reaches. "Tell me, Wentworth, what is it like over in Ireland, where my brother is working?"

Wentworth tries to ecplain; "If it is Londonderry, where your brother is, there is a great dissension towards the King, and that when the Earls took flight, this left a vacuum of the power structure that the McDonald's of Scotland were only too happy to fill; and since so many Scots were being sent over, given homesteads in the Roe Valley; who else would they look to for direction than the McDonald's who were already given a strong presence from their castle Don Luce. As far as King Charles having an advantage over the rest of Ireland, it's quite a toss-up.

"This is very interesting, what you say Wentworth. Is the King aware of this situation," asks George.

"I myself have tried to find a way to tell the King," answers Wentworth, "and only hoping that the situation would improve, but really, I don't think that Hamilton is having any more success in Scotland. But hold on, what has the King's stable master to do with the politics of the King's northern Kingdom?"

"Well, let's say that perhaps King Charles is looking for a 'Stable' Kingdom in the North."

"Wait just a minute," exclaims Wentworth, "If your brother is indeed building ramparts in Londonderry, I would wager that he is not Spanish; by God! You are Scottish. I believe that I have uncovered a deception on your part. No wonder you have been so close to the King these last few days." "Just; who are you?"

"Everything Wentworth, will be explained when and if the King himself feels as though he shall let it be known. But remember, both the King and Queen now have taken you into their confidence; I, on the other hand, am not sure of what I can tell you yet. What I can say, now that King Charles has let it slip, of my brother's work with Major Phillips in Londonderry, is, yes, my brother and I are Scottish, the sons of a Grand Master Mason, who has worked on many estates of the higher court counsel. But officially, as you know, I am just one of the King's Stable Masters. Have you seen them yet? They're a nice set of Ponies."

"Yes, I have seen them, and they are definitely Spanish," answers Wentworth.

"I must correct you," George adds, "they were a gift from the Portuguese." But that wasn't exactly true. George needed to keep secret; just how the horses arrived, and who they were from, and just for the reasons he had mentioned. "Technically, yes, the horses originally are of the breed that comes from the South of Spain; but are we to look a gift horse in the mouth?"

Wentworth answers, "You do have a way with words, not typically found among stable masters, as far as the horses are concerned, they do not please parliament, and added ammunition to their case of King Charles having Spanish sympathies."

"But truly, it's more of the other way around," explains George, "as, for Spain, looking to amend its relationship with England, and to show no remorse of the King to have chosen Henrietta as his queen. It is true, and let's not underestimate the value of the then-prince's visit to Spain; even though he did not return home with a bride; even though we all know better, and that King Charles did indeed return with a bride, just not a Spanish one."

The trust of the Spanish had not yet returned to Charles's court. Spain's attempted invasion was still a negative influence in the minds of prominent members of Parliament. Personally, James had set the groundwork of a truce, and peace with Spain.

"I do believe this must be your apprentice at the river's edge," Wentworth exclaimed.

The barge had now made its destination up the Thames to Westminster, and the oarsmen, finding the dock where the apprentice had been waiting, pulled up to secure the barge at the Westminster dock. The oarsmen, recognizing the stonemason's apprentice, took charge of seeing that the wheelbarrow got ashore Another two, volunteering to see the selected stone along with the wheelbarrow, are loaded into the awaiting wagon; Wentworth, having no clue that those were the Spanish horses that were hitched up to the wagon.

On its way towards Westminster, George and Wentworth followed along to meet up with the King and Queen, as they approached the Abbey, George motioned for the wagon to stop alongside the adjacent cemetery. With the apprentice's help, they quickly unloaded the wagon, then George dismissed the apprentice after paying him for his service.

Wentworth asks: "So, are we here? I thought we were to meet the King and Queen."

"They should be up ahead, says George: "We shall proceed with the wheelbarrow, to the side entrance. Charles and the Queen might already be inside."

When they reached the side door, George instructed Wentworth to stay by the wheelbarrow; and, if anyone asked, to say that you are waiting for the Mason; as you are setting up a memorial in the cemetery. George knocks on the door; as it opens, he steps inside to find the King and Queen standing at the right of the altar. As they catch his eye, Charles motions to come forward.

The Queen tells him that everyone has gone, and they have at least the rest of the day to finish what they're doing. She says that Charles has arranged an assembly in the banqueting hall that will last all day. It includes a grand banquet, and that she doesn't expect anyone to return until well into nightfall, which will give them all the cover they'll need to move the Stone to the chapel. George asks if they have brought an apron for him to wear. The Queen says that they have, as she points to the apron, as well as the other supplies George had asked for; including a square with some tacks, and some strips of bright dark blue satin.

"I have to measure the Stone first," George says. "then, outside, I'll shape the stone. I left Wentworth outside with the wheelbarrow, on the pretext of putting out a Memorial in the cemetery."

"And which of your names, is-on the Memorial," the Queen asks; with some signs of fear and loathing.

"It might be all of ours," says George. If we're ever found out, or worse; caught in the act tonight, moving it to your fine chapel. Which is another reason that our friend Wentworth is outside; guarding the wheelbarrow."

"You don't trust Wentworth? Is that your first impression, as you hardly had any time to get to know the man?"

"Well, that is just the point; I don't know him. But thank you for giving me the opportunity to question him. I assume you felt that I had questions about Ireland when I found out that my uncles are working over there. Should I be worried?"

"No, I don't think so, Derry or Londonderry, as my father calls it, everyone sees it as hollow ground anyway. It's a Holy site, not just for any faith, but for the Irish and their Kingdom. Will it take you long to fashion the stone?"

"It shouldn't take me long," says George, "the apprentice helped me to pick out a fine piece of stone to work, but first I need to get the measurements. Let's take the square and get the measurements from the Stone. Can you show me where it's at?"The King shows George up to the side of the altar, where the coronation chair sat. Almost immediately, they noticed a draft; as if someone had opened the side door, but they could see that it had remained closed, as it had not allowed in any light.

As George got closer and closer to the chair, the draft was now swirling around, and seemed to be traveling about on its own, inside the abbey church. You could see the look of fear on their faces; and Henrietta turned away, as if it were a dust cloud, which it might have actually been. Charles seemed to be starting to hyperventilate.

George asks, "Charles, are you still doing that? We should all go riding every morning; and open up your lungs for the rest of the day; we can take Henrietta with us too." George took the square that the King and Queen had brought; out from under his belt, and commenced taking the measurements he needed. "All right," he says, as he starts to walk back towards the side door. The King mentioned the strange draft and asked George, "what do you make of all that strange wind?"

"You would think that such a large building to have an atmosphere or a climate of its own," explains George, "I have seen it before in some of the larger cathedrals on the continent. When somebody comes in from the cold, a thermal within the building is formed. But on second thought, it was strange indeed. But it seems to be gone now."

George, Charles, and the Queen had made it outside and rejoined Wentworth, who was now taking his bows before the King and Queen.

"I can see that obviously; this stone is way too large," comments the King.

"In itself, yes," George explains, "it is, but with the apprentice's help, I was able to pick a stone where I could easily fashion what we need."

And at that, George proceeded to cleave off what pieces he would need to make the replacement. And of course, having a father and brothers, who were all Master Masons, George himself could have readily picked up the trade himself if he hadn't chosen the path of the clergy. And so it took George no time at all to cleave off the four pieces of stone they needed.

Next, he and Wentworth moved what was left of the stone block and set it down over by the cemetery, where it looked quite natural, blending into the other memorials. Now returning with the empty wheelbarrow, they headed back towards the abbey.

The King, thinking the wheelbarrow to be empty, questions George:

"Oh no, have you lost the Stone?" Thinking that George had made a critical error and split this stone, rendering it useless for the task at hand.

"Not at all, your Majesty," explains George, "I have all I need now to render the facsimile we require."

The four then return to the abbey through the side door, this time bringing the wheelbarrow in with them."

As they approached the coronation chair, Charles once more asks George, "have you any idea, as to how we shall remove the stone, without making it look obvious that the chair has been tampered with?" George replies: "Yes, I think so, let us first open the back, taking the framework to allow the stone to slide out."

The atmosphere inside Westminster Abbey had the feeling of reverence and anticipation. The King led George toward the old coronation chair; while the grandeur of the ancient masonry walls seemed to whisper secrets of all the monarchs of the past, today there was an undeniable sense of tension that would make even the most reverent of souls shiver.

As George stepped out onto the old stone floor, he couldn't help feeling a sense of history. Yet, almost immediately upon reaching the side of the altar where the chair sat, a draft of air brushed past him; sending a chill down his spine. He glanced around, trying to locate the source of the breeze and saw that the heavy oak door to the side of the altar remained firmly shut; giving no indication of light or what might have been an entry from the outside.

"Strange," George muttered under his breath, instinctively clenching the square of parchment that Charles and the Queen had given him. It contained all of the vital measurements for the meticulous task. George felt overshadowed by the eerie ambiance of the abbey; each step he took the draft got stronger, until it was swirling around him like an unseen whirlwind.

"Alright," he declared, more to bolster his nerves than anything else, "I'll just take my measurements and be done with it."

He could hear Charles and Henrietta conversing softly behind him; their regal grace rather unbothered by the strange air. "You all right," he called back to ask the King, who was just then adjusting his posture, glancing over George's shoulder; looking at the chair that had been the throne of the English kings for centuries.

"What do you make of that strange wind?" Charles asked, raising an eyebrow as he stepped in beside George. "It's odd," replied George; now taking a moment to steady himself beneath the flicker of candlelight. The aged wood of the throne had a regal presence, the carvings depicting tales of glory and struggle.

"You would assume that such a large building would have an atmosphere of its own; a climate formed by the many souls that have passed through here over the generations. When someone comes in from the cold, you often feel a warm thermal rising. But this is different, isn't it?"

George concentrated intently on the measurements, the draft continuing to swirl around him as he went on to complete his task. "The presence of a draft in such a closed space… It's strange indeed."

As he finished jotting down the final numbers, George then took a deep breath, he felt his heart pounding from the atmosphere inside the abbey. Charles nodded his gaze wandering about the magnificent sanctuary. "Indeed, it seems we're not alone in here," he mused, his voice low and contemplative. "This Abbey has seen countless ceremonies, but it feels like the air itself has a story to tell, doesn't it?"

Just then, the draft shifted again, rustling the parchment in George's hands, causing a shiver to run down his spine. He turned, and through the side door, he caught a fleeting glimpse of movement. A flutter of something bright-white, darted past, too quick for him to comprehend fully.

"What was that," George blurted out; his thoughts, racing. Henrietta, who had been standing quietly, approached with an expression of fear and intrigue. "What do you see, George," she inquired, her voice soft yet filled with anxiety."I thought I saw angels… it was just a flash," George stammered, trying to articulate the inexplicable anomaly that had caught his eye. "A brief flicker by the door."

"Perhaps it's just the light playing tricks on us," Henrietta suggested, glancing toward the doorway. "I could swear I saw them too."

"Or perhaps," interjected Charles with a twinkling smile, "the spirits of our forebears are curious about our plans. They were once crowned in this very chair, after all. If not having the knowledge that you are the Guardian, I would not feel safe,"

George chuckled nervously, but warm laughter didn't dispel the mystery in the air. The unease persisted, a lingering question hanging like a delicate thread in the vastness of the abbey's darkened corners. Wentworth, the royal attendant, entered the main aisle with a flourish, bowing deeply before the King and Queen. He was oblivious to the strange occurrences as he began recounting tales of the coronation chair's storied past. With grand gestures, he spoke of events long gone and those yet to come, while the draft continued to swirl gently around George and the royals.

"That chair has witnessed history, has it not? It holds the weight of destiny within its structure," Wentworth said theatrically. George found himself captivated; the earlier unease fading slightly as he listened. "Indeed, it does," Charles remarked with a knowing smile, while George jotted down additional notes, now pondering both the physical and historical significance of the throne and the precious stone placed underneath.

As they prepared to leave, George cast one last glance at the coronation chair, feeling a connection that reached beyond time. Whatever force had stirred the air, whether real or imagined, had woven itself into the fabric of the moment. He couldn't shake the sense that they were being watched, but somehow, it filled him with a profound feeling of belonging.

In that ancient abbey, where the echoes of royalty entwined with whispers of the past, George turned to follow the King and Queen out again into the crisp evening air, and motioned for Wentworth to follow. George had the sense this might be the door to see heaven's guiding hand, and more than just a knowledge or understanding of God's word, but a strong present of God there too was overwhelming, while giving a peace of mind and a deep sense of relief that God was there too.

George then went to removing the back framework then he and Wentworth tip the chair backward, having the chair resting on the floor facing upward. Then it was just the simple task to lift the chair straight up and let the Stone itself slide out, resting on its back edge and pulling up the Throne.

"Wentworth, let us now prop the stone onto its side edge and stand it up, to allow us to then tip it forward and back into the wheelbarrow. It was the Queen who first seemed uncomfortable, and then the King spoke,

"Wentworth, did you leave the door open, or did you notice that someone has come in?"

Wentworth, who was not in a position to see the side door, suddenly looked around and then said, "Your Grace, I cannot see the door, but wait, did you see that?"

"What, do you mean, that wisp of smoke above the altar?"

"Yes, I saw it too," adds the Queen: "look, there is another; just above you-two now. How completely unsettling."

The King, not unfamiliar with a place that was used a lot for debate outside of Parliament, the tense feel he had, he didn't want to show and making a well-informed statement to dismay any fear, he said; "Perhaps just another trick of the sparse lighting and the remnants of dust particles that were brought up when we entered and then caught by the draft we all feel."

Wentworth: "I suppose, but we have now been inside almost twenty minutes, and I'm assured that that side door has remained closed; indeed, I have noticed no one since we have arrived to enter."

The King: "Strange, I felt the same thing when we had first come in."

"That's right your Majesty," George said, "but I'm also hearing something that sounds like a swirling wind; do you hear it?"

"No, I hear nothing; Wentworth, do you hear the sound of swirling wind?"

"No your Majesty," Wentworth replied, "I am amazed though how much sound we generate from the shuffling of our feet when we came in. This is not some kind of religious ceremony is it; I'm not sure I should be here with all the trouble with the Catholics in the North. Is this leading to a ritual?"

"Maybe so," George replied. Not wanting to say what he really heard was a faint cry ; 'unite the kingdom.' A mission of his Father and so made George wonder if his father had heard the same faint cry too. "You want to know the truth, most of your Scottish settlers were at one time Catholic believers, and rather than banished to the continent, agreed to change their belief and settle on the plantation in the hopes that they might get a chance to return home someday. You need to show some pity on those who are under servitude; give them a break, and it might serve you well in the future,"

Just then, George had the stone up, and sitting down on branches that he had picked-up from outside. From there it was easy enough to flip it into the wheelbarrow. He motioned to Wentworth to get the door and started his way out. What they had just witnessed seemed only an oddity; nothing more was said, and in fact, didn't seem to garner much interest now that they were on their way outside. Once outside, the wheelbarrow was stationed near the side door, and once again, Wentworth was put in charge of looking after; and guarding the Stone.

"Thomas, we wanted you here for a good reason," says Charles.

"Aspects of our shared reverence for God are bigger than the congregation we serve; do you think it matters to God exactly how you show your devotion? And just in case you're thinking how this would ever matter to God, anyway; , . Tell him George."

"Thomas, I wanted you here to witness what happens, so keep a sharp eye out because we need an objective observer, and the King and I will want to question you and get the facts of what has happened."

"And remember that God might just be looking after us all," says the King. "And is always just an arm's length away."George and the King finished up on their work inside. They planned to make a facsimile of the stone inside the chair so that no one would notice it had been taken. George had made up four stone tiles to fill in each of the four sides of the chair where it would be visible. And to just reinforce the deception, a drapery of velvet would be tacked up along the outside of the chair, making it impossible to see the stone from afar.

To notice any deception, you would physically have to draw back the little velvet drapery that they had put in place to even see the stone in order to form some kind of opinion whether the stone was real or not. The chair itself was now a lot lighter, but who would know as there were not those who sat there and would be seen as distasteful as if they were to do so. The chairs sat back in place; the King, Queen, and George now made their way back out to rejoin Wentworth who had been appointed to guard over the stone. The King motioned forward, and the group took off towards James's Palace and the Chapel.

The Stone of Destiny, Coronation Stone or the Stone of Scone. Furgus M'or an early king of Dál Riata, and later of Scotland brought the Stone from Ireland bringing it Scone Scotland around 1234.

Testing the Stone

Chapter 10

"As it is now approaching midday," remarks the King. "Still I think we should not be bothered as we make our way; I made sure to schedule the first round of refreshments to be brought out well before midday, as for those in the banqueting hall should be well busy enjoying the activities that I have arranged for them and hopefully admiring the fine luncheon that I have served."

The stretch they had to travel along the Pall Mall and to the chapel was just a little under a half-mile in distance; the closest they would come into view of the banqueting hall would be when they crossed alongside the southern exposed parade-ground behind the horse guard and stables. The vast open parade-ground would actually make a fine buffer zone, for if anyone did happen to notice them, and tried to approach. When you finally passed the horse guards Parade Grounds, it became clear the strength with which George possessed, with an enormous girth and muscular build, King Charles would comment on George not yet breaking a sweat.

"George, I'm sure you ask for help in your labor with the wheelbarrow, and so please, ask if you are tired out."

George replies, "Oh no your Majesty, it's more about controlling the wheelbarrow. I dread the idea of being approached by bandits; nonetheless, whereas I would have to run off and try to hide it before it's detected, we can't have it go missing for another 300 years."

But then they were already approaching the chapel. The Queen looked annoyed as if being bothered by a pesky fly, and was about to hurry up the King so they could get inside when she remarked, "where do they come from this time of year?"

The King: "I do know what you mean, strange I've never seen anything like it."

As Wentworth got the door, the King and Queen rushed in, followed by George with the wheelbarrow. There was still enough light of the day, and that time of day let the light shine through the elaborate stained-glass windows that were installed above the back end of the Chapel. As the light shone through, it streamed across the inside and over the center aisle and seats to either side. But there was something going on quite strange that immediately got the group's attention. "Good Lord," cried Wentworth, "it looks like an infestation I hope it's not a wasp's nest."

"Of course not," the King said, "Wentworth, the chapel gets a regular cleaning once a week."

"I think that it is the same thing that was so bothersome outside," remarks the Queen. "George, do these look anything like the water flies that you have in Scotland?"

"Oh, you mean the midges. ."; answers the King, " but I think it's the wrong time of year for that, but again, that was in the Highlands, but I've never seen them this far south."

"Unless it's a swarm that has come up the Thames," says George, "and have decided to make your quaint little chapel their home,"

"So where do you suppose we should put it," asks the Queen.

"There is a pedestal that holds the baptism bowl. let's try to see if the bowl can be moved aside."

George and Wentworth then went to the baptismal bowl, one on each side, attempting to lift it off its pedestal. The bowl was empty, and so it was quite easy to lift off. George then took the wheelbarrow, moving it closer to the pedestal.

George instructs; "Wentworth, I am going to lift the wheelbarrow tilt and roll it over onto the pedestal. I want you to hold it on that side and help guide it onto the pedestal. Your Majesty, maybe you should help him; we wouldn't want the stone to crash and break while we are attempting to move it onto its pedestal."

So, as George tilted up the wheelbarrow and allowed the stone to roll forward. Wentworth and the King were on the other side of the pedestal and catching the stone and directing it to its place .

The group stood in amazement, having placed the stone on its pedestal on the left side of the chapel's altar. Just then, the Queen notices that the group of water flies or whatever seemed to start maneuvering up above the altar, directly above the stone, the sunlight still shining directly over the altar, just where the swarm of flies was shown. Flashes of light were what they saw, how the lights were moving made it look like a swarm, it seemed only that it was getting brighter and brighter.

"Now I wonder, what has stirred them up so," remarks the Queen.

"It must be the acoustics in here," says Wentworth, "plus the vibration caused as we moved the stone in place."

"I'll go and move the wheelbarrow now that we're done, outside," says George.

Wentworth opens the door as George takes the wheelbarrow outside. Upon his return, the Queen had noticed that for that brief moment George had stepped outside, that all visible traces of whatever kind of flying insect it was, had disappeared. And now that George has returned, the insects also seem to have returned and were again swarming some distance above the Stone and again could clearly be seen in the light that streams from the Windows at the far end of the Chapel.

"Strange,- thing," the Queen says, "George, is it common for you to be followed by the flies? Do us a favor and step out once more, please."

George, following the Queen's request, promptly steps out through the side door, and just like before, the flies disappear.

"Wentworth, ask George to please join us and come back inside."

"You see," just as George returns from outside, the insects return. As strange as it seems, the insects must be attracted to our friend George."

The King: "George, are you wearing any kind of scent, something that would attract the flies?"

"No, your Majesty, that is, I don't think so. I've gotten into the daily habit of bathing every morning."

Wentworth, who is now standing next to the Stone, remarks, "wait a minute, these aren't insects at all; looking at them closer, they look more like shards of light that are moving independently; and though I believe what I am seeing, I can offer no explanation as to what's causing this."

At this point, the four, the King and Queen, Wentworth and George, are all standing and encircling the Stone where it now sits, gazing at the strange phenomena of light that swirls above the stone. "Okay, so if what you say is true," George says, " I would like to try something else that might explain what we're seeing."

George then tells Wentworth to bring forth the old lantern that they had found at the Abbey.

"Now bring me the incense burner the chapel uses now, take incense when it's out, and put it into the old lantern, and replace it on the chapel's incense burner chain. Wait, better yet hand it to me."

Wentworth retrieves the old lantern and hands it to George. checking to see what incense had been left there in the Chapel's incense burner, and gives that to George too.

"Okay, let's make a match to light the incense. I'm anxious to see these two relics of the old religion," explains George, "and what happens when we put them together."

George instructs Wentworth to retrieve a candle from the altar, and as George lifts the old lantern, then tells Wentworth to bring forth the candle and holds it underneath to light the incense. Instantly, as a cloud of incense rises, the shards of light begin to slow down, as they seem to grow larger and larger.

The shards of light could now be easily seen as four individual objects swirling around above the stone, and still growing bigger. Then all at once, they turn into four Angels and what appears to be a central beam of light, which then turns into what could clearly be seen as a ladder ascending upward.

As the group, in their amazement, are staring up at the Angels, the Angels seemingly stare down at them. The Angels, saying nothing, but motioned with one hand to join them.

"Charles, I'm scared, please make them go away," pleads the Queen.

"Wentworth, get me that chalice that sits behind the altar, and bring it to me," asks George. "careful, as it should be filled with holy water."

Wentworth brings forth that chalice , as George goes over to the old lantern, now an incense burner, and now holds it up.

"Wentworth, carefully hold the chalice of holy water beside the lantern; I am going to tilt it, and have the incense roll out into the chalice, and that should extinguish the incense. Let us see if this goes away."

Wentworth, following George's instructions, holds the chalice underneath the lamp as George drops out the incense. Then, in an instant, the Angels, along with the beam of light; looking much like a ladder, instantly disappear. But now they notice that the sun no longer shines through those back windows, in such a direction directly over the altar, and so in an instant, everything they had seen previously has vanished. Awestruck, the four of them stand speechless and amazed at what they have just seen and experienced. And for several moments, they seemed to be frozen, all having their focus towards the altar.

"So, this is what you wanted me here to see," asks Wentworth.

"I'm afraid not, in fact, I'm not sure of what I did see," says the King, "even so, Wentworth, you should keep this in strict confidence and tell no one of what you did or what you saw today. I keep you in the highest confidence, just as you are my emissary to the northern regions."

"So, about that; your Majesty," George hopes to explain, "Wentworth here, has some misgivings on sending Hamilton to plead with the Scottish assembly."

"Even though Hamilton's position with his family and the Scottish assembly is diminished," explains the King, " he would still have the right to attend, but then this has little influence. And taking that into account, that whatever he would say, would have a diminished leverage; having no voice of his own, his appearance at the assembly was to go to waste; and so, I appoint him the emissary of my voice. Naturally, as their King, I should preside over the assembly, whereas Hamilton stands in my place, and has my voice. And by God, George, if the Assembly has a problem with this, I instruct Hamilton to close the assembly, and I will personally travel to Edinburgh and establish the Scottish Star Chamber."

"Oh, I see, Hamilton's family still has power in Scotland."

"But, the question is," asks Wentworth, "will they accept Hamilton as an emissary, when they have readily been demanding presence before their King?"

"Scotland's regency has been intact since the days of William the lion," explains the King, "so their acceptance of me as their King is not in doubt, but again they should realize, that this is a united Britain, which is ruled from London, the chosen seat of power and so I prefer to take the council of my Star Chamber and dispatch injustice throughout the realm. Those at the assembly are just going to have to realize that, and this is how it will be; their concerted efforts will guide Scotland, where I have a much more difficult task, and that is to guide a United Kingdom; both in England, Ireland, and Scotland."

"Yes, and if you were to ask the Archdeacon," Wentworth says, "he would say the Kingdom should be ruled from Oxford."

"So Wentworth, what does Loud think of Hamilton's prospects with the Scottish assembly," asks the King.

"The Archbishop is confident that Hamilton is the correct choice to bring the King's voice to the assembly, he himself being from a prominent Scottish family. The only thing he does see that might be helpful to persuade the assembly, of course, is a visit by the King himself."

"A visit is not totally out of the question, but more of an inconvenience."

"You wouldn't have to travel across country," explains George, "and expose yourself to all your enemies that are lurking behind the bush or along the roadside; if and when your presence is needed in Scotland, why not take that journey by sea, for you have quite a merchant fleet at your disposal which must make sea travel quite safe, as I am witness to upon my arrival in England just recently."

"And you'll have me believe that you'd be happy with another sea voyage," asks the King, "after having spent almost two months aboard ship to get here. Anyway, you have brought me such a fine string of horses, I would feel that it would be a dishonor to you if we didn't travel up to Scotland on the horses."

"Charles, I'm glad you thought of that, for it would not be my place to have done so;" says George, "and you're right, these are the finest of horses you'll find anywhere on the continent, I would estimate from here to Paisley a four-day ride, with another two days to reach Aberdeen. Of course, if we were to test the horses, I would say we could make Edinburgh in a day's ride."

"Splendid then," says the King, "I do believe it to be the right way to go, this will give me a chance to find my true allies, then North of England and along the borders of Scotland.

I do think, though, it best not to push the horses, and plan a three-day ride to Barwick."

"I believe it would also be in our best interest," says George, "to take the entire string, ensuring us, that we can have fresh horses if need be."

"If we keep it to a small group," the King adds. "say ourselves and four Knights, we can travel in haste, while not arousing suspicion."

Again, The King had taken his position carefully; to be able to reach the Scottish border in two days on horseback, but if they boarded one of the newer designed sloops; a smaller one masted boat much like what the Northern Scots would use to get from one island to another, they could reach all the way back to Turriff and Fyvie castle in the same two days. George knew of one such fleet that would take the men from the quarry to jobs across the kingdom. Somewhat larger in size were the Sloops that they used, but just as swift and seaworthy, and able to take on a good-sized cargo; too.

"This is that assessment though of Hamilton's that we get from Wentworth that troubles me," says the King, "I would think as my appointed adversary Hamilton would get the respect qualified of one who is to lead the assembly."

"You have made a good point," answers George, "as if Hamilton brings little respect upon himself, how much respect is he to garner for us towards your Majesty. I think we should look at what assets we shall bring to the assembly, and surely our presence upon such great stallions can be seen as an asset."

"Yes, might they remember, the service of your father, as a Captain of Calvary in the protection of my grandmother Queen Mary; this is an asset, as they also served her father well."

The Queen's Chapel, built between 1623 and 1625 by Indigo Jones for King James having it constructed for his Queen; Ann of Denmark. Located on Marlbough Street on the Pall Mall across from St. James's Palace in London

At the Queen's Chapel

Chapter II

The king arranges for two of the gifted stallions to go with Hamilton and have them shipped from Berwick to Aberdeen, from there they have taken across country to where he and George would take them. George would take the King to Fyvie Castle, a place where the two spent their early childhood both as wards of Leslie. George and the King would then follow Hamilton when the time called on them to make an appearance before the General Assembly in Scotland. Most of the Assembly had already known that Hamilton, as the King's main representative, would immediately call for the Assembly to gather.

What they really wanted is to have the King appear; those who had just recently signed on to the Covenant; the assurance that the Assembly should make policy in Scotland, and to hold the King accountable.

The King was taking a chance, leaving England in the hands of Parliament as they were sure to take advantage of his absence. Matters of the Crown will be left to the Queen. And if she is anything like her sister Elisabeth the Queen of Spain, or just a bit like her Mother; Marie de' Medici who ruled France, it's more likely to have the members of Parliament trying to keep a low profile.

The King and Queen, after dinner and crossing the street, headed toward the chapel adjacent to St. James's Palace. Looking across the street, they noticed that the Queen's, her confessor, (sent by the King's mother-in-law who would still guide her daughters and influence world power) was already across the street and headed towards James's Father's Palace on the Pall Mall.

The Queen's mother had a hand in sending George, back to Britain; it was only natural, that of course the confessor that she and her mother relied on in France, would be sent on to still serve a daughter and the Queen of England. The Queen couldn't help but to call out "George, come walk with us".

The Three had only been into the chapel twice before. Both times they had been interrupted by the strange occurrence of what they thought to be birds, that had somehow become trapped inside the chapel. This now would be the third time all three had been together inside the chapel.

When they first moved the stone from Westminster's Abbey: on that occasion the three all concluded that someone had left the door open in the haste to get the stone inside. All three then swore to the fact that it was birds, and nothing more than birds that had flown in the open door.

As the three got into a carriage that would take them around the mall, and over to St. James, this would seem like a good time to talk together about how they were, and how the Crown was to support efforts up in Scotland. Scottish society had gotten so fractured, with the influx of different national and international cultures; taking up roots in the major cities, and ports that drew new residents from Europe and abroad.

Though the Council or Highland Council stayed strong in support of The King, a royal presence in Edinburgh had been absent for way too long. Most urban residents were following the signals that they got from Parliament; way south in England, and look towards what was being laid out by their own Scottish "General" Assembly.

And so, this is what spurred a dilemma, on how the best way to deal with Scotland now. Wentworth who was the King's representative in the northern region was not that effective in Ireland and had an even slimmer chance of getting through the King's policy in Scotland. It was the counsel in London the King's star chamber representatives, whose idea it would be to send the Duke of Hamilton, up to attend the general assembly when they next would meet. Hamilton, who was tasked by the King to make a point to the General Assembly that it had no authority unless directed At first hand by the King. But then in the King's absence, the Assembly would be obligated to be overseen by the King's representative, who is now to be Hamilton.

The King still looking to gain support for the Common Prayer, in its defense, putting forth that it was nothing more than the revised edition to what his father had put together in part to unify the three nations England, Scotland, and Ireland. It was his father's plan to put together a United Kingdom under God's grace. The General Assembly's reluctance to accept the King's book of common prayer went against his father's insight into the formation of a United Kingdom under God and therefore regarded as treasonous actions under the Crowns' authority.

The other problem the King would have, would be; how to mobilize his support and establish a standing army, troops that would maintain and uphold the King's authority as needed in Scotland. The main problem was with how to raise money to support the troops established in Scotland. Separate from the English coffers, which seemed to always be scrutinized and controlled by the parliamentarians, there was the Scottish treasury.

This treasury it seems had been drawn upon by his father James I, and brought down to London, and added to the King's treasury there at hand. There, of course, were personal accounts, and the small treasuries, that of the Scottish gentry, that could be relied upon in times of need by the crown. These personal treasuries were often hidden and kept out of sight away in special rooms and hidden places.

They were also gathered together and put away by the Barons acting as a local banker who would dole out monies on account. And so even though the Royal Treas. In Scotland have officially gone to London, there still was the existence of the Royal Treasure. still in Scotland, land-barons, or the bankers for the local accounts that were still held intact by the Scottish treasury. This also included the Templars, who had after the crusade in the Holy Lands, followed Alex Sinclair back to Scotland and started an Annex; that would allow those patriots who had also come back from the Crusade, to join after participating in a ceremony that would document their time in the Holy Lands.

The problem that the King had now is that the Scottish Treasurer, who in essence was the Crown Treasurer for Scotland; would be influenced by the parliamentarians in London, and hold back funds that were needed to raise the guard he would need to be able to safely travel in Scotland.

"There was always, the treasury of The King's at Fyvie".

"I saw the plans of that once," says George, " when my father was doing in addition to the castle. He had pointed out to me, a special room he said for the King's treasure. This is when the Leslie's were the court treasurers."

"Very well," says the King, "we shall travel to Fyvie Castle, there we can meet with the captain of the Templar Knights, and I will pay them for an expeditionary force to ride with us into the lowlands of Scotland to raise the standing army that I will need."

"Truly, why not just ask for their support, are they not indebted to the crown," asks George.

"George, if I come out and ask them now, I would likely have to pay them, with funds I do not have. And if I pay one, I'd have to pay them all. I don't want to confuse my purpose, if found out, I don't want it to look as though I'm calling on the Templars to support me in a war against Cromwell's parliamentarians. It would be much better if they were to come to me, I will make my plea to one of their Captains, in hope that they will support my cause. There is such a Captain of arms who lives not far from Fyvie at a place called Barclay, do you know of such a place?"

"I do," answers George, "it's not far from Fyvie, and just a half day ride out of Aberdeen, but I say we look into Fyvie first; we will have to get a look at the plans, those are kept under lock and key at the quarry office at; Del Gotty Castle; next to the quarry, located about a mile north of Fyvie. The Templars of course are faithful, they believe that Sinclair had found in Jerusalem, plans for a new Temple, thought to have been written out for Tai Tempi for her escape from the Assyrians, it might just have been written by Jeremiah himself".

"I have always wondered what fascinated the Templers about Sinclair," the King says, "the fact that he is the exchequer of the Scottish Crown, I find troubling and wonder if I should have left the job to Leslie, would things be different. Won't there be a problem getting the plans?"

"No, I know my dad's filing system. I doubt that anyone else would know it other than my brothers; only that the keys needed to access his office and files are at my brothers' manor, just north east of the quarry. The problem we have with the Templars goes back to the declaration of Arbroath when the nobles petitioned the church to recognize Scotland as independent from the English; hence Scotland is back in the graces of the church and recognized as a special daughter. This while the Templars are still at odds with the church, while Sinclair starts the building the Temple at Rosslyn, and infatuated with rebuilding the Temple, and that this would be held in God's grace under a new Jerusalem. James V then gets the Papal decree to build the temple at King's College in Aberdeen. The Temple at Roslin was never completed. Sinclair, who had influence within the Templar society would be at odds ever since.

Although Sinclair had an idea as to how to rebuild the Temple and thus establish the new tribe of Israel, he really had no clue as to how it was to be done, even though he never discovered exactly how the Stone of Scone was actually connected. But I suspect that Richard the Third, who had taken the Stone out of Scotland, knew more about how it would be used, and of course, continue to have it be used in the ceremony of the coronation.

"All right," says the King, "we shall send Hamilton to Aberdeen; to contact with our allies in the Shire, and to make sure that all is ready when we arrive and clear our way to Fyvie Castle".

James Hamilton, son of the second Marquis of Hamilton, his father had come to England with Charles his father James I. Fought alongside Alexander Leslie the Mortimer of Fyvie Castle, once allies, their friendship would take its toll over their losses fighting in what would become to be called "The Thirty-Year War" between the French and the Holy Roman Empire.

They had both come back to Scotland nearly disgraced, licking their wounds and blaming each other for their defeat. Both men though, like their fathers before them, were high standing members of the Scottish Court, and at times They had both served together in the King's chamber of the Privy Council. The question of whether they could be trusted to work together would never fully be realized by the King.

For this was a big mistake; with Alexander Leslie siding with the General Assembly. Alexander Leslie was the illegitimate son of the captain at Blair Castle, and even though the Murray's of Blair supported the King, Leslie who was a mercenary and had gone off to fight in the 30 year war, would answer the call of the Scottish General assembly to lead the fight against the King. Charles sends Hamilton North to secure Aberdeen and waits for the King along with his guard to arrive.

The King is resolute; "Now we must make our way to Aberdeen. What shall we do with the Stone, George?"

"We dare not move it now," fearfully pleads the Queen, "I believe it's in its place; at St James's"

"You both forget that I am the son of a Grand Master Mason, and I can just as easily craft a replacement Stone, as I did by making the tiles we used in hiding the fact that we had taken the Stone away."

"As for the money you need," says the Queen, "you know that my Mother would be glad to give towards your cause, as would my sister."

"Yes, and I would greatly appreciate any and all support given by your mother and sister," argues Charles, "but this is an issue that concerns only Scotland and they and only they should be the ones needed to come forward in support".

"Yes, you would have all of France, and Spain," George adds, "with their support purely out of devotion, and what I hear from my brother; that the Vatican police, to come to your side in support, but where we would most need it, would create its own set of problems."

"Your brother, from what my sister says, the Vatican police, were given your case after O'Neill died and that they are just waiting for an excuse to pull you back to Rome."

"I will take it that my passport then is in order," George playfully replies.

"Please George, don't take it for granted; if this whole thing does not work out, we might just be joining you."

"How nice, a trip to the continent," the Queen jokingly comments, "I hope we will have a chance to visit Paris, I would so much, like to see my mother there too."

Little had she known that her older brother, King of France, would have a son of his own. Her mother would then be forced to relocate from the Netherlands, and abandon any hope to installing her youngest son Gaston to the throne of France; and for Marie to act as a vice ruler. The carriage arrives at St James's and pulls around to the front of the Chapel and stops, the three passengers hurry towards the side entrance.

"Now my Queen, why is it that you bring us here? You say there is something I must see; I remember what we saw or what we all think we saw the last time that the three of us entered here."

"No, it's not that," replies the Queen, "please come in and see."

As the three approach the chapel, they find waiting there is the Archbishop Loud, and Wentworth, who has been in Oxford and fascinated with George's library. Hamilton is also there; the three waiting for King Charles and his company to arrive. They greet one another, and all go in. The group goes inside where they find a strange portrait of The King.

"You know how my mother can be," explains Henrietta, "she has been the patron of a quite popular artist and sculptor whose work has adorned many churches and chapels and even fountains. She has commissioned that busts be done of the both of us. And I asked if we could include you too; George. And so, I had Van Dyck do a study of Charles, and apparently, he has enough sketches for myself and George to get started on those right away.

"This is wonderful Henrietta," Charles exclaims, "the three of us immortalized in stone."

"From what I hear," says Henrietta, "he works exclusively in white marble."

No one knows, what ever became of the Queen's bust, perhaps it was never made, or instead sent to her mother, who had commissioned the work to be done in the first place.. The King's bust is said to have been lost during the great fire of London in 1662 that devastated most of London at the time, and all but destroyed the King's Palace at Whitehall.

George, interested to see just how much Wentworth knows, asks, "Wentworth, what is this that Hamilton has told me, about strange apparitions seen at the altar?"

But before he can answer, the Queen spoils it, asking, "yes George, would you please explain just what is happening, in my beautiful little chapel?"

"George, I think it's time we tell them the truth about what we think is happening"

"I think the best way I can explain," says George, "is to show them; don't you think so?"

"But we have tried that with the Queen, and only got the wisp of something."

"A wisp of what," asks the Archbishop.

"I guess you would call it an apparition of a sort" Hamilton tries to explain.

"I am not sure," states the Queen, "to what we saw. But between the squeaky wheelbarrow, and what we thought to be a bird that was frightened by the aforesaid wheelbarrow, or that it be spirits, or Angels, it was not clear."

"This time we're going to try something a bit different," explains George. "Check each side before the altar, the row of chairs down along each side; try the fifth or sixth chair and see if it will not pull away from the wall; check well, for they might be latched."

George had seen similar Alters in Rome, and since the Chapel had been built by the famous Indigo Jones, it might have a similar feature. "See how expansive the front is before there are seats for the congregation; I think that there is supposed to be another altar here."

When they check, they find indeed in between the seventh and eighth chair along the wall there is a latch, that releases the chairs to be pulled out from the wall; thus creating a type of screen and dividing the altar from the rest of the Chapel, making in sort the holy of holies in the Temple, as the stone is placed in front of the altar. The problem they have is in finding the release. Wentworth then shouts out, "Yes, there is a break between the chairs, and it does look like there is a latch holding the chairs in place."

The Archbishop answers, "There must be a catch release somewhere, check underneath the chairs to see if there is not one there."

"No, I don't see any type of latch at all." Wentworth says.

"You really have to hand it to Jones," comments the King, "his design to make a unique answer to unlatching the row of chairs on each side. I had always thought the cross on the altar here had been constructed odd, let me try something here."

The King steps up to the altar, where a modest cross is set in a base open on its backside, as each rise to lay the cross down onto the altar, he pushes it forward, as a lever and it gently lays down upon the altar. At that, was heard a click of the latch on each side to the row of seats that flanked the altar. The chairs now were free to swing away from the wall cutting off the altar from the rest of the Chapel.

"Look! In the center of the floor," says the King, "another altar is rising up."

"And look," adds Wentworth, "there seems to be a separate vault below the altar,"

"That looks just about the same size," adds the Queen, "as that rock we moved in here with that wretched squeaky wheelbarrow."

"Oh yes, clever man that Indigo Jones," says George.

"And what rock was this," asks the Archbishop.

"That is precisely why I had all of you here today, and that is to act as a witness to what you are about to see, and on the threat of death," commanded the King, "talk to no one about this, ourselves excluded"

The Chapel now has been made into two separate areas, divided by what looks like a screening, and having the seats that were once along the sides of the Chapel, now facing directly towards an inner altar: with a new altar standing now before the congregation seating.

"Now we go to work," states George, "your grace please approach the altar, while the rest of you remain behind our newfound screen.

"Your Majesty if you would please light the incense burner, I will pull it up by its chain, so that it's above the altar."

The Archbishop asks, "your grace, shouldn't I, as head of the church, the inside the inner sanctum?"

"Technically Archbishop; I, am head of the Church. But we are talking about a tradition that goes back almost one thousand years and before there was even a Bishop of Rome; way before the assemblage we know as, religion. George here, is the descendent of the high priests of Ireland, whose ancestor had brought the very stone to Scotland. By his lineage, he is the Guardian, and the defender of the faith and such able to take his place as high priest.

For a united kingdom

Part Three

Scotland and The Bishop's War

Al Ponte'

First folio ~ MMXXV

The Quarry Secret

Chapter 12

"Lord Archbishop, believe me, this is nothing I sought, and only by sheer coincidence, I was thrust into this position. But as a priest, I am well aware of its formidable responsibility and hence, Guardian, whose secret my ancestors did convey, as such have always been a defender of the faith. So let's see, what secrets have been guarded over the generations."

So as George raised the now lit incense burner, and it started to rise and set to swing over the altar, the beams of sunlight came streaming fourth from the stained-glass windows overhead. But there was nothing really strange or odd, as this would happen naturally around this time of day anyway. It was the way the beams of light came directly over the stone, which made it seem strange, and now the way the smoke came from the incense burner swinging now high above the altar, has started to engulf the chapel.

The way that the smoke danced around, it really did look like angels ascending a luminous ladder, which was suspended over the stone. But what would happen next had everyone there questioning, just what exactly had happened. The next thing was heard although calm voice saying, "unite my Kingdom, unite my Kingdom on earth as it is in heaven."

Of course, because George and King were well separated from each other, as well as from the rest of those on the other side of the newfound screen; King Charles thought that he was hearing George, whereas George, new better, and himself knowing of the legend of the stone, in a better way to accept what he heard, still just initially believed it was King Charles who had been overheard. George initially was to say nothing about the incident, and King Charles did not want to pry, thinking it was only part of a prayer that he overheard. Indeed, everyone thought it had been a prayer that they had heard. Later, Wentworth would ask the Archbishop what it was that he thought he saw.

"Wentworth, although it might seem unbelievable, but I think, what I saw was Jacob's ladder rising up from the Stone, and I heard then the word of God. But we are both bound by the promise we gave King Charles not to talk to anyone about what we saw. "Unite my Kingdom, unite my Kingdom on earth as it is in heaven."

"Oh yes, I see it now," Wentworth says, "but how can this be? And who would believe such a story?"

King Charles now instructed that Wentworth return to Oxford with the Archbishop that they were to retreat from London, as it would no longer be safe for them to stay. So, in the middle of May 1639, Hamilton with five ships loaded with arms and close to 300 soldiers sail off to the northeast corner of Scotland to where King Charles would pull in his alliance from the Scottish Highlands. And while Hamilton and his troops secure Aberdeen, George and King Charles would find their way to Fyvie Castle and look for the treasure trove, that once was the bulk of the Scottish treasury. With Aberdeen secure, the word went out for the king's ship, that it was safe to enter Scottish waters and head for Berwick, just north of the border between England and Scotland. Once the King's ship could make out Berwick from the Captain's spy-glass, they would veered north and out to sea as if heading to Norway and Sweden.

Then at the point it seemed to leave the furthest point North; it rounded the point north of Fraserburgh and headed in closer to shore. Arriving at the quarry's port at Crovie; coming in at high-tide, giving it only hours to load up and head back out before the tide changed; or wait till the next high tide. Just north of the larger surrounding town of Garden.

It was where usually a barge would be ferried in and out of port, full of the quarry's product of cut stones, doorways, and window treatments; all sorts of cornices to adorn the roofs, as well as a large assortment of the mason's tools of the trade; all to be pulled behind a ship heading south, sitting just outside of the port. Smaller boats would often tie up to an incoming barge and be there ready to bring in the traveling free mason to the dock. At the incoming tide, ships could come right up to the dock and tie up in the deep water port; here they could stay as long as they needed and then go out on the next high tide.

As their ship tied up to the Crovie dock, George and Charles were able to look over the dock and see if there might be any trouble there waiting. The Port was busy with the bustle of activity; teamsters, dock workers, and a flock of apprentices; hard at work, you could see the trying look of strength on each and every face. As they stepped off on to the dock, George turns to King Charles and says: "Watch what happens when I show my face; even though I doubt that anyone here has ever seen me before. You keep your face covered and watch the workers and teamsters."

As George pulls off the hood of his cloak, showing his face in the bright morning sunshine, the steady bustle of activity seems to have skipped a beat. All activity now slowed to less than half of what it once was, while the focus was now on George, as he was clearly now their center of attention.

"It's the family resemblance, they probably think I'm a son, or brother, even though they've never seen me ever.

"We should do just that," says The King, "and not be discovered. How far is it did you say to Fyvie Castle?"

"It's less than half a day's ride, but we shall have to do some discovery first on our own, so we shall ride to just east of Turriff and to the house of my father's.

Just West, and before the town of Turriff, is the Quarry and his office; where I hope we shall find some records of when he did the additions at Fyvie."

"Do you think we will see many troops between here and Turriff," asks Charles.

"I think not, but I'm not sure, both Leslie and his brother, are off on the Continent, fighting for what has become, the Holy Roman Empire, operating outside of Rome, in what the Pope calls the great recovery of the Catholic Church."

What the two didn't know was that the great general of the 30-year wars: Alexander Leslie had returned; not alone, but with men and armament; horses, arms, and armor for 150 men; given to him, as a supposed payment for his services by King Gustavus Adolphus of Sweden.

But, it was Leslie by means of the Scottish treasury, had bought the arms and armor, when he first went into support of Gustav, Emperor of the Holy Roman empire. And it's not quite sure he was given equitable estate, upon his return. Leslie, and his brother, both would command vast armies on the continent unbeknownst to others all paid for part and parcel; man, horse, and sword, out of the Scottish treasuries, whether it was part of Templar money, that was brought back after the Crusade or actual money from the Scottish treasury cannot be verified, but George and The King, would soon find out.

"Watch this," says George.

Looking around, George sees one of his uncle's masons there on the dock, and drawing his attention, gives him the sign of the Grand Master.

"Do you see that man over there handling that cargo that I suppose is sand; over there," George asks the King.

As George directs The King's attention towards the man, the man hurriedly steps away disappearing among all the activity at the busy docklands.

"Did you know this man? Has he now ran off to betray our presents? How ever do you know it's sand that they're loading in to that wagon?"

"I've never seen him before in my life. It's sand because the Mill uses a lot of sand; see how loaded down the wagon looks. As an apprentice mason who works at the quarry, they sometimes work the docks too. I showed him the sign of distress where he will bring us a Templar knight to escort us to the quarry. I believe that is why he ran away so quickly."

"But how did you know he was a mason?

"Simple; by the color of the stone dust on his clothes, its no-doubt come from the quarry.

Suddenly the man appears with two saddled horses and says that he would arrange for our escort to the quarry. George says that there would be no need for an escort, as he knows the way very well, and trusts that their safety would be assured, due to the amount of traffic to and from the quarry by brother masons. George mounts a dark horse, while King Charles gets on a rather large bay, one expected as like what King Charles is used to; one used to carry an armored Knight, but actually is one used regularly on the docks and in the quarry.

"Am I wrong," asks the King, "but isn't that the ship's horse? Are we to come back this way?"

The horse now in the bright of day, was now a shiny dark black, all over except a white diamond blasé on his forehead, which readily identified the horse.

"Not exactly your Highness"

"This is my horse; like the one's I had brought you it's also from Spain, and also an Andalusian stallion."

"I was taken to believe that all Andalusian stallions were white."

"Your right, most all of them are. This horse comes from Seville where they raise a rare breed of the Andalusian stallion that is black. Where most of the stallions are born grey and after time turn a solid white, these are born brown and turn a solid black and stay that way for the rest of their life. It's a gift to my Uncle who with all of the horses used at the quarry has acquired a love for them, but never had a one special horse of his own."

"I can see now how your family became somewhat famous at commanding cavalry."

"Bruce was so reliant on their cavalry," explained George, "that he claimed they would always be at his right hand.

He gifted this land to my family here in recognition of their essential contribution at Bannockburn to turn the English troops around. And again in the defense of your Grandmother, for delivering a victory at Glen Livet."

"So it's another war horse. When I first saw them together, when you brought them to White Hall, I noticed that they were similar in stature, but just thought that they had all came along with you from Lisbon, and so were all of a similar Spanish breed."

"It was the one horse that wasn't hidden during their trip here from Lisbon, the so called 'dark horse'. It was stabled in the ship's hold in plain sight, as it would have been impossible to conceal all of the horses because of the smell; and then said it was the Captain's horse, and essential to work the hosts on the ship's crane and used in port to arrange for supplies."

"It's kind of small for a work horse."

"Yes, but what would a coastguard lieutenant know about a Portuguese pony."

"I thought that these lands here of your family were gifted by James IV, for some building project they had done?"

"Those are the lands adjacent to Fyvie Castle, Rothiebrisbanc, on the other side of the Aberdeen to Inverness road. You could say it was for the civic projects done in Aberdeen, in lieu of pay, work that was paid for by my Uncles."

"But you were thereby able to collect rents on the lands, didn't they?"

"Only a few wad setters who farmed the land to grow rye for the Whisky distillers up towards Inverness. We did make a profit from the grain and was always kept in a good supply of spirits."

"On that, I can't wait to get there; is it close by, I hope?

"I'm interested to try this Scottish Whisky."

Just under half a day's ride, to where the two came ashore, they would ride on to George's family home.

"It's close by, and an easy ride."

Just as soon, as they started out, they could see there was trouble; there were fires in the fields and great billows of smoke that could be seen for miles in the horizon south. Seeing this, George felt that it would be much safer, to not stop at his uncle's house, who was the Grand Master Mason and ride straight through to the quarry, whereupon with the sign of the Grand Master they could enter the quarry and find refuge amongst the Mason community.

And it was quite easy, for George bore out a striking resemblance to his uncle, and once showing the proper signs was shown past the guard at the entrance to the quarry. Here, they would find new clothes and take on the new appearance of working masons. From there it would be easy enough to walk over to where his father's office was and to look for what records there were that were saved from the additions that were made to Fyvie Castle.

What George knew was that his uncles had built a secret way up and out of the quarry. They were always well guarded, of course. Some of them would at just seeing George would not say a word, letting us pass while others George would signal to. As they both started up the narrow passage way, up the stairs alone, the King asks again; "Your uncle, kept the records for the work he did at the Castle?"

"I'm sure there is, I can remember seeing them here when I was just a child. I can even remember my uncle showing me them, he might have even shown me the vault, and where they put it. I would just like to be sure before we start poking around at Fyvie.

"I remember talk of a secret room," says the King, "and that everyone thought it was on the third floor where there's a den, but if it was there, it was well hidden.

"It was the entrance that was on the third floor. I'll need to check but think that the vault is actually on the second floor; you have to enter it from above. I do hope that we can find the plans that will show how to enter from that third floor den. Usually, any plans of a secret nature would be given to the owner, and he would either hide them well or destroy them. I think that there was a reason my Uncle showed me the plans, that maybe he saved a copy for in case there was trouble, just for the reason we look for them now. Let us both hope that we can find them."

They reach the top of the quarry, and after just a short walk they reach the quarry offices. The King finds it strange there were now no guards in sight, none anywhere, asking George;

"Where are the guards? Have you seen any about?

"The guards are posted around the perimeter, and told to stay clear of the offices. They guard the stairway and know we are here. They might decide to double the guard."

The quarry offices looked like any local fortified manor house, with the main part of the house being multi leveled and having several stairways. George's uncle's office being on the third floor. As they approached George led the way to the front entry and turning a statue around operating like a screw that worked a fulcrum; and when George pushed in a stone near the door which unlocked it and allowed them to enter.

Once inside George finds a wall that had carved wooden

paneling and finds a section that when pushed opened to a lift; one that would take them directly to the office on the third floor. Small only enough room for maybe three men, a design of George's Uncle that worked on a counter weight or a large stone and could be easily activated by just a pull of a chain from inside the lift. Slowly the lift carried them up to the third floor, but still a bit faster than if they would have taken the main circular stairway located near the front door in the entry way.

As the lift stopped at the third floor, and they step out to find the office surprisingly well-lit; having the natural light of day filling the large open office space.

"It's surprisingly bright up here, is this also a design of your uncle's?"

"Yes, it's the windows placed above, and the large windows along each side that let the natural light fill the office."

George begins to search thru a large cupboard filled with drawers of files and drawings.

"Do you have any idea where the plans to Fyvie might be?"

"Yes, I have found them here, but there seems to be more than just a single addition done; I have found not one, but three additions done by my uncle. One for the Forbes, another for the Frasers, and then one for Leslie. I think it best, that I make note of all three additions."

"It seems that we have definitely set into our enemy's camp," replied Charles.

"How do you mean, your Grace?"

"They are of those who have signed up in support of the covertures cause, and now we find ourselves in their lair. If I find that they have used up the Scottish Treasures to finance their armies, only to fight against our friends in France.

"What? They don't realize, that you, yourself have just spent the last fifteen years to do; something that the last four King's could not do and bring us to live in peace with the continent? Can't they see, that by your marriage, you stand in good relationship with France, Spain, and Italy?"

"George, my good friend, I'm afraid that they only weigh in the account of our religious differences; afraid that we would try to convert the rest of England. Anyway, it only adds to why, with Leslie's help, Scottish mercenaries were over in Europe, fighting for the Protestant cause in Bohemia, and against my own nephew at that."

"Even though we have both, whenever the subject comes up, adamantly deny our cause is to try to convert anyone. Maybe so our enemies, if we can. The Templar loyalty is firmly with the crown, having taken them in after the crusades; when they were abandoned by the church and the rest of Europe."

"So you don't think they see us as the Catholic threat? I'm sure that Leslie's made it known of my supposed Catholic tendencies."

"I think that by now they know Leslie, and who he is. If it were a contest between yourself and him, they would have no second thoughts as to where their loyalty lies. I have by a trusted account, that most who ride with Leslie, are something other than connected with the Templars, and we're not sure just what kind of mercenaries, that Leslie had brought back with him."

"Well we know now that he might just have returned with his own private army, and instead of turning in all the arms and armor to the Crown's Armory, he's decided to turn treasonous. No doubt to cover for his and the Assemblies' larceny."

"Do you really think that they might have taken irresponsibly from The Kingdom's treasury?"

"Maybe so, but irresponsibly; probably not. They probably made the case the money would be well spent, that is to protect our interests on the continent, in the Palatine. Knowing of my good cousins need for fresh financing, saw it like taking a lump of sugar from a baby. And not knowing of my intentions in the Netherlands; as any support from Spain against the Dutch they just wouldn't understand."

It lays heavy on my heart to think of our poor friend Buckingham, having some defeats, but still having done given it an honest effort."

"Well if what you say is true, we must be ever so careful now as you say we are in the enemy's camp. But don't despair; no less than a mile from here is my family's land and estate; we can be safe there."

A Treasury uncovered

Chapter 13

“And what about our friends close by in Temple Brae?”

“You mean the Templars in Turriff? Hard to say, how sympathetic they are to our new French allies, and how much of a grudge they still hold or whether or not they have let their older wounds heal.”

“But I would think they would naturally have a strong alliance of course when they understand our special task, and moreover, our taskmaster.”

“And what about your men of the Quarry; how far can you trust them?”

“Ah, your majesty, they are our insurance policy. All Masons hold a special truth amongst themselves. But they would also hold on high, the up most loyalty to that of the Grandmaster.”

“What; above that of their King?”

"And that's just it until we know better, I think we would be better served by an allegiance towards the Grandmaster. Believe me, when I tell you that they have a special place in their heart for Scotland and the Stuarts for taking them in when no-one would. Be assured we'll have no trouble at the quarry, or in the offices. We will be; Master and his apprentice. Can you now become the Apprentice, your majesty?"

"Whatever in the devil do you mean. Shouldn't I be the Master? I am so much better qualified."

"I'm afraid Charles, not this time. They will see the master's face in mine, and we might even run into someone who actually knows me. There it would be most easier to explain you away as my apprentice."

"I see your point, but just don't let anyone see me bowing down to you. That would be quite inappropriate. And for my own sanity; please don't over-play your role."

"Don't worry; we don't do that; bowing and such; it's left to ceremonial events only. But don't ever look me in the eye."

"You've got to be kidding me; right?

"And you're right again, I couldn't help myself."

"Always the joker George, but even though then, we must make our time at Fyvie quick, is there any indication on any of those records of revisions where the vaults are located?"

"No; these are just the records of accounts, I know because my Uncle would have me go over them when I worked here, but once I have the account numbers, I can look in a special place where he would keep such plans. It was just my good luck to have seen my two of my uncles in Ireland on my way here to see you.

And they told me of a special drawer in his design table. They have to be there; I just need the correct account numbers to make any sense of them."

"Is this the table over here?"

"Yes, look along the side just under the tabletop for a carved acorn; it should slide forward and release a drawer again just under the edge of the tabletop. Do you see it?

"Yes I've got it"

"Good, pull out everything in there and bring them over here closer to the lamp."

"These looks like they're in code, can you read them?"

"We'll see, if he hasn't changed the code, I used to read it all the time, and even write it too.

"Do you see the vaults listed? And maybe just as important any accounts leger?"

"There seem to be several ledgers, but their mostly of weapons and armor with a mention of

several vaults."

"That's what we want, if we find the vault, we find the treasure."

"Only these don't seem to have anything to do with Fyvie Castle, but OK then, there is a mention of a treasure inside one of the vaults."

"Fyvie? Does it say where?

"It does mention a vault, though it's not at Fyvie, but hidden away in the back of the Quarry, apparently there is some trick to open it."

"Do you think that you know where it is, can you get into it?"

"Wait a minute I think there's something here about vaults at Fyvie, yes there are two of them, one marked lower and one smaller marked Higher."

"Do you think you know where they are."

"I know exactly, where they are. The trick will be getting in past the guards, but first, let's go back to the quarry and see what we can find there.

If this is what I think it is, aw what I believe to be the map; this should help quite a bit. I'll feel a lot better going back to the quarry; It'll be a lot safer for us there anyway. Fancy a spot of tea old man? We can elect our strategy and relax a bit before going back."

What they didn't know is that Leslie's forces were starting to gather at Fyvie. Whatever they were going to do had to be done fast. Safe back at the quarry the two took time to rest, George found some biscuits, and a teapot, and wondered where it was that the master masons stashed their tea.

Looking around and letting his nose lead him in the right direction, he found himself standing in front of what appeared to be an empty mantelpiece above the fireplace.

Noticing that there was nothing on the mantel he surmised that something must therefore be behind it. Seeing that one of the panels behind the mantel looked loose. When he goes to see that it is; he easily slides the panel to the left, and it opened to a small cupboard.

Inside he sees something that is just what he was looking for, something he hasn't seen in many years, and remembering having to fetch when he was a very young man, still only a child; His Uncle's tea caddy, a clever puzzle box with sliding square and rectangular pieces on the top. George had opened the box a hundred times for his uncle, so without really thinking, he opens the box right away. Having found the tea, George and the King set down to take a break and look over what they have found.

"You don't suppose that they'll miss these," asks the King.

"It's the week's end, and only a skeleton crew is working. Only apprentices would be here now; doing what needs to be caught up on. It's not likely the time for an audit, but yes they'll have to go back as soon as we are done with them."

"Are there any clues, that you can see, as to how to get into that second-floor vault, the one which is supposed to have the royal treasury?

"The drawings of the second-floor, show what looks like a door, and an arrow pointing to the right. Ah, here's a diagram which looks like a latch, it looks like it's on the wall, on the right of the fireplace, there on the second floor."

"Good, we'll try getting in, after we have return the charts. What did you say about a vault that contained arms?"

"It was that riddle that I found in my uncle's puzzle box, I think I know where it is. Let's go see if we can find it now."

"Do you think that it might be the treasury?"

From there, King Charles and George found their way to the quarry entrance. As it was a Saturday, only a skeleton crew was working, still it wouldn't be too much out of the ordinary to see a Master Mason in the quarry at this time of day; looking for a mass of stone to quarry in the coming workweek.

"Now, according to my uncle's riddle, we should take the right path and follow it back to where we find the sentry; a sculpture of sort; one who watches over the vaults. This should be an arms store, one that goes back to when the Templar knights were welcomed to Scotland."

"Yes, a marriage of convenience, as at the time they've just been excommunicated from the Church, and hunted all over Europe; so, what you're saying is that there were two separate vaults?"

"Separate, yes, but I've always felt that this one in the quarry was shared. Because, as a youth, I admired those who had come back from the Crusades. This is a Templar region and Township. There was always the thought that they were made to put down their weapons, but in storage, ready to be uncovered only in defense of the Scottish Kingdom, or for the King; himself."

"Yes, I know of their store of weapons, and that they would come to my aid, but had no idea as to where they were or where on earth they would ever have stored them."

"I can remember, two columns at the back of the quarry, but that was years ago. That part of the quarry should have been cleared of stone by now. Of course, I was to know nothing, of the vaults, but of course, I did. It seemed very strange to me as a child watching them put the posts up, and it seemed like they had also laid out a trench that went back right up to the stone. And there they are!"

King Charles and George had walked what seemed to be all the way back to the back wall of the quarry. Here they came upon two columns, both of classical design, one had about two quarters of the way up was split by four smaller decorative columns that held up the rest of the original column.

At the top of one of the main columns, there was a small figure of a man carved in stone. Directly across from the two columns was the back rock face of the quarry. But of course, the quarry didn't end there; they had just continued in another direction. As George looked the place over, he told Charles that he needed to go over to the center work area, to find one of the mason's fulcrums; a large shaft of hardwood that the masons used to move around the stones.

George knew enough not to follow the path along the back wall, that would lead to the center work area; the area along the back wall was dangerous and there was always a chance of being hit by falling rocks. The center work area was where most of the masons, along with their apprentices, would cut and then rough out the stones.

The Master mason would have set up his office here; normally a small shack where he would keep drawings, and plans of the projects they were working on. Here he could find a fulcrum to use, as they were usually lying about the worksite. So, finding the sturdiest amongst those that were there, he ran back to find The King and explain what they needed to do to open the rock vault.

As they together now turn the column, the rock face behind them starts to move, revealing the vault built behind. The little man was the key that allowed the column to turn and open the vault. Inside was a cachet of swords and targes, smaller swords, and a large metal chest that was roughly five feet by four feet; with a large padlock on it.

"If this chest contains part of the treasury, it should correspond to what's in the castle vault also," said the King.

"This looks more than a Templar cachet. Some of these weapons could have come from the Crusade, but look at that Blazon on the staff, this is not from the Crusade, but much earlier."

"That resembles the Blazon of William the Lion, but without the double treasure."

"The Rampart Lion, the Roman symbol of power and authority. I've seen some of the Roman Legion battle standards when I served in the Vatican in Rome. But I believe it to be much older than that. Your right, it does bare a resemblance to the battle standard of William the Lion, minus the double treasure, there is a legend that Somerled had used such a Battle Standard to raise the army of men he needed in Scotland, perhaps given to him by the Alban Lords to help him recruit the men he would need when he came over to Scotland.

It would have been hard for a foreigner, who spoke with a foreign tongue to raise the force he would need. And when Somerled was betrayed, the Battle Standard was then handed over to King Malcolm for an agreed upon price. Malcolm then gave the Standard to his son, and heir; William, who from that time onward would be known as William the Lion. You see, it's much older than a Roman Standard; a crimson Lion on a field of gold; that, perfectly describes the Battle Standard of King David, who was called the Lion of Judah. This must be another relic brought from Ireland; that of the Guardian, the Defender of the Faith, who would have in his possession."

"Yes, it does look like it, but how did it get here? "Legend has it being brought over by Somerled, and used to rally an army, given to him by the Alban Lords."

"I don't see it; how could just this raise an Army?"

"I would think that many a man would literally give up his right arm to stand and fight under the battle standard of David, the lion of Judah. There was always a question as to how Somerled, a definite foreigner, could have raised such a great army in so short of time."

"You can't be serious about this, can you?"

"Well, look at it; as a battle standard, it's not of this century, it looks more Romanesque, a blazon hung across a cross beam and not flown like a standard. And taking a closer look, the threads of gold are in the different shades of very high quality.

"You're right, this is of the highest quality, and I must say that I have never in my life seen anything like it.

Even the French, and you know how they are, have nothing close to this craftsmanship."

"Look at these, I thought them to be lances at first, but after a careful examination, I'm amazed to realize that they're solid gold and appear to be lamps, and very old at that."

"You don't suppose they are more relics of old, something brought back from the Crusades?"

"Wouldn't that be something if they were from the First Temple?"

"Then I guess they would be more of the relics you seek."

"You could be right; David's Standard and gold lampstands from the Temple."

"What's that over there? It looks like a silver candelabra. Perhaps something else from the First Temple in Jerusalem?"

"They're a pair of flintlock pistols."

"Pistols? What kind of man would carry something so fancy into battle?'

"As you must have noticed, there is a shortage of wood here in Scotland; that's why the pistols were crafted in silver. And from what I can see must have been quite a craftsman at that. We can use them; can you see any of the primers over there?

"But how can this be? they look brand new? Those primers, what do they look like exactly?"

"I think they are new. There's a gunsmith outside of Perth in the burgh of Doune; half gunsmith and half silversmith, known for his elegant design of pistols. Look for a small box or bag filled with a lot of tiny silver hats. Can you still handle firing a pistol?"

"Sure, deadly at eighteen yards, but I'll have to admit my eyes are not those of a young man anymore.

"Quite a piece of equipment they are. Even has a belt clip on the side. Here are your little, tiny silver hats, and what looks like the musket balls, too."

Next, they had a look at the trunk, which was a large chest that measured roughly 5 feet long by 4 feet high and about 4 feet deep. It also had handles that looked as though they were just a couple of pieces of pipe attached to each side, just large enough to get some sturdy poles through to help move the chest.

This was a large wooden box secured by a lattice of iron straps that bound it together. The heavy chest was also supported off the vault floor by what first appeared to be a pair of heavy wooden ties, but with a closer look, they were actually made of the local stone of the quarry. This area of Scotland ran a thick layer of so-called Pink Sandstone; the regular type of sandstone would be a grainy, sandy beige. However, in parts of Scotland, there would run vast areas of this kind of pink sandstone, made pink by the large amount of iron content found in the stone itself.

As the sandstone was cut and exposed to the elements, the iron in the stone would literally rust and turn darker, turning it into the color of weathered wood. But this iron content also made this type of sandstone an excellent building material; stronger than regular sandstone, but still soft enough to shape and even finely carve into geometric shapes and figures. And this was the work that was done in and around the quarry at this time.

The Stone was a superior stone to build the type of fortified manor houses you see in the Northeast corner of Scotland.

At the quarry, the Master Mason would usually set up a little office shed and from there would keep all of his designs and work contracts, if not usually working for the Grand Master.

There were church restorations and civic projects paid directly by the Crown or a Royal Architect who would also have to work out of a little shed of an office, like all the rest of the masters working inside the Quarry. There could normally be as many as ten Master Masons here at work, and a small city of little sheds in and about the quarry.

Fyvie Castle south of Turiff in the upper Aberdeen-shire.The boyhood home of both George and the King.

The Turriff Trot

Chapter 14

As it was Sunday and the Sabbath, most if not everyone, was neither at home or at work; so George and the King were quite safe in going through the vault and making an assessment of its contents.

"This seems to have a rather large padlock on it; it will take quite an effort to break this off. Have any ideas George?"

"We might try the key I found in my uncle's tea box. When I came across it, I thought it might have something to do with the vault."

George then tries the key that he had found to see if it will open the big padlock on the chest. And with a click, the big lock opened, and they were then able to lift up the large lid of the chest. Inside, they found what they were looking for; the emergency treasury, the needed funds that would be required to sustain the Kingdom, and enough to raise and pay for an army of men, might that be required.

"Take out five thousand merks to pay off your Templar Masons, while the rest should be safe if left here for now."

"Loyal, they are these Templar Masons, their numbers are growing to include bankers in London, but there are council members that secretly want to return to the Vatican authority, and find Templars an embarrassment."

"And their unbounded loyalty has my Scottish ministers at court very nervous."

"Could it be that they might have something to hide, like what they are trying to do in America, controlling the trade in Tobacco and East Indies rum. I hope that you can continue with adding to the plantations that your father had started."

"You say that they're trying to control the trade, how do you know that it isn't me who wants to control it?"

"Well, that would certainly stand for your looking after your father's interests."

"And you would think that expanding the number of plantations would benefit my efforts over there? I think you're right; George."

"A healthy competition will always ensure a better quality of merchandise in the end."

The question now was: were there still matching funds in the hidden vaults at Fyvie? The problem was that the chest in the vault at the quarry contained much more than money; there were jewels, ingots of both silver and gold, and also what looked like land deeds and landlord contracts. But as for gold and silver coinage, having both made it count, they agreed it to be roughly five hundred thousand marks. The jewels, rough gold, and contracts, who knows what they might be worth? This cache of treasure seemed more to be that of the main treasury, although it was not yet known what the vaults inside the castle might contain.

As this was Sunday, even the staff in the castle would be at a minimum and easily avoided, especially if one appeared to be of the priestly order out on a Sunday. Still, there was a heavy presence of Leslie's troops gathered outside of the castle.

There's always a good chance that they could be stopped and questioned by the castle guard on duty as they approached. Their best way to avoid the chance of being stopped was to casually, and nonchalantly enter through the back of the castle closest to the Castle's Chapel. No one would even think of stopping a priest from questioning his business. The two easily slipped into the castle, and according to what was depicted on the plans found in George's uncle's office; they made their way up to the third floor.

"According to what was on the drawing, go to the right side of the fireplace mantle, there should be a lever on the end, it should pull up."

Searching the side around the mantle, King Charles quickly found the lever and was able to open the passageway; it was dark, and only when George produced a candle could they see that it had been totally blocked up with brick, the staircase going down to the second floor was gone.

"It looks as though there have been changes made; let us look on the second floor, to see if they might have put an entrance down there."

The two then made their way down to the second floor, and what they found astonished and seemed to upset the King. It seems that the vault must've been moved to somewhere else because it certainly wasn't on the second floor.

The space where the vault was supposed to be, was open to the rest of the room, creating a side room, and there was nothing, not even a suggestion that there ever was a vault there. Instead, there were two chairs placed across from each other up against the opposing walls of the alcove with a small side table under a window, perhaps a card table, suggesting a pleasant nook under a window; a place to sit and play cards.

"This is quite odd, there was not a mention of having the vault moved; I wonder what they did?"

"Well, for some reason, they moved it. We need to find our escorts and tell them to send word to Montrose and Lord Graham that their presence is required under the threat; of the Scottish Star Chamber Court, to meet the Lord Treasurer here within a fortnight."

"I don't remember that window there being so large the way it is now."

"You were in the vault?"

"I must have, though I was still a little boy, I remember when my uncle built it, I was here; and I strictly remember thinking how small the window was."

"I'm certain there was no window. Could that have been the way that someone entered, having broken in from the outside?"

It could be done, on the pretense of enlarging the window. It was likely done in broad-daylight, on an off day.

"You saw it watching your Uncles building the vault, and I never saw it. I do remember seeing it from the yard and always wondering where it was because I thought I knew every room in the castle. "So, do you think it's true of the rumor that Leslie had taken from the Scottish treasury monies to finance his efforts on the continent?"

"Frankly, I don't know what to think. I'll wait to form an opinion after I've met with the Scottish Star Chamber.

Better yet, I should call for a meeting of the Earls, the Council of Ten, and see what they know of this. I rather found it odd that the vault in the quarry contained so many jewels and gold, other than coins. It makes me wonder if some part of the treasury, from the vault inside, was moved and put into the quarry vault.

George: "You don't think that by calling them here is not going to reveal your presence? Your father had serious reservations about some of the Earls and their loyalty, which goes along with his resentment of how they treated your grandmother."

"In times like this, it would not be unusual for one member or another to call a meeting of the Council. And you're right, I don't think it would be wise to reveal my presence here right now; Ogilvy is the Templar Captain, he shall stand in my place, and will see if we cannot get the truth from Leslie. Hamilton is my representation here, and though they haven't given him the due respect, that one would expect to be given to the King's Councilor. With Hamilton there, and having Ogilvy as his Captain, they should take the request to answer some question regarding the treasury as a serious request from their King; even if I'm not present."

Meanwhile, George arranges to have the cachet of weapons found in the quarry taken to the royal Armorer at Barclay Castle. The masons at the quarry would often use the grade of the land to move large consignments of the pink sandstone, most of which had been worked at the quarry mill and shaped into door and window dressing.

Using the grade of the land below the quarry, George has the arms put on a wagon and simply rolls it downhill to where he'd arranged with the quarry pond to flood the small channel located at the bottom of the hill. So the word went out to flood the lower creek, up to the point to where it met with a bridge, where a hoist could be set up to unload the barge, and from there, put on to a wagon. From there the wagon could travel west, towards the main Inverness to Aberdeen road; below Terriff. Avoiding being detected by traveling on the road above, having to go through Turriff to get to the main road. The road that would take them south, to the Armorers at Barclay Castle. And of course, it would have looked like just another barge load being moved by the quarrymen.

Barclay Castle is situated on the main road between Banff along the northern coast to the southern port town of Aberdeen; was a perfect place for the Armory, then having the men assemble in force at Turriff;

Turriff is commonly known as a Templar township. As Montrose rallies men to join the Covenanter's resistance, King Charles enlists the Second Marquis of Huntly, George Gordon, to start to gather men from the Highlands to support the King. Hamilton, by then, had had a limited success, raising support based down close to the English border in Berwick.

When the Covenanters hear about the scheduled meeting and that his supporters were to gather on the lower green field below Terriff, they naturally assumed that King Charles would attend the meeting, even if there was nothing said that he would actually be there. A fortnight has now passed since King Charles put out the request to have the council of Earls or Star Chamber meet at Fyvie Castle.

The meeting is to be held on the second floor to ask about the missing vault and crown treasury. And even though King Charles would not be at the meeting himself, he would be close by and be able to listen to what is said and hidden safely away.

George and the King, now hiding out in George's Father's office at the Quarry, are planning how best to question Leslie about the Scottish Reserve.

"I think that it would be a grave mistake for you to make your presence known by attending such a meeting."

"But I need to hear from these men, to find out just what happened to the treasury. And just what would they have to say about your presence? "

"There may be a way for you to, not just listen, but to actually see what happens in the room. I remember seeing the plans, years ago, and remember a very strange addition made to the second floor; a closet of sorts with a section cut out opening to the Second floor. My father had said that it wasn't uncommon to have such details worked into such a place to spy on one's adversaries."

"And I do remember just such a place, we would sneak up there to listen to what was being said in the gallery below; the both of us as kids. Remember?"

"Yes, let's hope that we can get in there before Hamilton confronts them, and make sure that there is a tapestry hanging in place. If not; may we have the chance, to put one up ourselves."

Looking out over the Great Hall onto the second floor is a Gallery that would usually have Court Musicians. Now it was hidden behind a large sized tapestry that ran the length of the entire eastern wall. The tapestry has a weave that could be seen through, yet hides one from view from the Hall floor below.

"That sounds like a perfect solution, do you think that there is such a place, there on the second floor?"

As the night of the meeting rolls around, a group of men arrives at Fyvie Castle, answering to the request of Hamilton, who had come up from his assignment in Berwick. George and the King are now dressed as some kitchen servants, taking their place in the hidden gallery above where the meeting will take place.

All were in attendance except Leslie, who must've been so scared that he forcibly took Edinburgh Castle, breaking through the main gates with a petard. Lord Davies speaks to the others present before Lord Hamilton arrives:

"I hear that King Charles seeks the treasury that was once in this room."

John Stewart, the First Earl of Traquair answers, "it's plain to see by having us assemble here, that he presumably wants to know what happened to the auxiliary treasury. So, gentlemen, just what do we tell The King?

"Who is to argue that it was spent in defense of Scotland's allies," answers Lord Rothe, "It was voted on by the Council of Estates; we were all there."

"My office serves the King and not the Council of Estates," says Traquair, "let's not forget about the deeds, land rents, and promissory notes that have gone missing. This could be the demise of all of our families.

"If indeed King Charles has them, and uses them to show a breach of promise," says Rothe, "it will be the ruin of us all. While we haven't been made aware of those yet by The King, he may not even have them."

"I heard, that there was much more to what we had found in the old vault. Gold and gems along with over two hundred thousand merks," adds John Lindsay; the Earl of Lindsay.

"That is what worries me," says Rothe, "if they weren't here; then where? Does King Charles know where? If he is up here searching, we need to find it first."

"Leslie believes it must have been taken to Edinburgh," says the Earl of Traquair, "and he has now traveled there to take over what Arms and Treasury that's there. He knows the real importance of finding the Notes and Deeds."

"Do you think that the King would use these things against us," asks the Earl of Lindsay.

"Let's face it," answers Lord Rothe, "we all owe our titles, our lands, and estates; in a promise to support the Crown. By our refusal to support the King when called upon; by all legal grounds, could be seen as treason."

Lord Davies looked around the room, sensing the palpable tension among his fellow lords. He knew that the arrival of Lord Hamilton would signal the urgency of their situation. "We must act with discretion," he urged, lowering his voice. "Our survival depends on how well we navigate this crisis. We can't afford to show weakness to the King."

John Stewart, 1st Earl of Traquair, shifted uneasily. "Discretion is one thing, but if the King learns of our mismanagement, our feigned loyalty looks suspicious at best. We must prepare for the worst."

Lord Rothe leaned closer; his brow furrowed.

"What if Leslie's information is correct? If the treasury indeed went to Edinburgh, and if it was moved to safeguard against our actions... We don't know how deeply the King suspects us.

He could already be laying plans."

The Earl of Lindsay cleared his throat, the weight of their collective anxiety evident in his tone. "What's done is done. If we are to convince the King, we must have a united front. We must weave a story that intertwines our actions with loyalty to the Crown."

"Loyalty?" snorted the Earl of Traquair. "Hypocrisy more like! Declaring it spent on allied defense may buy us time, but it's a thin veil. Should Charles demand the accounts, we shall be found wanting."

Lord Rothe nodded. "Perhaps we can propose that a full accounting be prepared to present to His Majesty. It could show our intention to protect the Crown's interests while buying us space to recover what we've lost or hidden."

"I'd caution against it," Earl Lindsay replied, glancing toward the door. "What if the King presses further? If he senses our desperation, it could provoke his wrath. We must remain calm and let him come to us before offering anything of substance."

Lord Davies fixed his gaze on Lindsay, considering the dynamics at play. "You speak wisely. Let Him come; however, when he does, we must be ready. If we admit to wrongdoing, he may choose to dispense with our lives as easily as he would soldiers in a skirmish."

"Then what course is there?" asked Traquair, desperation creeping into his voice. "We cannot afford to be at odds with the King, nor can we afford to lose the trust of our peers. Each moment we delay truths being unearthed is another moment for suspicion to grow."

Lord Rothe stood tall, the resolve fanning the flames of his ambition. "We play the cards we hold. Let us stand together, united in our loyalty to the crown, while we retain leverage. For now, we must appear as loyal servants, and the streets of Edinburgh provide cover for those seeking to hide their treasures."

The murmurs of agreement rippled through the group, though apprehension hung thick in the air as they braced for Lord Hamilton's arrival. Each lord knew the stakes were higher than mere finances or titles; loyalty to the crown and their lives were entwined in this dangerous web. The weight of silence lingered, but among them, decisions began to form in the shadows—a pact forged by fear and driven by necessity as they dared to tread deeper into treachery's embrace.

"So it's up to us, to save ourselves, and at all costs find these promissory notes and Deeds," remarked Lindsay, "to ensure our titles and protect us from the ensuing liability we may incur. What do we know of The King's Captain George Gordon, The Marquis of Huntly?

"The Marquis of Huntly was seen on the Aberdeen to Inverness Road," reports the Earl of Traquair, "and he's heading north towards Inverness. He was last reported to be enlisting troops south of Elgin in Aberdeenshire.

"He was said to be traveling with a good-sized wagon," adds the Earl of Lindsay, "presumably carrying arms.

My question is: had he accomplished his task just south of here, and is he planning to arm more troops in the North? He may be looking to squeeze Leslie's men here at Fyvie."

"If I hear you correctly," asks Rothe, "we could have come into a trap. When did you say Huntly was seen on the Aberdeen to Inverness Road?"

"I believe someone saw him today," answers Traquair, "I don't think he could have organized anything yet."

"What if he had a waiting force," questions Lord Rothe, "one that is ready to go and ready to ride?"

"And that this meeting itself may be a trap, and that any minute the castle could be raided and all of us captured," the Earl of Lindsay says with a touch of fear in his voice.

"Once they learn of Leslie's taking of Edinburgh Castle," adds Traquair, "Fyvie will no doubt be on the defense of Royal forces; with its centralized location in the overwhelmingly Royalist Aberdeenshire. Soon Leslie will return in force, and here at Fyvie will be the safest place to be."

"And what do we say to Hamilton about the auxiliary Treasury," asks Lord Rothe.

"We just need to tell him the truth," answers the Earl of Traquair, "and that what we found in the castle's auxiliary Treasury came to no more than a few thousand merks. We just say that when the Treasury was uncovered, nobody knew of its existence and saw it as a divine intervention and sought the best way to invest it."

"What if there are more than just arms that Huntly is taking to Inverness," asks Lindsay, "he may also be carrying the deeds and notes that we're after. We need to stop him before he reaches the Castle."

"I think it's time to assemble Leslie's mercenaries," answers Lord Rothe, "let's see if we can't flush out The King's advocate to find what we're after before it's too late."

"Right," agreed Lindsay, "have them assemble on the open plain below Terriff; this will make sure that they're not confused with Leslie's mercenaries, thought to be quartered at Fyvie. Leslie will have to go after Huntly, have him put under arrest and taken to Edinburgh; his father will know just how to deal with Huntly."

"Excellent idea," says Lindsay, "I see where you're coming from on this; so it's seen as more of a civil action than a rebellion; carried out by Leslie's men.

"Sure, and if we come across the King," argued Lord Rothe, "he can be swept up along with the rest and later held for ransom; for the notes and deeds we're after."

Building the Kingdom

Chapter 15

That was enough heard by George and the King as they silently left from their perch above to signal the reception committee to come forth and enter the Castle. Hamilton arrives with the Royalist Sir George Ogilvy of Banff and his second, his cavalry commander, and a leader of the area Templars. Immediately, they're recognized as all highly positioned local authorities. Only then did the others realize that King Charles would not be there.

"I believe you know why you are here," starts Hamilton, "and that King Charles wants to hear the accounting of an auxiliary treasury that used to be held here at Fyvie. Where is the Earl of Leven? Does he plan to take charge of the Castle here? I don't see Montrose either; I rather thought he'd attend."

"As Scottish exchequer," spoke up the Earl of Traquair John Stewart, "and it's my duty to report and clearly explain as to how this auxiliary treasury had been found and subsequently invested. The others here are senior members of the General Assembly of Glasgow and represent the Assembly."

And so it's as simple as that; this auxiliary treasury, all of a couple thousand merks, was simply stumbled across, even though I knew not of its existence. Leslie felt that he was free to invest it as the Assembly saw fit to do so. The Assembly felt that it was in support of Scotland's and mainly the Assembly's best interest, to fight on the side of our Swedish allies.

"We knew nothing of any Royal reserve," says Rothe, "It was literally a small half cask barrel of coin, not something you would consider as a reserve treasury.

The investment was brought before the Assembly, and the Earl of Leven stepped up to take the offer of support to the King of Sweden. King Charles was presently fighting for the control of the Palatine, the Rhine Valley in eastern France.

"So it made no difference that the present Elector of the Palatine is the King's own sister's child," asks Hamilton, "The King's own nephew, if you hadn't realized. When the Assembly met to allocate its newfound fortune. Why didn't you ask for the King's attendance, as it is written in the Assembly's bylaws, a stipulation put in place allowing the Assembly itself to take place?"

"So where is King Charles anyway," Traquair asks, "Here we are again; meeting with only a few of the principal parties in attendance."

"King Charles is in London," answers Hamilton, like if they had any right to know, "He awaits the arrival of his Mother-in-Law, who plans to visit King Charles and the Queen. He has much on his mind, such as where his Scottish auxiliary has gotten to.

"His Mother-in-Law, keeps the King in London," asks Lord Rothe, "The Regent de' Medici, Queen of France, and an Italian Catholic; not the best company to have."

"What would you do, if it were your Mother-in-Law?" quickly asks Hamilton.

"He makes a good point, John," adds Traquair.

Even though neither Leslie's Father Alexander or Montrose bothered to attend, King Charles hears what he came to hear, in that what treasure held in the vaults at Fyvie; monies that were allocated thru the General assembly and used to finance men and arms to fight in the thirty years war; useless to say though, as they were fighting on the wrong side that would have been supported by the Crown.

It's hard to say which way Leslie's mercenaries will lean. Thinking that the King would attend that night and not wanting to see a royalist rally in the adjacent town of Terriff (Pronounced 'Turra') the Covenanters decide to rally there themselves and rout the town, demanding their support. Their plan was really to kidnap the King and force him to appear before the Assembly, charging him with sedition against the General Assembly of Scotland; some members had wanted to demand a ransom from the King.

Within a week, Leslie would meet with some of the representatives of the General Assembly; again, the meeting would be held at Fyvie Castle.

After their clandestine appearance and overhearing what was said at the Fyvie Castle meeting, the King immediately dispatched a message out to Huntly, warning him to look out for the Covenanters' men, and that they were out to stop and arrest him.

"Leslie's back," George tells the King, "and it seems as though he's meeting with members of the Assembly tonight, and I'm wondering if we might again try to listen in?"

"I don't know, it would be taking a dangerous chance, seeing that they're after us both."

"Yes, but it would be to our advantage to know exactly what they have in mind, wouldn't you agree?'

Even though reckless, as The King's own mother-in-law, had taken residence in Denmark, and was doing well to present their other daughter's side, that being Spain.

The Covenanters thought to have had the West Coast covered in case of an Irish reinforcement coming across to support the King, but didn't fully understand that King Charles could have just as easily recruited forces from either France or Spain and have had those forces be readily at hand.

Leslie, upon hearing of the meeting, has now decided to attend while gathering his forces on the greens below Terriff and deliberates whether or not to go in and try to capture the King. Leslie's action is relayed to the Earls Council at Fyvie, where it is discussed what capture and measures they should take against Leslie and his mercenaries.

The question goes out to muster up a Templar force to go in and deal with Leslie now, sooner rather than later, sending a clear message to the General Assembly that covert action will not be tolerated by the Crown. But, as the Marquis of Huntly who is the leader of the royal forces in Scotland, confers with, Hamilton who is the King's magistrate in the North; he directs Huntly, for now, to stand down, and instead send in a cavalry of mainly older Templars; to route the mercenaries from Terriff, and make sure to have the town swear an alliance to the King; all of which was readily easily done, if not done already.

"It seems, on that, we have a split in the loyalty with the Crown," the King tells George, "I wish there was some way to unite those who have chosen to side with the Assembly instead of staying faithful to the Crown."

"I will contact some of our best quarrymen," says George, "most of them are the old Templar knights who are working at the quarry; and have them appear along the road into Terriff above where Leslie's mercenaries are gathered. Have them under a flag of truce, present the town's petition of their loyalty to their King, saying that they wish to avoid any sort of a confrontation and wish that they disband so to satisfy the wishes of the town. That should free up Ogilvie to secure Aberdeen; there is one thing that I wanted to try in Aberdeen at the old chapel in Kings College. There is a theory that the Stone was much larger than it is today, there are stories, that originally the stone was split in half and then in half again; with a quarter given to Bruce, and the other quarter shipped back to Ireland."

"You think that you might have one of those pieces? May be a piece of a piece? Or perhaps the Stone was switched. But everything is too strange, and it has to be one of the pieces."

"We will try again; this time at your Great Grand Fathers Chapel at Kings College."

The King had sent the Marquis of Huntly with a wagonload of arms to Inverness, but they needed to secure Aberdeen to ensure the ship could dock and pick them up along with the horses to take them south to Barwick. However, the gentry in Inverness had voted to support the Covenanter cause earlier that year. When the Covenanters learned about the arms destined for Highlanders who supported Charles, they had to act quickly to stop an invasion.

"As much as I have faith that Huntly will succeed in raising the troops you need here in Scotland, it are those in Inverness I'm worried about."

"As much as this northeast part of Scotland has traditionally given its full support; Aberdeen is something quite different. It has drawn those from the central, bigger cities, those who have trade with England and with Parliament. They look for support from London and have let this alliance influence their full support of their King."

"Without a strong presence here I think that they know they won't be challenged. They hear that the Assembly has now voted to reject your efforts to unite God and Country and to lead the nation to a more prosperous outcome. If we can have the same result we found at the Queen's Chapel, that might be enough to sway their support and be more willing to come together as one nation under God."

"And do something like we did in London and invite several members of the assembly to witness. But what about the incense burner, don't you need that as well?"

"I find that it happens well enough when I am alone without the incense burner, but with the presence of others, it helps to have it."

"Well, don't tell me, that you have taken the incense burner with you."

"Yes I brought it with me just in case we might need it. For all I know, there might have been a piece of the stone there in the little chapel on Iona. With all the Kings that were buried there, it does make sense; and I did feel the presence of Angels when I had first walked in, and I was alone."

"I've sent the Marquis of Huntly with the wagonload of arms to Inverness, but after that, we will need to secure Aberdeen, so the ship can dock and pick us up as well as the horses to take us south to Barwick."

But what the King and Huntly didn't know is that the gentry in Inverness had earlier that year voted to support the Covenanter cause. Not much later the Covenanters learned about the arms and that they were destined to fall into the hands of Highlanders who supported Charles, not so much as that he was now sitting on the English throne, but that he was, first of all, their Scottish King. The Covenanters would have to act quickly if they were to stop an invasion of heavily armed Highlanders.

How the Covenanters knew about the arms probably had to do with the Highlanders themselves. Of course, most of the Highland clans, were all in support of their Scottish, now English King. Owing to the fact that the Stewart dynasty had gone back almost one hundred years, there were still others that have contested the way that the Scots were electing their Kings. Yes, as always it seems, there were those, as always claiming rights to the Crown and others who thought it was wrong to have the Council of Ten be more or less in control, rather than having a more traditional King.

Of course, it seemed to the latter who were also the ones that were claiming their rights to wear the crown themselves, so of course, they wanted to do away with the Council and have a more traditional Kingdom where it was much more based on what power they could show within the kingdom.

The Covenanters were soon to discover the arms shipment and so stopped what they believed to be an onslaught of a Highland invasion. It was common knowledge for some time that King Charles would try to rally his support, that what he had in the Northeast and the Highlands. In the Northeast were the most powerful of Clans, that of the Gordon's, or the Marquis of Huntly, who he had himself arranged for the arms to reach the city of Inverness. Inverness though was not controlled, and not part of the Gordon's lands, but mostly controlled by the McDonald's friends, and sometimes in the past were enemies, the two clans always bickering between themselves.

The McDonald's, whose title of chief, had been stripped from its founder Donald, chief of the Clan Donald, Lord of the Isles, and that of Ross, which incidentally was exactly how Donald had lost his title, and which was handed down to his cousin, who would take the title Chief of the McDonald Clan. This was, of course, decades prior, but it's kind of ironic that he would lose the title, and just ten years later the lands of Ross would also be given to the McDonald Clan; as part of a legal judgment in civil court; it just took ten years. After Donald, then defending his wife's claim to the lands of Ross, had confronted a loyalist contingent, mainly made up from the Lords who had an interest; wanting to control the shipping trade out of Aberdeen; mainly to English ports. But after a day of fighting, Donald had a change of heart and couldn't find himself to slaughter fellow Scots and withdrew.

After finding the arms The Covenanters quickly put Montrose onto the trail of how and where the arms had come from. Montrose found out not where or how, but what was of a major importance, and that was where another cachet of arms, and where they were to be held. Charles had no choice but to defend the arms intended to raise the army that he would need to be able to stay there in Scotland; for if there was no army in Scotland, King Charles could not remain there. Charles's plan was to confront those in the assembly before their peers, and demand that they show their loyalty to the Crown. The problem was that King Charles had presumed that they would honor his choice, that of Hamilton, to represent his voice at the assembly.

Hamilton had in the past, had troubles with the some in the assembly, but had resolved to relocate to Ireland; with the reputation, that Hamilton had to bear more or less insured that there would be a measured resistance, not so much as to the Crown, but to Hamilton himself. King Charles would have to confront the assembly himself if he was ever to maintain control of the church in Scotland.

Another problem was that the Stone had not been used inside Scotland for generations and might have well just been forgotten by too many. Now it was time for Montrose to raid the cachet of weapons that were stored at Barclays Castle. It had all gone like clockwork with utterly no resistance, except that of the Page teamster that had taken the wagon loaded up with the crates of arms. During the raid he had tried to escape and was killed; the very first one to lose his life, to a misunderstanding of why Charles needed to raise a force in Scotland.

When the news reached the King that the arms sent to Inverness had been taken, King Charles quickly dispatched Ogilvy's light cavalry force to Barclays to quickly guard what was left of the weapons. Ogilvy though was a little late getting to Barclays, as the Castle had already been taken by Montrose. But Montrose decided against a confrontation and fled. Ogilvy was to find only the cachet of weapons guarded by one single dead page.

"Do you think that our plans have become known by the assembly," George asks the King.

"I'm not sure, but I've been advised that it is not safe to stay and that it is not yet the time to retreat to Aberdeen."

"It is a half days ride to the High Constable's Castle Slains, located just north of Aberdeen; It's situated on the coast, where if we have to, we could board a two masted sailboat, that could quickly take us all the way south to Berwick."

"And what about my precious ponies, shall we have to give them up and leave them behind?"

"By no way would we leave them; they will simply, when ready; be taken to Aberdeen and loaded on to the Sovereign, remember they're after you, not a pair of horses."

"So what am I to say about my Scottish ministers and my friends of the Privy Council?"

"I had advised your father to be coronated here in Scotland, but he decided to instead to have only your mother crowned at Holyrood, which really makes no sense at all. With all of his strongest allies in Edinburgh, why he didn't choose to rule from Holyrood, I don't know."

"What happened to my loyal set of lords? Their titles as Knights of the realm; should they not assemble when called upon? And if not, then should they stay as lords and landlords, or see themselves in a tenancy instead? And as tenants, they would have the responsibility to hand all money received from their wad setters or sub-renters, over to the Crown as well as their own rent, which I have up to now ignored due to their oath of title, and promise of support when needed, which now they have now failed to do."

"I'm not too ready though to blame Hamilton for failing to get the support of the assembly. Your Scottish Lords of your Privy Council should have made your wishes be known to the Assembly but instead of leaving it to Hamilton, which wasn't that well received by certain members of the Assembly. There were those that had still a resentment that goes back to way before his family had moved to Ireland and were members of the Scottish Royal Court, and subsequently disgraced so as to have to move over to Ireland."

"Was it not enough that he was acting as my emissary?"

Just then a Templar Squire approaches and asks that they both take heed; the Captain of the King's escort needs to have council urgently. The Squire turns and points towards the edge of a nearby field and the barn sitting there and says that Knights have assembled there and await King Charles and George to come forth. As King Charles and George make their way towards the barn they see Sr., George Lennox, one of Charles's privy councilors and a cousin of the Marquis of Huntly. When George and the King get closer, Lennox comes forward, they can see the anguish in his eyes and fear that something terrible has happened.

"Your Majesty, George, something terrible has happened; Huntly has been taken by force after his meeting with Montrose at Fyvie Castle. At first, we thought it was just for safe passage back to Aberdeen, but then when he didn't return, we thought the worst. It seems that during their meeting at Fyvie, as a Covenanter force gathered just below Terriff on the green. They were set on taking the King, and then when they were routed by Ogilvy and his troop of Templar cavalry, that Montrose duped the Marques into going off to Aberdeen under the arrangement that he would be given free passage to come and meet with the other Covenanters leaders, our sources in Aberdeen say that they were told that the Marques, by his own free will, has boarded a ship going to Edinburgh."

"The Marques knows that I now seek a settlement," says the King, "but he was supposed to try and contact Leslie, and by no way deal with him directly."

"With Leslie so heavily committed," says George, "he is hard pressed to put down a concerted effort, for his new over lords the English Parliament, who now has enlisted his own brother."

"And I believe that we too have been betrayed, as they suspect that you are here in the vicinity," adds Lennox.

The group then makes their way into the barn and is met by Ogilvy and his Templar commander.

"It seems your Majesty, that we have been betrayed, says Ogilvy, "we are surrounded by traitors, those who have signed up with the Covenanters, giving their alliance not to you, but to the parliamentary forces under Cromwell."

"Yes it seems as though we were betrayed," states the Templar commander:." Montrose was sure, that you would be there at the meeting at Fyvie Castle and had assembled a force at Terriff to capture you."

"It seems that Leslie thought that you would be there, and upon telling Montrose, devised a plan to capture you," added Ogilvy.

Montrose entered Edinburgh, using a petard to burst through the front gate.

"He's essentially taken the Castle, either looking for the crown jewels, not knowing that they had been already moved to Dalkeith and looking for the missing treasury."

"Both George and I were there at the Fyvie meeting. We saw and heard everything hidden above in the gallery that was completely covered over by a large tapestry. And with George's help, we found the hidden treasury and the cachet of weapons."

"Our only downfall being that we would be betrayed again," George explains, "and Montrose would take such lengths to keep us from calling forward men to defend The King."

"So with Huntly gone," Lennox adds, "Ogilvy now wants to know who is in command of the royal forces here in Scotland."

"We have to do something to stop this madness." Says the King, "make arrangements for the release of Huntly, on the promise that a Treaty is made on the conditions of the Assembly.

Tell them that we'll meet them in Berwick, and I'll sign for his release.

"It would be better now to plea for peace," argues George, "that one man die: the Paige 'David Prat', is it now the time that the Guardian come forth, I think it not"

"You both must bring charges, to those who betray you." Lennox adds. "Go to the High Constable and prefer charges and furthermore, make charges on those who have not stood up to their commitment to the King in regard to their Titles."

"George, your family's associated with the Earls of Errol; are they not?" Says Ogilvy. "You could easily set off towards Berwick from there."

"Yes, I could contact the Earl," George says, "you're right; a Sloop two masted sailboat could maneuver around the rocky coastline of Cruden Bay. And I'll admit as I would much rather sail on one of the quarry ships, it would be faster and just for a short way; we could reach Burwick straight away."

"So I'm to sail to Berwick, and you back to Rome." Replies the King. "Please if you go by Spain, give my best regards to your brother. How many brothers do you have anyway? If you do go by Spain, give my love to the Queen's sister but dare not let the Queen know of your plans, she'll understand if you don't, but she'll want to come with you if you tell her. There again you could go with safety by way of the Netherlands and if you know who asks, you haven't seen me. O.k.?

"That wouldn't work," answers George, "she knows all about us, who would be so vain as to have us all sculptured in white marble?

"What about the; You Know What? Asks The King.

"What are you two talking about," asks Ogilvy, " is this a

private conversation? We all would like to know who is now in charge, now that Huntly is gone?

"Don't worry," says George, "I put it back before we left. The one left in the Queens' chapel is a copy (saying this under his breath) Sorry though the key is mine. As for me leaving, it would probably be better if right away, even though I seem to have some estate matters the need to be taken care of around here."

But George had already literally taken away what he was after; locked away in with the King's treasury, the family's title deeds to their land holdings here in the Aberdeen shire. George wanted to pass them off to his Uncles who were working for Commander Phillips and had taken up residence in The Kings' father's plantations in northern Ireland. Thomas and his brother James would later be able to sell off what land holdings they had in Scotland.

"What key," asks Ogilvy, "Shouldn't the key be given to whoever is in charge? I am sorry but are you two having a private conversation?"

"A private conversation, no," answers George, "we never do seem to have time for a private conversation. The rest of the Scottish ministers on the council would think we were plotting."

"Yes and when do we plot? And so you ask; who's in charge," the King explains, "Hamilton is and has always as the Crown Minister to the northern territory, been in charge. George and Myself will need to visit the High Constable before I go on to Berwick. Send on a message to Montrose, my terms for the release of Huntly.

For a united kingdom

Part Four

Escaping to the Continent

Al Ponte'

First folio ~ MMXXV

Bowness or New Slains Castle near Cruden Bay Scotland

New Slains built by Francis Hay the High Constable of Scotland around the turn of the 17th century. Exiled to France, Patrick, George's father was able to negotiate their return that allowed him to rebuild the family seat and retain his title. (shown are some small boats along the coastline facing the English Channal)

A Hasty Convenient Truce

Chapter 16

"The key that you ask is at this point lost to us all, and a great unfortunate loss it is," says George, "my hope now is that it won't be needed. There was a story that Bruce broke a good size chunk off of the original and shipped it off to Ireland; Blarneys Castle and hence given the name 'the Blarney Stone.' We never thought to give it a try when we found it. We just assumed that it was a relic, and rightly property of the Guardian, and of course thought it would come into use when brought together with the Stone. You've got to admit that when we used it both at Westminster and again at the altar in the Queen's chapel that some strange things did happen."

"I now can see that it's not safe here," says the King, "and if not for Ogilvy's group of Templar cavalry breaking up a Covenanters assembly at Terriff, whose intention was to take George and me into custody."

"Ogilvy's forces are now holding the docks in Aberdeen," says Lennox, "The Sovereign waits just offshore and set to sail south to Berwick on your say so."

"Excellent," says the King, "make sure that the horses are loaded aboard, but don't do it right away, wait five days, that should give us a good deal of a head start. George and I thought we wouldn't be sailing with The Sovereign, but it will serve us well as a decoy, and while she waits in her moorage just outside of the docks in Aberdeen, George and I will take off in the other direction."

"And just how are we to get to Berwick," asks George.

"The Sovereign is quick for its class," the King says, "but how fast can it be when carrying over one hundred cannons? There's a new ship's design that's smaller, faster, and can get us or me into Berwick quicker and undetected, and I won't have to go all the way back to Aberdeen."

"You have a good point," says George, "but maybe it would be better now if we split up, if we have been discovered, they'll be looking for two. I grew up around here, and with the quarry still going strong and the area storming with masons who will know the sign of the master mason, I'll have no trouble getting around. let's see if I can't find one of your fast sailing slips and sail back to Londonderry. Once I'm back in Ireland, I can safely, with the help of my two Uncles, wait to find a ship heading to Italy; I'll have the Guardianship secured as long as I continue to stay in Rome."

"Isn't that what O'Neil did," asks the King, "and tried to get out of the deal that he had made with my father?"

"What was the deal that your father made, George asks, "do you know? Why did O'Neil then try to back out?"

"All I knew was that O'Neil was given his own island up in the western islands," explains the King,

"The problem was that it was a smaller island than what was described; the fact being that despite being located in a central spot in the western island chain, it was a very small island."

"Right now," says George, "I think just about anywhere would be better than staying around here. To see what I saw in Spain and their program of counter reformation or the Inquisition as it is called, what it really comes down to, is that you can't force someone to believe something that they don't want to.

"The biggest setback to any unification that people have to want to believe in it; the same belief as in faith and hope; So establish a learned Society which could someday be able to invite a united Kingdom into Gods' Kingdom established here on earth, and of course, you can always trust and rely upon those Templar knights, they have always known or simply believed in what secrets that they had brought back with them from the Holy Lands."

"So, what you are telling me," asks the King, "that these secrets brought back from the crusades, that the treasure they possess is in the knowledge of these certain prophecies? And that they are all linked to the Stone? That kind of makes sense, you know."

"But that kind of puts me at odds," explains George, "because they will never reconcile with the Catholic church. And all those who are on the outside will take any offense at my position as defender and guardian."

"And you say that these masons," asks the King, " are reluctant to open up on this knowledge, and share all of this with society?

"They feel that it's not their place to inform anyone," explains George, "but quite the opposite, as they have all been sworn to its secrets, that they stay secret. And of course, all must have the faith that God's Kingdom is at hand and will all soon be shown into Christ's Kingdom here on earth. But will all remain silent until that time has come."

"And should I now take that position," asks the King, "one of the Templars, or masons; as I wait for the guardian to return? What shall I do, George?"

"Look to building," explains George, "and not so much into rebuilding; following the scripture in Jeremiah to build up. And you know with all we had done with the Stone, and its rearrangement in Westminster, you could easily become one in its society of masons."

"You really think so," asks the King, "I'd like that, I think that my father would have liked that. It's something to always arrange for others, but to be accepted in by others, and a secret society at that is marvelous. haste. Henrietta's mother mustn't know; we need to return right away."

"I really doubt she would hear about it from her majesty; Hamilton has her convinced that it was all just a trick of the light and nothing else. The Archbishop, though, is sure it was a divine inspiration. Both of them could see it as a one-time phenomenon."

"Maybe you're right, her majesty has ordered that the front windows be blocked. So you think that we should put it back and take it back to the Abbey and into Richard's chair."

"Like nothing ever happened. We will always have our own secrets, and I don't just mean that of all our shenanigans we did concerning the Stone, no one but us needs to know. Build up and keep building; go forward and follow your father's enthusiasm in Virginia and establish more plantations; friendly competition will only make them stronger."

"And you, what happens when you go back to Rome? My connection there says that they consider you as the English Bishop, which by the way was one of the Assembly's requirements, they wanted the Bishops turned over."

"I have to disagree; anyone in Rome who really knows me, I mean really knows me, would know that I'm a micro manager and have not the practice it would take."

Of course, George had no intentions to leave; the stone had to be created, sitting back at the quarry, locked away with the deeds and titles he would need to also take back to Ireland on his way back to Rome. At the quarry, he can have what he needed created up and done right; the quarrymen were always shipping stones off as far away as Ireland, even as far away as London on occasion.

Plans were commonly sent right along with the creation attached and shipped. And so, to escape from the abject Covenanter forces, a so-called force because it was to force a policy which differed from that of the King's Royal obedience was not so uncommon even in the central lowlands; a loyalty to the Stewarts was still going strong, having the span of over a hundred years.

Even if there were the well-trained forces that were now starting to come back to Scotland from fighting in the Thirty Years War, there were plenty of older and wiser old soldiers who, as young men, fought in the last crusade; many who were Templars and could be assembled quickly, as Ogilvie had at Turriff. But was it, really, over a religious policy or the way that King Charles had pulled back on the gifted and chartered lands, which often came with a title, and then went to collect what rents were due?

After several attempts to have the Assembly turn over a certain number of its members due to their failure to supply men and arms, A requirement which was always a duty that went along with having received their title, King Charles was ready to charge them with High Treason, and then also to label the Assembly illegal, banning their meeting. But this didn't stop the Assembly from meeting; a large majority of men on the Assembly continued to meet and knowing that the Covenanter forces had the upper hand. They proposed to meet the King on natural grounds and negotiate an armistice at Berwick.

At this point, King Charles didn't trust several men on the Assembly, and the way they had tricked Huntly, and not stopping to have an assembly as demanded by Charles, and undermining his authority. Holding an assembly without inviting the King to oversee its proceedings where anything else would be considered illegal.

The Assembly would meet despite what threats that Charles would make; in fact, at their very next meeting, they would call out King Charles, stipulating that they would not accept any changes or additions to the Scottish church.

George, having then made it back to the quarry and to the relative safety of his father's home of Red Castle, called so because of the brick red sandstone he had used in its construction. George had grown up only minutes from the quarry and the town of Terriff. Seeing that his father, Patrick, was home,

George makes his way straight thru to his father's study, hoping to find him there.

"Good God, George, is that really you? I returned when I heard from one of the workers. He had returned to his work at Londonderry, saying that you were in danger.

"No one is to know that I'm here. where was this worker coming from exactly? Did he mention The King?

"Oh!, The King! Yes, he's sent a message for you. You were there in Paris when the King married your devotee. Your Nephew said he was on his way to Paris, as an advisor in the Royal Court.

"His office is now under the First Minister, Cardinal Richelieu."

"I've met Richelieu," George explains, "and he's a man who is not to be trusted. He turned on Queen Maria and secretly works against the Church. He's the Devil and a thorn in the King's side. If Charles knows that my Nephew is now his advisor and in Richelieu's office, I'll wager that is what is in his message."

"What did you say? Priests don't wager, do they? And if the Cardinal Richelieu is, as you said, working against the church, what in God's name is my son doing there?"

"Wagering, of course not, but you would be surprised what goes on between the Brothers. As for my brother and his position, I believe that I might have unknowingly been responsible, because of my past position in Court and what influence I might have with the Queen Mother. Let's see what our King Charles wants."

"George, don't tell me that the rumors are true? That you have been running around here with the King, and he's out there hiding somewhere and has left his horse in our stables."

"No, I'm sorry. No one is to know I'm here. I have been traveling incognito as a Stable Master, and the horse is yours; kind of a tribute to you and Grandfather's action as a Captain of Cavalry."

"So the King's gifting me a horse? Where is he, exactly?"

"The horse is my gift to you. King Charles, I suppose it is where he should be; back in London, at his palace in Whitehall. Let me read the message; perhaps he's accusing me of horse theft."

"First your brother's position at the French Court, and you now accused of horse theft; by all means read the message. And let us hope to God that it's good news, we need some good news right now."

"As I thought so., The King's back at Whitehall in London. He mentions his mother-in-law, and how he wishes he could send her back to France."

"When you say 'Back in Whitehall' that would assume that you knew he was gone. Tell your Father the truth now; were you with The King?"

"OK, yes, we were here, and at Fyvie looking for part of a Royal treasury. We opened the quarry vault and tried to arm the King's bodyguard."

"You say you did what? Breached the Royal Auxiliary? Distributing weapons? This does not sound like you, and so where was King Charles while all of this was happening? Wait I don't want to know, but please thank him for the horse.

"Father, it was I who gifted you the horse."

"Well thank you, no mention of horse thief then? Does he mention your brother?"

"No father, but I was given all the Deeds to our lands here in Scotland and was on my way to Ireland so I could give them to you to keep."

"Give me those; there's a perfect place to hide them; over at the quarry offices, mixed in with all of the other deeds we have there. Is there no mention of your brother? I wonder if he knows?

"Well I certainly didn't tell him. By the way, most of the money we left in the vault, along with many other deeds. The King plans reprisals against the Scottish Lords who are refusing to stand with him, using the deeds to call in their land grants and titles, demanding that they instead now pay rent to the Crown."

Upon finding his father, George would change his travel plans and head towards London hoping to catch Maria before she arrived at Court. If he was lucky, he would find both the Queen and the Queen Mother together.

The last thing King Charles wanted was for the Queen Mother to find out about her daughter's husband, King Philip of Spain, and the ghost fleet he is building off the Southeast coast of England; with Charles's help of course. If this was ever to be made known, Charles could be charged with treason. But then, it really wasn't a Spanish fleet, only a ghost fleet; there to lure the Dutch Navy out of their port in Amsterdam. And so there was no time to lose, George would have to say goodbye to his father, and travel with haste to London.

The King's letter had said that Marie, although already having visited her daughter at the Queen's Palace in Greenwich, she was yet to have made her formal entrance into London, and she was staying with an old friend and clergyman; some 30 miles on the outskirts of the city.

George in confidence had already told the King that he has Louie's ear, and that not only had he approved his marriage to Henrietta, but was responsible for having Richelieu placed into Louie's court by Pope Urban the eight; Vincenzo Barerini; another Florentine and early supporter of the artist and sculptor; Lorenzo Bernini. At the time Bernini was working for Marie's brothers in Rome; he would later give Vincenzo a bust he had done of George, only to say it was a gift from his work-shop, wanting his apprentices to share in the credit, the Pope knowing better, as something close to both their hearts.

George and King hoped to persuade the Cardinal Richelieu to lift Maria's exile and allow her to return to France. George thought that with the help of his Nephew, who was then placed in the Cardinal's office, could help in Maria's case. Earlier known as a

Stable Master, it was easy for George to slip into Whitehall and find his way to The King.

"So you think your Nephew can convince Richelieu to lift Maria's exile," asks the King.

"If Louie sees her as an enemy, we can have my Nephew suggest that it's better that she's kept close at hand, and at that way, keeping her away from the rather embarrassing adversary; his own brother, Maria's younger son Gaston."

Maria had earlier supported her younger son; but now after years in exile she seems more likely to reconcile her differences with Louie. Whereas blood is thicker than water; her desire to return to France is greater than putting one son against the other.

Charles on the other hand, was looking forward to having Louie give support by way of reserve troops when needed in Scotland. What Charles had not realized was that Louie's troops were fully engaged in the Palatine, fighting Frederick the fifth, who just happened to be Charles's Nephew. He became King of Bohemia and the Elector Palatine just as Louie the thirteenth took control as King of France. Pulling his troops to then support Charles in Scotland would be a conflict of interest.

Already Charles's one time adviser Buckingham, who had traveled to France with the Prince of Wales, would later have a disastrous campaign fighting on the side of the French Huguenots; a protestant rebellion; fighting the Catholic persecution by the French troops.

Buckingham returned to England in disgrace; twice he had been rebuked by Parliament and twice King Charles had to come to his aid by shutting the Parliamentary proceedings down.

Finally in 1628 Buckingham's past would catch up with him when he was assassinated by a disgruntled army officer who had served under him.

"We need then to set up a meeting to catch them together," Charles says, "It seems that she only visits Henrietta at the Queen's Palace in Greenwich."

"Maybe it would be more prudent if I was to stay there," George replies, "since Berwick, it's not safe to be seen at Court anymore. I'm afraid someone will see who I am and give me up to the Scottish Assembly. Not that there is publicly a price on my head, yet you can be sure that privately there is."

"Yes, even though most around Whitehall would still see you as my Stable Master, it takes just one to recognize you and alert our adversaries. As my privy council has many from Scotland, they come with their own entourage which might see an advantage to turn you over."

"At Greenwich, I can become again the Stable Master. Henrietta as much as yourself enjoys to ride; may I take two of the Iberian Stallions to help me to better blend in."

"That's a fine idea," says the King, "but can you be sure that Henrietta and her Mother will keep your secret? They know nothing about the Guardianship, but how would their loyalty change if they knew the truth?"

"It's not as much about loyalty as it is about respect. Where it's much different on the Continent, men of the cloth are given much more respect. Over there they realize that Priests marry into the church and become part of the Holy family and are over seen by the Lord God. To transgress against a Priest would be an unforgivable sin."

"It's a shame that there's not more in the Assembly that feel that way."

"Such is the problem when Scotland left the Church. When Bruce committed the unforgivable sin, of killing his rival to the Crown on hallo ground. The Church had little choice, after Bruce then Crowned himself at Scone, but to excommunicate the entirety of Scotland. On the contrary, there are some that know of the old Scottish traditions and that of the Guardianship and Defender of the Faith; both concepts that are separate from the Roman Church and unique to Britain, and so, they are faithful to the ones that hold the Title of Guardian.

"I need to know what my Queen and her Mother are talking about. I can't afford them wondering about Spain's intent in the Netherlands. I'll need all the support I can muster in Scotland. I wouldn't fair well inviting troops from France or Spain, but if I could convince Gaston to send some of his mercenaries into north eastern Scotland to organize the militia I would need for my return, I would have a better chance of putting down any resistance. But as to a question of truth, when was the last time you heard the Queen's or her Mother's confession?

"It really hasn't been that long ago, I would say in the last couple of months."

"Is there any chance that you might influence Henrietta's Mother to move on and go back to the continent."

"The question is, will Richelieu listen to reason. I believe Richelieu is a reasonable man. And he will see that there is more of an advantage of keeping her close by and resolved in an arrangement to where she can live comfortably in peace, safely away from Europe's conflicts."

Escape to the Continent

Chapter 17

The next day they decide to put their plan in place, as George and the King ride to Slains Castle and secretly depart. Taking one of the two masted sloops belonging to the High Constable that he regularly uses to travel to different locations around Scotland; it would be highly unlikely for them to be stopped and searched. Charles would transfer to the Sovereign sitting outside of the docks of Aberdeen; that will take him directly to Berwick to sign the Treaty with the Assembly. George will stay on the sloop and race down the east coast to the River Thames. Sailing down to the navel docks above Greenwich, George was told to access Queen's House by way of the maze of foot paths from behind.

George knowing that he could evade anyone that might be following him, using the foot paths through the woods that opens onto the well-guarded open field behind the Queen's House.

The Queen's Palace in Greenwich along the River Thames, was originally built around 1616 for Charles's Mother; the Queen; Anne of Denmark. Built by the master builder Inigo Jones; it was his first major commission upon his return from touring the Palladian architecture in Italy. His sprawling example would overlook the Thames just miles downstream from the heart of London. Its refurbishment was completed in 1635 for use by Queen Henrietta. Although any conventional act of confession could have been done at the Queen's House in Greenwich, it's more likely to be performed as part of a service held at another one of Jones's Palladian buildings that were part of James's Palace on the Mall. With the Stone still hidden away in the Chapel, it was now more or less off limits and under guard.

After Henrietta's last experience in the Chapel, she had the western windows blocked off, and she was hesitant to go in after that. So the best chance for George to hear any confessions would be at Greenwich anyway.

It was a bright morning at the end of July, and George was hoping to catch the Queen and her mother out having breakfast; in the morning sun. As he came down the Royal Walk, situated behind the Palace, he would be in clear view from the second story veranda.

"Mother, there's a man out there on the walk and it looks as if he's coming this way."

"Does he look familiar to you," Marie asks with a tinge of fear in her voice, "maybe we should call the guard."

"Wait, there is something vaguely familiar about him, what do you think?"

"I think we should call the guard, how on earth did he get out there? He must be trespassing."

"He must be lost, but the way he seems to be just idly strolling, is he trespassing, or does he really have business here?"

"Well you will never know if you don't call the guard."

"Wait, we know him, isn't that Father Conaeus"?

"You know, I think your right. But he's not in his normal attire. We both know that walk of his. I wonder. Early for him; what's he up to?"

"Maybe he's come for breakfast?"

"We really then should call the guard, before they find him and take him as a trespasser."

Henrietta then shouts out: "Father George is that you?"

George now stops as though he's heard her now standing directly below the veranda. Actually, he has stopped because he now sees the guards rushing towards him. Just before the guards reach him, a shout from above This draws the attention of everyone down in front of the veranda. "Wait"

It was the very recognizable stout voice of the Queen; Marie de' Medici. The guards froze as if turned off with a switch, as they were fully aware of who had shouted out the command from above.

Next it was Henrietta who commanded everyone's attention. Not shouting but with a big voice asked: "Father Conaeus, would you care to join us for some breakfast?"

"Not wanting to impose," promptly replied George, "I did want to speak to you both."

"Guards let him thru, I'm sure, George you know your way up."

The guards then lead George through to the inside of the Palace and he makes his way to the magnificent Tulip spiral staircase.

Designed by the architect Indigo Jones it was in honor of the Queen Mother's planting of the sloping hill behind Greenwich Palace a vast field of tulips. Leading up to the first floor and taken thru to the veranda; The two Queens seem excited to see him, as he greets them both with a gentle kiss to the cheek.

"Where have you been," asks Marie.

"He's been up in Scotland with Charles, trying to convince the Estates that they need to unite in a common religion, to please God and bring peace to this God awful place."

"Henrietta you would be careful to watch your tongue and not use our Lord's name in vain."

"I guess we should be thankful that we have such a representative to guide us towards righteousness. Mother the way Charles listens to every word with such enthusiasm; as if Father George was his personal Prophet.

"George what is this hold you have over Charles," asks Marie, "and these strange goings on in the Chapel on the Mall?"

"Wait, he's got the hold on me," argues George, "with all this unruly commotion up in Scotland. I tried to warn his father that it would have been better to have ruled from Edinburgh and have grown a firm support in Scotland than have a waning support from both ends of his Kingdom."

"And can you tell me why Henrietta's afraid to enter into her own chapel? She says that you and Charles have set up some archaic ancient Scottish alter stone; she says is creepy. She's had to block the western windows; what's going on?

"Well we're not quite sure; it's the coronation stone, and it's thought to have spiritual powers of its own. When we used an old incense burner, an old Holy relic, we saw something strange happen."

"My God, the Archbishop thought he saw the Angel Gabriel," cries out Henrietta, "he left there white as a ghost."

"I don't know why he was so scared; did he really think that he saw the Archangel? There's really nothing to be frightened of; now if you heard him playing his trumpet, then I would be fearful."

"You, scared of anything? Charles says you are a Defender of the Faith."

"Well I'm more scared and have less faith in the Scottish Assembly right now, and they have become a thorn in The King's side,"

"He should not be worried about how they think, these Scottish Estates,"

Marie says, "my family in Tuscany would just ignore such insolence. Once they realize that they are being ignored, how quickly they begin to fall in line."

"Oh come on Marie, in France, you would have little patience and send in the troops at the first inkling of trouble."

"So I'm less diplomatic, I'm a woman. I could go back to my brothers in Rome. They have Lorenzo working on a grand plaza in front of St. Peters, a little like the design inspired here. But life with my brothers there in Rome would be such a bore."

"Do you think that you will ever go back to France?"

"Of course, I'd go back tomorrow if I could, but the Cardinal Richelieu betrayed me to my eldest son Louie. Banished by my own son and had to leave Paris and my beautiful Luxembourg Palace.

Like Paris's Notre Dame, I feel I am the Lady of Paris and will always be so. And poor Gaston; now that he is no longer heir, is finding it difficult to finish the work he's doing at the Château de Blois."

"What a beautiful Château, there in Blois," Marie says, "your father loved it, I hope that Gaston can reconcile things with Louie his brother. I just learned of the birth of Louis XIII. So now, Gaston is no longer heir, he is only now Louie's brother; I would hope that Louie now would display Brotherly Love and welcome you too, back at Court. If I could help you capitulate with Richelieu, would you move back?"

"Of course, but would the Cardinal agree to do so? He's in Louie's pocket now, and I think they would hardly want me back there."

"But if you could reach the Cardinal," asks George, "do you think that you could draw a truce with him and Louie?"

"What you suggest is near impossible," Marie says, looking somewhat puzzled, "what makes you think that they'll even entertain the idea."

"It's my sister's boy Thomas; as we speak, is in the counsel of the Cardinal Richelieu; He's part of a contingent sent by the Vatican to Paris and the Royal Court.

"So you're saying that your Nephew, has the means for me to start a conversation with Richelieu? You know that what you say could be very dangerous for your young Nephew. Richelieu is dangerous, he can't be trusted, you know. How do you know that he won't betray him, just like he did me?

"Marie, he's an envoy of the Pope, he's there on a Catholic mission. Who's to say that's not to find a resolution between you and Louie, can't it be part of the counsel he brings.

"He knows who to thank for his position in France and so does all of Rome; and he would hate to fail"

"What a brilliant thought George," says Henrietta, "you'll one day be Pope or at least a Cardinal. Do you really think that you can help my Mother return to France?" It would surely be a miracle."

"And Marie will be free to plant her tulip bulb collection finding a new home for both. How many were there Marie?

"I had barns of bulbs and others stored away. I heard it said that it was once over a million bulbs, but of course I sold more than half of them to finance the move I was forced to make. I've given Henrietta a good bunch to plant on the slope behind her palace at Greenwich. The rest I take with me; close to 9000 I think, they are quite valuable, and no doubt I can sell off some when I get back to France. As usual you have come to our defense, if you and your Nephew Thomas you say, can plea my case to Richelieu, will they listen to you?"

"I know Richelieu, and of course, I don't trust him either. But I think I know his weakness, and that is to serve Rome, which actually puts us in a better position to suggest a resolution between you and Louie. I've talked to King Charles about this wanting him to grant a stay of exile for my Uncle and Frances Hay who desperately wants to return to Scotland."

"So could you also help my beautiful son and brother; Gaston? He has lost all of his direction, and I'm afraid that for him to stay in the Netherlands is a bad really bad decision. Phillip is all ready to go in there to confront France."

"Now Mother, isn't that what Gaston has wanted, even when yourself were staying there in Amsterdam? I wouldn't worry about Gaston teaming up with Phillip either, and neither should you."

"No, I can't see Gaston going into an alliance with Spain; that would of course spoil him in the eyes of the French people," explains George, "as for Richelieu, he has much to answer to. I was in Pope Urban's office when Richelieu was given his post on

Louie's Court. My Nephew Thomas is there now serving in his office as a Vatican commission. I couldn't imagine a more direct method of persuasion than my Nephew holding the purse strings."

"You see mother, everything will be alright, you of all people can put your trust in George.

If we say here in London, it wouldn't be safe right now. That is why Charles wants us all to move to Oxford, for the time being.

"That's exactly what I'm worried about. Did Charles put you up to this, or is this all of your idea? I have the feeling that Charles wants me to return to France."

"I'm sure Mother that Charles is pleased that you're here; didn't he arrange to have us married at the Notre Dame Cathedral? So at least we could have members of the Church that you loved so much witness our vows?

"You will come with us to Oxford, I don't want you to say no."

"Yes, that was very thoughtful of him, though, it would have been nicer if it could have been inside the church; than held outside on the front steps."

"It was such a beautiful day," says Henrietta, "and you know that your brothers planned everything perfectly, God bless them.

"I'll admit that I brought this scheme to Charles, and at first didn't want the involvement or anything connecting him with France and was doubly concerned that Gaston would then show up at court; and that's the last thing he wanted. Parliament is looking for a way to find some kind of involvement with France, or Ireland, and say that he's recruiting mercenaries from abroad and raising a foreign army on English soil. Or something of that sort, that they could charge him with treason."

"Charge him? Charge The King," cried out Marie, "I would have had nothing to do with that in France; their claims would have been found seditious, and they would be all thrown into the Bastille, and that would be the end of it."

"Yes that would be wonderful. It would certainly scare the Hell out of Parliament, to see a newly installed Guillotine in the Tower's center court. Don't be surprised if Charles does just that, he has become at odds with certain members of the Parliament and is seriously thinking of charging them; arresting them and pulling them off the floor of Parliament itself. So yes, God bless your sons Marie.

"If it was not so much for their diplomacy," says Marie, "it wouldn't have worked; no thanks to Rome, all talking up a storm that the Pope would want to stop it. If not for their connections, Henrietta's brothers and their quick resolve; Thank you for that George, as we all know it was you to blame; God bless you too."

"Mother, Charles should make you Chancellor. Phillip certainly knows Gaston is his wife's brother and will act accordingly when he invades the Netherlands "

"I wouldn't be surprised if he decides to stay there and lives to a ripe old age," states Marie, "I'm done with that George, if I may change the subject, the painter Van Dyke is mesmerized with The King's new horses, and I agreed to commission a panel from him, on the promise that he includes King Charles and yourself. He already has your likeness from the sketches he gave to Bernini.

He wants you two to think of a situation that he can paint but remember it's going to be about the horse; of course. I've been told that this will reflect on your gift to Charles and Henrietta.

They are magnificent really; I can see how Lorenzo is so in love with them. My daughter also is very pleased with them, and when my lovely daughter is happy, so am I, Thank you so much for the very nice gift. I have a gift for you too, Henrietta. When I left Denmark I had planned to bring with me the vast collection of priceless tulip bulbs, I thought you could put in a field of them behind your palace here at Greenwich. I have much more than I can take with me back to France. I had the gardeners put the tulips still in their pots arranged around the back here: you have noticed them, haven't you?"

"You're not going back to London, are you George," asks Henrietta.

"I'm not now sure that it would be safe, but I need to retrieve my things, some personal things, some that I had sent on to Oxford. We had gone to celebrate the opening of the Archbishop's new wing of the library at St. John's to commemorate his residency and later as President of the College."

"I've heard of this Archbishop Laud," says Marie, "and of his opposition in the House of Lords. Is he an ally of you and The King?"

"Mother, George has donated a whole wagon load of books for the new library."

"Yes, though outspoken," replies George, "he has generally supported the King, and in the King's Privy Council and Star Chamber. Whether the Archbishop will now support raising a force to allow the King to return to Scotland is uncertain, as every attempt to raise a local security force to protect the King while in Scotland has failed. But then most of those personal books and manuscripts were to be sent on back over to France, to the Scots' College at Douai.

"I had given a lot of books to the Scots College in Paris. Why Douai and not Paris," asks Marie.

"My direct relationship with Douai, my family connection, and personal friendship with the College Chancellor. Paris now is getting all of the overload of books from the Château of Saint-Germain-en-Laye, which has become somewhat of an outpost of the Scottish and English living there in Paris."

"I can help you get to Oxford," says Henrietta, "but I'll be sorry to see you go. If you can help my Mother to return to France,

I think I will join her, just to make sure that she arrives safely. Charles also worries and wonders if the children and I would not be safer visiting my brother in France. Perhaps you could join us on our trip across to France. Wouldn't that be wonderful, Mama?"

"I've already sent a letter to my Nephew and should receive an answer any day. I think that a visit to your brothers' is a good idea and would go a long way in facilitating your Mother's return."

"And does that mean that you will be going straight back to Rome?" asks Henrietta.

"Family business requires that I deliver some land deeds to Ireland before I return. I'll be sure to go thru Paris on my way home."

"Charles says that your family intends to leave Scotland, and resettle in Ireland; I hope that they weren't being threatened there in Scotland, for your position with The King?"

"I hope not, but I will know more when I see them. Nobody is supposed to know that I'm present in The King's Court; I am just the lowly Stable Master. I believe that some have an idea that King Charles and I talk too much; those of the Scottish Estates."

"Well, I hope that your family is safe in Ireland, we will have to keep our eye out to see that all goes well," says Marie, "Isn't that so, Henrietta? So you think that your position with Charles has been discovered? Something about the Scottish Estates?"

"Charles and I visited Fyvie Castle, a place familiar to both of us in our youth. We had wanted to talk to the Assembly, but arranging for a guard turned into such a disaster, and an innocent young teamster was killed. King Charles will have to arrange for a guard now, here in England, before he can return and attempt to speak to the Assembly. He believes it's up to the King's prerogative to lead the General Assembly, and if he has to raise an army to do so he will."

The Tulip Staircase; designed by Inigo Jones located inside the Queen;s House at Greenwich

Visit to Glastonbury

Chapter 18

There was just one more thing George had to do before he left England: Register with the country ministers in the old capital city of Winchester, this is how he could legally possess the property and be able to transfer the family's land deeds and promissory notes.

Winchester was a medieval city, and where all of the most important records were held, birth records, death certificates, and marriage licenses alike. Once George registers, he will be legally a peer of England and able to appear in Parliament. Though he had no intention of doing so.

George asks, "Henrietta, could you arrange for me a safe passage to Oxford, and then on to Winchester."

"So you do intend to leave us? Of course, I will make the arrangements for you. Will you be staying in Oxford?"

"No, I'm just picking up the wagon I left there. I'll travel over to Glastonbury, where I'll visit the Abbey and its wonderful Cathedral. From there, it's down to Winchester where I can register myself as a peer, as I have some family business to take care of. I'll then try to arrange for a passage out of Southampton over to Ireland.

"Good; I can give you a royal book of lading that will take you all the way to Ireland and back, that is, if you still would want to travel back over to France with us?"

"Yes, I would feel much safer in France."

"I've heard that the Assembly has a warrant out for you now," says Marie, "how dare they, and how ridiculous is that; just who do they think they are anyway?"

"They think they're Parliament Mama, they have gone against their own tradition and culture insisting that they become England's bastard stepson and make up their own rules on how they trade with the south."

"The Estates have then risen up have they," asks Marie, "it sounds like a merchant's revolt. We would always deal with such at the docks or before the marketplace. This would always seem to keep the merchants inline."

"After James had left to come to England," explains George, "Scotland sort of unraveled going their own way; smuggling increased from the continent so much so, that it has taken over the economy and with no accounting to the Crown it has made some individuals up there very rich and powerful. And so to delegate their power have formed a union amongst themselves calling them the General Assembly."

"And now they're after you," asks Marie.

"They're after anyone that sees thru their treachery, and they know that I'm an adviser to Charles and a Scot at that."

"And if that was not enough Mama, there are those right here in England who would turn him over just for being a priest."

"How on earth have you been able to survive then?"

"I've taken on the role of a humble Stable Master, No one is supposed to know of my true identity. Actually, outside of Charles only you two really know who I am. Unfortunately, this will all change when I register at Winchester.'

"Oh I see now why you have chosen to register at Winchester, says Henrietta, "something you can easily do here in London."

"Yes. there are fewer of those who know who I am in Winchester than here in London, where if I were to register here, it would surely be dangerous and too much of a chance that my adversaries will be tipped off and I'd be captured and sent back to Scotland."

"But then why do it," asks Marie, "and just stay with us, and join us when we leave to go back to France. You might have to change your allis persona though, but I'm sure that we could put you on as a Gentleman Squire acting as our escort on the voyage."

"I thank you for the offer, and it sounds like something that would work to get me out of England. But I need to visit my Brother Patrick in Ireland. That is if war does break out in Scotland, as I think it will, it would be prudent to protect our land holdings there. By transferring the land deeds and titles over to my Brother in Ireland they will be safe. As I cannot inherit; as a priest unable to sire an heir, all such deeds and titles will go to my nephew Thomas who is already working for Captain Philips in Londonderry.

Thomas has already convinced my parents that it would when the time comes, move over to Ireland where they will be safe.

We are already looking at a retaliation towards our family, as with the Scottish title of Lord of the Isles, that was in danger of being corrupted went into receivership by James, in fact, he was essentially keeping it pure and clean."

"But won't you be taking a big chance by then coming back," asks Henrietta, "maybe it would be better if you didn't come back with us and go straight on to Roma from Ireland?"

"And how much fun would that be? Yes, it would be a risk coming back, but I couldn't miss the opportunity of having two of the most desired of traveling companions. It will be my utmost pleasure to meet you again in Dover upon your return to France."

In Henrietta and Maria, George had the best of allies. They would help him get to Oxford and then along to Winchester, where from there he was able to arrange passage over to Ireland. Charles was busy in his continued fight with Parliament; calling out the traitors looking to arrest a bunch, right off of the floor of Parliament.

They had already started writing the death warrants of his supporters; as if they had any right to do so, so King Charles thought. But this was more than a tit for tat ongoing conflict; they were there by building a case to go after Charles himself.

George woke the next morning, having stayed as a guest of the Queen and the Queen Mother. He had slept well; perhaps the best sleep he had in quite a while; he was much safer in Greenwich than at the Palace in London; where there was too much of a risk that now someone might recognize him knowing how much time he had spent with King Charles recently.

As hard as they had tried to keep it a secret, that is for George to continue to play the part of the Stable Master, there were those outside of The King's privy council who wondered what King Charles was doing spending most of his day talking to a lowly Stable Master, and it being nowhere near a one-sided conversation one would expect to hear between a servant and master.

Although for most of the time no one would suspect George and King Charles having such a developed friendship, one that had gone clear back to when they were children set to running around in the woods besides Fyvie Castle; and needless to mention the great friendship that he also had with his Father. And then there is also Henrietta and her mother and sister; Gaston and Louie, that he had got to know well when he had served in Paris when Louie had begun his reign as a young man.

As for him and Charles; most of the time they would spend in the saddle, riding out in the countryside. The brief times they were even seen together would be in the mornings before riding off for the day. The real suspicions though came from those in Parliament, who needless to say were uncomfortable with so many Scots given a position on the Privy Council, and the suspicion that George too was another Scot would be in itself enough to turn Parliament.

That morning George says his goodbyes as he gets his letters of travel from Henrietta and is ready to head off towards Oxford. He's assured that he will be safe there, as most of his Majesty's ministers as well of most of the Privy Council have already relocated there too. His letters from the Queen will help George to also make the travel arrangements he'll need to get him to the continent all the way back to Rome; Henrietta relying on the connections that of her Uncles; the Medici Brothers who were in Rome, over seeing that of Bernini's construction of St. Peter's Square.

George arrives in Oxford before noon and the city is busy and a rush of people; Professors from the different colleges; students, craftsmen, and store owners mix with all other members of society. He's hardly noticed as he makes his way through town as he finds his way to one of the oldest of Colleges, St. John's, and the site of the Archbishop's new library wing apply named 'The Canterbury Quadrangle.'

Not quite a year ago, he had visited here with King Charles and the Queen when the Library opened. He'd arranged to have the wagon that he had loaded with books along with others from The King's own library sent as a gift given to the Archbishop's new wing. Mixed in alongside all the books George had the documents he needed to go on to his family in Ireland with his personal belongings hidden away. True he would be safe while he stayed in Oxford, easily overlooked amongst the vast population that was Oxford; but when he would decide to leave; all security he would have would stop and leave him vulnerable. Even though his next stop; in the old English capital of Winchester, as a municipal township it could be just as dangerous as if he had stayed in London.

Having left all of the horses that he had brought with him in London, his disguise as a lowly stablemaster was no longer an option. He would now have to register himself as a peer to legally transfer the family deeds of their land holdings in Scotland so they could legally be sold off later by what family members who remained there in Ireland.

He would then have to make what was then the most dangerous part of his journey back to Rome; to the seaport of Portsmouth, where from there he could board a ship to take him over to Ireland. He could rely on the family there to find safety.

Having sorted all that he would have to take over to Ireland, and then on to his final destination to Rome, George now loaded a smaller wagon of sorts, more of a cart; something that was more typically seen on the waterfront docks; something to be shipped. That morning he had arranged to have breakfast with the Archbishop, and Thomas Wentworth who was now staying there along with others from The King's Privy Council. He wanted to say goodbye and thank them for the help they had given him while there.

Wentworth remarks: "We are troubled by the thought of you traveling alone to Winchester and then on to Southampton. Who knows what waits for you between here and the docks."

The Archbishop Loud adds, "we both feel that it would be best if you had an escort to see that you get to your ship safely."

"But I have yet to make any arrangements and thought that I would stay in Winchester," explains George, "Until I can find a ship to take me on to Londonderry."

"It seems that we're not the only ones that worry about your safety." Wentworth adds. "Henrietta and the Queen Mother also has concerns."

"So, with the help of the Earl of Strafford," explains the Archbishop, "we have arranged a surprise for you, and arranged an escort, that we are sure that you will approve of."

";Hello:, Nephew!, did you think that you would go back to Rome without saying goodbye to us?"

It was George's two Uncles from Londonderry that had served him so well while he first traveled across Ireland and up into the Northern Plantations.

"I was going to Londonderry to see you both, and say goodbye," explains George.

"I have some papers that I have to register in Winchester before I plan to hand them over to you; It's some titles and land deeds that I was given charge of in Scotland by my Father your Great Uncle Patrick. I need first to travel northwest over to Glastonbury and make a visit to the Grand Cathedral there. I have asked the Abbot for a few cuttings of the Holy Thorn; I want you to plant one in the Roe Valley.

"Holy tree?" ;,asks Thomas?

"It's said to be Holy. Just after Jesus was crucified, Joesph of Arimathea came to Glastonbury set on starting an Abbey to train monks to serve in Rome. The first five Bishops there were from that very Glastonbury Abbey. It's said that when Joesph came to Glastonbury, he still had Jesus's walking stick. He thrust the stick into the ground and the stick bloomed later turning into a thorny tree. The monks knew it was special when it not only bloomed at Christmas but would also bloom at Easter too."

"Amazingly it's true," remarks the Archbishop Loud. "I have seen it. I'll always have a renewal of faith whenever I see its blossoms and think of the Christ, and Holy Redeemer."

"We can take care of all of those deeds when we see you again in Winchester," Thomas says. "But then instead of going on to Southampton; we can go then directly to Portsmouth, where the Queen has made all arrangements for a return to the continent."

And not just that," Wentworth adds, "but it seems that they will be joining you aboard ship and look forward to traveling with you to Paris."

"King Charles no longer wants Henrietta and the children in London," explains the Archbishop, "and since neither was thrilled about having to stay here in Oxford, they decided to go to the safety that Louie can provide them in Paris."

"Perhaps it would be better if we travel with you to Glastonbury," asks James, "just to see that you don't get into trouble, we can travel lite and send your cart on to Winchester where we can all wait for our travel arrangements to be made and the ships to arrive."

"The King said we could make use of a few of the stallions you gave him; as long as we promise to send them back," explains Thomas, "the good Earl of Strafford was nice enough to bring them with him from London."

"Strange ponies they are," replied Wentworth, "surely I thought that I. had picked up the wrong string; and the smaller size made me think that they were not yet fully grown. How would they ever make the long trip out of London to Oxford, and then to go from here on to Winchester? And now it's to include a side trip to Glastonbury."

"These Stallions ran across Ireland after being aboard ship for two months," replied James .

"Yes all the way from Portugal," explains George . "Wentworth, you'd be surprised to know that they're as big as they are going to be; they are full grown. They are bred to travel in mass aboard ships; they are exceptionally trained war horses. Trained to go long distances with little in the way of food or water."

The next day George travels towards Glastonbury with the elder of his two Uncles; Thomas. The Abbey as grand as it once was, could be seen from quite a distance; as could the Glastonbury Thor or the legendary Ile of Avalon. It was made famous as the birthplace of King Arthur.

It was a clear and sunny day, but if it were socked in with a low fog, the large mound or Thor would definitely appear just like an island; an island in the clouds.

"You said that there is a Cathedral there at Glastonbury? It must be old; is it? Have you been there before," asks James.

"No, I have not been here before," replies George., "I had a request to visit before my return to Rome. The Cathedral and Abbey have a special regard to the Church in Rome; even though it's been closed since the reign of Henry the eighth."

"Held in a special regard, Nephew?

"I don't understand."

"All it means is that they're held in high esteem as an elder Cathedral and Abbey."

"Aye, so there is nothing to be afraid of then."

"Well if anyone ever asked what we did; say only that we just picked up a couple of thorn cuttings and left, nothing else; You got it?"

"On my word, nephew; what are we going to do?

"I have to see the Abbott; it's on his request that I visit. That's all I know. There was given no inclination as to what it's all about. I have no idea what he wants. Perhaps the Abbott has a message he wants me to deliver."

As neither of them had been there before, they figured that the best way to find the Abbott would be to go towards the Cathedral not having any idea where the Abbey is located. The Cathedral was hard to miss and stood out above the town. They entered Glastonbury from the north, as the note had told them, in the afternoon when the town was busy. It was easy for them to blend into the crowd; looking like they had no time to stop and went directly towards the Cathedral, hoping to find the High Street.

When they finally found their way to Glastonbury Cathedral, it looked deserted. Reading off the last of instructions from the message he had received, they were to meet a Fr. Reading at a choral rehearsal at St John's Church on High Street. The note said "From the Abbey take the path towards the northwest corner taking the alley way through to High Street and you'll find it there. Crossing through the Abbey grounds, going towards the back, they find the alley that leads to High Street and St. John's. They can hear the choir, so at the first break George goes in and asks; "Would anyone know where I can find Father Reading?"

"Yes, how can I help you?"

"I'm looking for Fr. Reading, do you know where I might find him," asks George.

"You must have divine guidance; I'm Fr. Reading, and you must be Father George. I'm very glad to see that you've decided to honor our request."

"Good to make your acquaintance Father, I was intrigued by your offer of some cuttings of the Holy Thorn. Was there something that I can do for you?"

"Yes, you do plan to stay over, we have prepared a room, it should accommodate the both of you."

"Oh, let me introduce my travel companion, James, my Uncle from Ireland."

"Great, I'll have someone show you to your room and arrange for some refreshments to be taken there. We'll have a small celebration before dinner; there are some robes for you, and someone will be around to collect you when it's time for us to start. Since the dissolution of the Abbey, we will gather first at the bottom of the Tor and then walk back to the site of the Cathedral."

The accommodations were nothing like what they thought they would find. To their surprise, they were to be honored guests of the Cathedral and not of the brothers of the Abbey, but of the Cannon Fathers of the Cathedral itself. The robes that were set out were of an exceptional quality, even the one for James, the plainer of the two, was of pure white silk embroidered in gold. George's was the typical priestly black with a silk collar, and black silk-ribbon accents.

One of the Fathers came around with a pitcher of Honey Mead and two crystal goblets. Across the hall from them, the Fathers had arranged a bathroom for them to clean up after a long day's travel across the dusty roads from Oxford. When they were done and had changed into their fine robes and after one more glass of mead, a Father came in and said that the celebration would start shortly and that he was there to take them in.

"Is this an annual celebration we attend," asks George.

"It's in your honor, your grace."

"You give us short notice," says George, "what do I say; could I relay a message back with me to Rome? I can see that your request is seen by the right people and even the Pope on a good day."

"You should talk to Fr. Reading, I think that he's the one who writes down the requests that we send off, or it might be that he is the only one who writes. They seem to be constantly waiting for a reply.

After a while Fr. Reading came to take them to where the celebration would begin. At the bottom of a hill where on top a tower church was built called the great Tor, there was a natural spring and a well. George was surprised to be met by what looked like the whole Glastonbury church community along with many citizens who lived in the town or farms of the surrounding area. George was led over to 'The Chalice Well' where he was anointed. Then so were the Canons and also the Monks.

When the last of the Monks had been anointed; George was led off in procession by the Canons followed by the Monks and the rest who had come to see the celebration service. The Canons led George to what was left of the Cathedral where an altar had been placed, and many chairs were set up. The Canons had gathered at the Altar, and George was shown a chair and asked to have a seat while the service began.

"Fr. Reading, I hear that you have been sending requests to Rome. Have the replies been helpful," asks George.

"We wait patiently ."

As the service began the Canon Fathers led a prayer and recited a passage from Jacob in the bible. Next, the group spoke about the founding of the Abbey and the subsequent building of the Cathedral and its purpose to serve humanity. Another Canon spoke about Faith and Hope and about the Guardian; Defender of the Faith. At this, it was time for the Canons to introduce George as he was led forward and asked to address the congregation.

"I had planned to visit the Abbey before going back to Rome, and wondered what condition; the Abbey would be in," says George, "and I was saddened to see what has happened.

Thanks to St. John's Church for holding on, and helping the Abbey Monks survive after the Dissolution; losing one of the grandest Cathedrals in all of Britain. Thank you for your invitation to have me visit. Fr. Reading tells me that they have been waiting on a reply from Rome for a while now. I say Fr. Reading give me your requests, and I assure you I will see that all your requests are resolved and resolved quickly. Write them down for me, and I will see that they get done. I've been looking forward to my visit here, as I've gotten homesick from time to time;

I have worked for the Vatican many years now, and upon receiving a sabbatical after the death of Pope Gregory, I have come here to visit with family and friends. I regret that I have to leave here now, and that England or as much as all of Britain seems to be working towards a break down in civil society. Policy is now more opted in the Public House on Saturday than from the service on Sunday.

The question I have myself is; is there a role for the Guardian to play in this account, and should we rely on the teachings more, now that a more secular arena is stronger? I hope we can find a new definition of Guardian, one that will bring us all back together through common belief. I hold all of you in the highest regard. I thank all of the Canon Fathers for their hospitality and will certainly take their requests back with me to Rome."

The Canons then gathered around the altar and placed a Mitre hat of the Cathedral Canons in the center; George was asked to approach where a Canon then placed; the Mitre hat, of the Cathedral Canons, on his head; he was made a Canon of the Cathedral. He was told to go back to Rome and work to open an English college, which they were in desperate need of one.

There had been no English college since Henry VIII had abolished his ties to Rome and the Catholic Church. One of the Canons then to close the service recited another passage from the book of Jacob, and then after a prayer closes the service. George was then asked to join the members of the Cathedral along with those from the Abbey for a meal.

The Cathedral had a large reception room that once was the Abbey's kitchen that had survived. They had set up a horseshoe shaped table and had given George the place of honor in the center; having the Canons and those from the Abbey sitting in two flanks on his right and left. James was given the chair on the right; next to George. A dinner was served, and before long an uncommon chatter of voices rose in conversation; any that hoped for a quiet meal would be disappointed.

There was a commotion of chairs moving into place as several Monks chose to sit directly across from friends. George and Fr. Reading gathered a crowd as the conversation quickly moved to the needs of the Abbey Monks; those older ones who would find it hard to be reassigned. George assuming that there was a large number of older Monks wanting to stay and not able to find accommodation now and thinking that the only thing now available would-be reassignment.

"I can help with accommodations; how many apartments are needed," asks George, "is there land the Church owns where we could build? Let me know, just how many rooms you would need, and perhaps I could show you something that could be built to accommodate them; like a building with separate apartments."

After much more discussion over building sites and where they could put the out-buildings they'd need, they were taken back to their rooms for a night of rest.

The morning came quickly as George was anxious to conclude his business there and be able to leave early as it would be an all-day trip to Winchester and then some, meaning they would arrive back after dark. So, after a quick breakfast, they were led out to find that the Monks had arranged to have another horse ready carrying the cuttings that George had asked for. Also, there was Charles and Henrietta; their children, James Wentworth, Archbishop Loud, and George's other Uncle, Thomas.

"Were you all there for the ceremony yesterday," asks George.

"We all were there; and with-you George," explains the King .

Loud adds, "I wouldn't have missed it, I'm so pleased,"

"I'm still not sure what happened," replied James.

Wentworth explains, "Your Nephew George was just made a Canon of the Cathedral and a member of the Abbey."

"Remember that the first five Bishops of Rome were members of the Glastonbury community."

"George, what will you do when you get back," asks Henrietta.

"It looks like today, they've already, made him Pope. Maybe someday, he could be the Pope in Rome," replies Thomas.

So now with the help of his good friends, George is able to travel safely in the King's entourage, on to Winchester. There he employs an advocate to have his identity registered within the Kingdom. Fortunately, George now has the King to witness his claim as a resident of the United Kingdom. After having his two uncles also act as witnesses, George sends them off directly to Portsmouth;

"Go now and arrange for the passage we will need; Henrietta's ship is there as well; they should be able to help you find a ship bound for Greencastle. I need to travel back to Oxford, accompanying the

King and Queen, and officiate some documents to the Boadleian Library, and I will return with them to Portsmouth. Watch yourselves in this part of England, and remember that Parliament has taken control of the port of Southampton; so stay clear.

Please make sure that my wagon makes it aboard the Queen's, or should I say Queen's, Ship. I do not look forward to saying good bye; to you both. I'll write Captain Philips and thank him for allowing you two to see for my security and arranging the time for us to be together. I will send him an address where you can write to me. And I'll have an advocate in London, who will look after a small-estate that I will leave there to cover any more administrative fees, or land title transfers if they appear."

"How long do you plan to stay in Oxford," asks his uncle James, "I've heard about the Boadleian Library, what's the new one like at St. John's?

"That's the Archbishop's new Quadrangle, it's new and still filling up with books. Loud wants to make a deal with the King so he can have the same arrangement where any new book published in England; a copy has to be sent to the Boadleian."

"There has been a lot of building there in Oxford. Uncle Patrick has been sending Masters and Apprentices there for many years; some with the commissions they were working on at the quarry."

"Yes Oxford is wonderful, a beautiful city of classic construction, refined and a pleasure to behold. I was surprised to find some of the Masters who are still here and still working. It was good to see them, and they all ask about Patrick and how things are going in Aberdeen with the new docks there."

"More worried about their shipments, I would guess. "You did get a chance to see your father," asks Thomas.

"Yes, I presented him with one of the horses I had brought from Spain, A trained Stallion."

James says, "he's not going to like a white horse, tactically it's a disaster."

"White; no it's the one you rode to Greencastle; what did you think?"

"He was excellent! I was going to ask you about that very horse, I thought it was from the ship, or something that you had picked up outside of Dublin; Spanish you say?"

"Andaluciein, actually, and then trained in Portugal."

"I thought they were supposed to be smaller," asks Thomas, "and solid white; trained mostly for ceremony."

"They have actually been for over a century trained for battle. Some jet stallions are also picked to go through the training as well. The stallions are bigger, giving them presence on the battlefield."

"How about that," James says. "I got to ride the Grand Master's mount. But it will have to be our secret, as I know how particular Uncle Patrick is about anyone else riding his horse."

"Technically, it wasn't his yet," says Thomas, "But I'll never tell. Your secret is safe with me."

"Patrick's fame as a cavalry commander is legendary," explains George, "He certainly stands up to every aspect of that reputation and is very proud of the given opportunity he had to serve, whether it was for Queen or Country."

"As he's now a sheriff in Aberdeen, and Commissioner to the High Constable," adds James, "he will need a good horse," .

With George now officially registered, he could now legally transfer the titles, and deeds, over into the hands of his brother Patrick, the son of the Master Mason; also named Patrick.

Patrick, an old friend of the Hay family, traveled to France with Francis Hay, obtaining a pass from Charles I, upon their return dated; Oct. 28,1631.

Later, he would be made the Commissioner to the Earl of Errol, the High Constable of Scotland, considered Scotland's first citizen; second only to King Charles, himself.

Legally, having signed these documents over now to Patrick, they would be very hard to challenge. Land titles in Scotland were always even hard to prove in court; most were always conditional, where the actual ownership belonged to the Crown. Barons were established by the King to manage the land, collect the rents, and work the land.

With most land owned by the Crown, you can't sell what you don't own. In Patrick's case, his lands were gifted, and so he would have sole possession and be able to sell off if he so wanted. This would help his brother's family settle their estates, now in Ireland.

"George, I heard at Winchester that you will be made a Cardinal when you return to Rome," asks James.

"You have said something about serving as the Vatican's Vice Chancellor. As a Cardinal, would you have a chance to become the next Pope?"

"No, since I served as Vice Chancellor, I will be barred from entering the Conclave, from which the new Pope will be elected from one of the Cardinals attending there. Since I'm barred from attending, I can't be elected. Now, if the present Pope dies, and then, only then, could my name be considered.

"Ah, you're a shoo-in," replies Thomas .

George's Uncles travel with him onto Portsmouth with the King and his family. They all would gather in secret to say their goodbyes; all grief-stricken: the children's cries and gloom filling the hall.

Knowing now what their fate was in Scotland, the fracture of culture and the growing power of the General Assembly, their life outside Aberdeen would undergo a drastic change, a real tragedy. If it were not for the presence of George's two Uncles, the future would look very bleak indeed.

"Ï was glad to see both of your Uncles," says the King, "they should be just fine getting back home. To see that you, Henrietta and her mother, and the children get over to France safely, I will have the Queen's own ship, the Henrietta Maria, take you."

You could hear it in the King's voice that he felt full of sorrow to be left behind. Saying goodbye to Henrietta and his two children, he felt that he had little choice but to send them away where they would all be safe.

The weight of the decision bore heavily on his heart, knowing that this separation might be permanent. The children clung to their mother, their tear-streaked faces reflecting the pain of parting. The hall now echoed with the sounds of weeping and despair.

Soon the ship would set sail, and the King, now overwhelmed with grief, knew his heart would ache with every wave that carried his family away. The uncertainty of their future gnawed at him, and he felt a profound sense of loss. The once vibrant and united family is now facing an uncertain fate.

The journey to France would be fraught with danger; the constant fear of being pursued by enemies sent by a Parliament that the King once regarded as friends added to their sorrow. The children, still too young to understand the full gravity of the situation, sensed the tension and fear in the adults around them. Maria and Henrietta tried to comfort them, but their own hearts were heavy with worry and sadness.

Upon reaching France, they would be met with a cold and unfamiliar sense. The warmth and familiarity of the home and the Palace in London are replaced by the stark reality of exile. The children missed their friends and the life they had known, and their cries of homesickness added to the sorrow that enveloped the family.

George's Uncles did their best to provide support and reassurance, but the weight of their own grief was evident. The sorrow of their separation from their homeland was a constant presence.

To adapt to their new life, but the shadow of their past and the uncertainty of their future loomed large. The once close-knit family was now fragmented, each member carrying their burden of grief and loss.

The King, left behind in Scotland, felt the absence of his family acutely. The halls of the palace were empty and silent, a stark contrast to the lively home they once knew. He now was destine to spend his last days in solitude, with his thoughts consumed by the sorrow of their separation and the stark uncertainty of their future.

The End

The Glastonbury Holy Thorn Tree shown before it was topped by demonstrators in 2010. This was not the first time; it was first cut down in 1647 by a zealous Parliamentary soldier serving in Cromwell's new standing army. You can just make out St. Patrick's Tor; the hill shown in the background and the site of St Michael's Church destroyed by an earthquake in 1275, leaving only its tall tower.

Epilogue

The Treaty of Berwick and the Liturgy; An out and out rejection of the English hypocrisy

When asked about the Bishop, King Charles replied: "You don't mean the Queen and I's oldest friend, what did you say; 'The Bishop', I know no Bishop and never did know any Bishop." As far as George, he was more of a family friend; a friend of my father, and my father's family; one who wrote the biography of my Grandmother. But a Bishop, I think not, though he was my wife's 'the queen's' confessor.

I didn't see him, though, as a Bishop, and only knew of one time that he wrote to Rome with a complaint about the Jesuits; circulating pamphlets that they had printed in Denmark, so he thought. George was always in agreement that Rome had given the Scotts a special dispensation that was written out along with the Declaration of Arobroth, given to Pope John the twenty-second in 1320.

"I see him more as a Cardinal, and one who could have brought something really special to a united kingdom, if it were found united, and in peace. You'll never imagine what kind of a Kingdom, under God, as he had planned. "You want me to surrender a Bishop; I know of no Bishop. The one that you have apparently lost, seems that it is indeed a great loss to us all."

And in fact the comming years would be bleak and overstrained in conflict in London, in Scotland, and in Ireland too, Soon all of Great Britian would be involved in a civil war.Parliament would issue a death warrant for Charles and his allies. Hamilton had the good fortune to have gone to the American colonies and escape any prosecution by London. There was a different attitude in America towards the English Parliament, and for that matter there was a similar attitude felt in Scotland and most all of Ireland.

The division between religious beliefs grew and would fuel the fight and civil war for another fourteen years. The American colonies would continue to support Charles's monarchy even though he was deposed, and England and the colonies were ruled by the Parliament. George Gordon or The Marquis of Huntly another one of Charles's allies who had escaped the retribution of Parliament, would go on in his support of the King. In May of 1646 he would defeat a force of Covenanters who had taken Aberdeen.

Supported by the politicians of Parliament and Oliver Cromwell's 'New Standing Army', the War of the Three Kingdoms would rage on till 1653. It wasn't until the end of the war that the American colonies would have no choice but to give in to Parliament; the war dragged on for another year before it would be over. Parliament would then have their war from within and in less than ten years restore the monarchy putting Charles's son: Charles II, back on the throne.

Then again in 1688 the Scottish Estate would rise up again and side with Parliament to depose another one of Charles's sons; James II and VII of Scotland; giving the crown to a daughter instead who was a Protestant presbyterian and not a Catholic. Insisting that it was a legal question whether a Catholic could be the Monarch, in 1689 by an Act of Parliament excluded succession by a Catholic.

Was this legal? We only have to look into the Middle Temple in London; a society of barristers or trial lawyers. Situated near the Royal Courts of Justice it was given over to the trial lawyers in 1346 by a fashion of the Knights Templers'; the Knights Hospitaller who after the Templer's dissolution in 1312 had taken over the Hall. They were clearly in support of the Stuart Monarchy by the predominant display of their portraits there; both Catholic and Protestant alike.

London's Middle Temple

The Château of Saint-Germain-en-Laye Palace on the outskirts of Paris. This would become the official sanctuary of the Stuart family outside of Great Britian

Acknowledgements

The author would like to thank all of those who had the patience to work with a first-time author and self-publisher. Pictures, Graphics, and Artwork unless otherwise indicated are property of: Kingdome Graphics® a division of; For a united kingdom® a registered business in Oregon, USA 2025

LCCN# **2025927305**

ISBN# 979-8-9937486-0-3 Hard Cover

ISBN# 979-8-9976486-1-0 Paperback

ISBN# 979-8-9976486-3-4 E Book

ISBN# 979-8-9976486-2-7 Audio Book

Published By: For a united kingdom®
A registered business in Oregon, U.S.A.
Kingdom Graphics® a Division of
For a united kingdom®

www.ingramcontent.com/pod-product-compliance
Lightning Source LLC
LaVergne TN
LVHW090556110826
845146LV00001B/153

* 9 7 9 8 9 9 3 7 4 8 6 1 0 *